T0352345

africa pulse

SHE'S TO BLAME

BM Khaketla

Translated from Sesotho by JM Lenake

OXFORD
UNIVERSITY PRESS
SOUTH AFRICA

OXFORD
UNIVERSITY PRESS

Oxford University Press is a department of the University of Oxford.
It furthers the University's objective of excellence in research, scholarship,
and education by publishing worldwide. Oxford is a registered trade mark of
Oxford University Press in the UK and in certain other countries.

Published in South Africa by
Oxford University Press Southern Africa (Pty) Limited

Vasco Boulevard, Goodwood, N1 City, P O Box 12119, Cape Town,
South Africa

Mosali a Nkhola was originally published in Sesotho in 1960. This translation is published by
arrangement with Morija Sesotho Book Depot.

The moral rights of the translator have been asserted.

First published 2019

She's to Blame

ISBN 978 0 19 073160 1 (print)
ISBN 978 0 19 074638 4 (ebook)

First impression 2019

Typeset in Utopia Std 10.5pt on 15.5pt
Printed on 70gsm woodfree paper

Acknowledgements
Co-ordinator at the Centre for Multilingualism and Diversities Research, UWC: Antjie Krog
Publisher: Helga Schaberg
Project manager: Liz Sparg
Editor: Liz Sparg
Book and cover designer: Judith Cross
Illustrator: James Berrangé
Typesetter: Aptara Inc.
Printed and bound by: Delta Digital

We are grateful to the following for permission to reproduce photographs: Shutterstock/
mimagephotography/1039432687 (cover); BM Khaketla (Courtesy Dr Mamphono Khaketla)
(p. iv); CMDR (p. 296).

The authors and publisher gratefully acknowledge permission to reproduce copyright
material in this book. Every effort has been made to trace copyright holders, but if any
copyright infringements have been made, the publisher would be grateful for information
that would enable any omissions or errors to be corrected in subsequent impressions.

Links to third party websites are provided by Oxford in good faith and for information only.
Oxford disclaims any responsibility for the materials contained in any third party website
referenced in this work.

THIS BOOK FORMS part of a series of eight texts and a larger translation endeavour undertaken by the Centre for Multilingualism and Diversities Research (CMDR) at the University of the Western Cape (UWC). The texts translated for this series have been identified time and again by scholars of literature in southern Africa as classics in their original languages. The translators were selected for their translation experience and knowledge of a particular indigenous language. Funding was provided by the National Institute for the Humanities and Social Sciences (NIHSS) as part of their Catalytic Research Programme. The project seeks to stimulate debate by inserting neglected or previously untranslated literary texts into contemporary public spheres, providing opportunities to refigure their significance and prompting epistemic changes within multidisciplinary research. Every generation translates for itself. Within the broad scope of several translation theories and the fact that every person translates differently from the next, it is hoped that these texts will generate further deliberations, translations and retranslations.

BM Khaketla (1913–2000)

Bennet Makalo Khaketla was born in 1913. He started schooling in Souru, but after his father died, his mother sent him to Ramahlakoana School in Matatiele. He gained a teaching certificate from Mariazell College and began teaching at various places while studying for a BA at Unisa. During this time he began writing.

Khaketla excelled in three genres, publishing two novels: *Meokho ea Thabo* (Tears of Joy, 1945) and *Mosali a Nkhola* (A Woman Betrayed Me, 1960); three plays: *Moshoeshoe le Baruti* (Moshoeshoe and the Missionaries, 1947), *Tholoana tsa Sethepu* (Results of Polygamy, 1954) and *Bulane* (1958); and a collection of poems: *Lipshamanthe* (Astonishments, 1954).

In 1953 Khaketla returned to Lesotho to start the newspaper *Mohlabani* (Warrior), which established him as a highly articulate and influential intellectual with vast influence as one of the New Africans. As editor of *Mohlabani*, he published the full version of the Freedom Charter, and about the role of the British in Ghana, he wrote: "The English leech stuck its hooks into the black bowels of a black country inhabited by a black folk… The victory of Nkrumah and Ghana is a victory for the whole of Black Africa". Drawing the same lessons from the Congo Crisis as Frantz Fanon, Khaketla wrote about efforts of colonial powers to prevent the emergence of African intellectuals: "But they seem to have failed to reckon with one thing: that ideas – particularly political ideas in this age of sputniks – have wings; that Africa is today like a chain of mechanical contraptions which are set in motion from Cape to Cairo and from Morocco to Malagasy at the mere touch of one button."

It was this capacity for remarkable articulation that Khaketla used, whether constructing African Nationalism or writing literature. His work is vividly formulated, energetically presented and masterfully paced.

A literary opinion on the text

Mosali a Nkhola (1960) by BM Khaketla is set at the height of British colonial rule in Lesotho. What happens when a young educated ruler who values free choice is confronted with the possibility of losing his kingdom?

> ...the dichotomies between justice and injustice, educated and uneducated people, backward and advanced culture all contribute to one central idea, namely that if a foreign culture is imposed on a people, it is bound to disrupt the social fabric of their lives, thus causing mental dislocation, emotional displacement as well as confusion of self-knowledge among them. This is, in short, what deculturation amounts to.

T Selepe quoted in Attwell, D and Attridge, D (2012) The Cambridge History of South African Literature. *Cambridge: Cambridge University Press, p. 614*

Lesotho of *She's to Blame*

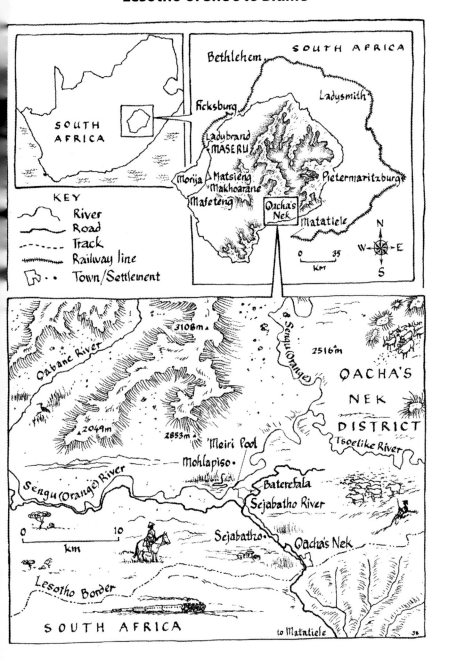

List of characters

Lekaota: a king in the Qacha area, Lesotho
Mosito: eldest son of King Lekaota
Sebolelo: married Mosito and became mother to Thabo:
    thereafter known as Mmathabo
Thabo: son of Mosito and Sebolelo (Mmathabo)

Pokane; Khosi: close friends and advisors to Mosito

Khati; Sebotsa; Maime: councillors of the late King Lekaota

Selone: herbalist

Tlelima: a man from the Bahlakwana tribe
Lipuo: Tlelima's wife
Senyane: Tlelima's friend, and one of the men selected by Khati
Bohata; Papiso; Letebele; Molafu: men selected by Khati
Maleshoane: wife to Senyane

Thebe; Tsietsi: men from Batarefala
Likeledi: Tsietsi's daughter

Maleke: fisherman from Nqhoaki
Motiki; Tefo: passersby
Seleso: undercover policeman
Thulare: undercover police sergeant
Khera: witness

Reverend Tshepo
Reverend Motete
Mokali: old man

SHE'S TO BLAME

BM Khaketla

Introduction

It is unusual for a novel to have an introduction, but I found it necessary for this one (*Mosali a Nkola*) and the reader will pardon me.

Although this book is only published now, it was written some time ago. I started to write it in February 1951, while at Nigel, where I held a teaching post for two years, and completed it in July that same year.

The story is original, based on events that were discussed widely, but it does not mean that I am expressing my own feelings about the pain the ritual murders caused the people from Lesotho. My aim is twofold: to entertain the reader, but also to enable readers to digest ritual murders, examine them carefully and try to see how they can be prevented.

Although the places mentioned in the story are known to many, especially the inhabitants of Qacha as well as those who occasionally visit Qacha, the characters in this book do not relate to anybody in particular and if anyone living here, or anywhere else, has a similar name, it was unintentional, and I do apologise.

BM Khaketla
Maseru
Lesotho
22 September 1959

Contents

TO ALL THE BASOTHO

"In Your name they rejoice all day long,
And in Your righteousness they are exalted."
Psalm 89: 16, 17

1

The 'initiation lodge' burns down

It was a Wednesday, at three o'clock in the afternoon. A lorry that delivered post between Qacha and Matatiele stopped slowly in front of the Qacha post office. Many people got off, took their luggage and dispersed in different directions, rushing to reach home before sunset; because, as the saying goes – nobody knows who could be hooked unawares by the neck!

Among the people alighting from the lorry was a pleasant looking young man, about twenty-five years old, with a light complexion. He was tall and moderately fit, but there were already indications that, when he settled down with nothing to disturb him, he would put on some weight.

The young man was dressed in a double-breasted brown suit, with a closely fitted jacket that showed off his physique. Bare-headed, his long hair well combed, with a parting on the left and the sides in a careful French cut, he sported a style that was strange to a traditional Mosotho. With him were two friends of the same age, also dressed neatly and appealing to look at.

As soon as he got off the lorry, a group of people crowded around him, welcoming him back. Among them were the police sergeant, a senior government interpreter and their wives.

After the greetings and some friendly banter, he went up to a tall, well-fed grey horse, with a strong round rump, and mounted it. His two contemporaries mounted the other horses that had been brought by ten boys who had come from the village to welcome the young man.

Once everybody was on horseback, they sped away, passing Ralefatla's store. One could see red dust being kicked up behind them, as if a strange whirlwind had risen there. From afar they looked like a group of cattle, trekking.

Who was this young man, so exuberantly welcomed? It was Mosito, the son of King Lekaota. He had returned from Lovedale, the famous college down in the Cape, where he had been studying. He had completed his studies by writing his final matriculation exam, and of course, nobody doubted that he would pass with flying colours.

Mosito was King Lekaota's first born. Since Mosito's birth, his father had ensured that he was in good hands. As one of the kings of the Qacha area, Lekaota saw that times were changing and kept up to date with the latest developments. Although he had never been educated, he made sure that his son was, so that Mosito could rule properly when his time came.

"These days," Lekaota remarked, "to be born a king, born as royalty, is no longer considered important. The king who wants to rule well should be educated. Times have changed. Our forefathers ruled the blind, and among the blind the one-eyed was king. That was how they ruled. Today, things have changed and we should change and move forward with the times. Communities and their kings should open their eyes. If the kings are blind, they are unable to govern those who can see a bit more than themselves."

It was on these grounds that King Lekaota sent Mosito to school to drink from the fountain of education, so that one day he would be able to talk with white people without the use of an interpreter.

"You see, Mosala?" said Lekaota to one of the old men who was always hanging around the court. "When I go to Qacha to speak to the Deputy Commissioner, I always depend on an interpreter, and so, whenever I say something confidential, the interpreter shares the secret with us. That is not a good thing! I do not want my son to be a fool like myself, or a person who needs somebody to speak on his behalf or who is nervous in front of British people, like we are."

Today, the things Lekaota had wished for had happened. Mosito had fulfilled his father's wishes. He had attended school, acquired European knowledge and prepared himself to take over his father's reign when it was time to do so. Mosito's education down in the Cape was now complete. Mosito, like the other 'initiates' who had just qualified, had left their boyhood in the Cape. He had brought his manhood, education, along as a precious gift wrapped in a blanket.

Towards sunset, when the mountain shadows were spreading, the horses stopped at home. Suddenly, ululation started; then it poured from all directions until the whole village reverberated and the sounds echoed and boomed off far away cliffs. Soon everyone came forward to greet the King's son – their future ruler.

It was clear that Mosito was loved by the whole community. Many remarked that, despite his high education, he remained humble. They openly said that he was not like the sons of other kings, who were frequently arrogant and disrespectful of adults – they seemed to assume that their fathers' subjects were also *theirs*, to be kicked around at will.

On the Saturday after Mosito's arrival, King Lekaota called for a big feast at his place. The whole community was invited to celebrate with him and rejoice in his son's achievement. His son was the son of the whole community and their future ruler had fulfilled his father's wish, as well as that of his people.

Because everybody loved Mosito, all those who could walk turned up. Young men arrived in groups from their villages, singing and dancing. Sometimes, unexpectedly, one of them would break ranks, run forward and then retreat, bending forward, with eyes large and staring, like those of a fierce bull. The moment women began to ululate, the young man would run amok, prance and pretend to be a lunatic, about to graze with cattle.

A short time later, young women began to join in, with their traditional dance, mokhibo. They were miraculous, the way they shook their shoulders so gracefully. Observers watched with bated breath – yes, in this form of dance, Basotho women surpassed everybody! Who would dare say that the Sesotho dance is barbarous? Only the ignorant or those who have never seen true experts in action! That day of the feast, each girl flaunted her skill. Around the next corner you would bump into a group of girls performing a moqoqopelo, a dance for young women about to marry. They were singing and tapping their feet lightly in a breathtakingly graceful and intricate manner.

At midday, the King appeared, his face genial with excitement. He came out brandishing a colourfully decorated gun. Some people got a fright, thinking he was about to shoot somebody, but he fired three blanks into the air and the crowd cheered loudly!

King Lekaota was not a Christian and had many wives, but he did not despise the Church. In all his gatherings he never forgot to ask a minister to say grace before a meal, to thank the giver of all gifts. All the ministers were, therefore, also invited and honoured the feast of their ruler.

By two o'clock in the afternoon, everybody had stopped dancing and sat down to listen to the King. When all was quiet, King Lekaota stood up and addressed the multitude.

"Nation of Mokhachane, today I am very happy to see you assembled here in such great numbers. You have gathered as if for a normal pitso, in order to discuss affairs concerning govern-ment matters. But today's meeting is different. This is a friendly get-together, like when our elder, Monokoa invites people to a party. Your attendance today has shown me something wonderful: I see it as a sign that you love me and that you also love my son in whose honour we are gathered here today. This is something great and very important.

"I have invited you to rejoice with me. I am not a Christian, but as you all know, I allowed Mosito to become a Christian when he asked permission from me. Because of that, I have not treated him according to our forefathers' tradition, as it manifests in the initiation school of the Basotho. If he had gone to initiation school, you would not be gathered here today, but I want you all to remember, although he has not been to that school, he has been initiated in the European way. I deemed it necessary to invite all of you because his presence today is a sign that his boyhood initiation lodge has been burnt down. You also see his classmates from school with him today, Pokane and Khosi. We are all very proud that Mosito and his friends have fulfilled the wishes of their parents. They have arrived among us with wisdom from the Cape.

"Before we settle down to eat, I shall ask Reverend Motete to say a few words and then give thanks for the food we are about to receive."

The happiness of King Lekaota was visible to all present. In addressing his subjects personally, he had done something very unusual. In Sesotho custom, a king addresses his people through a councillor, who conveys the message.

Reverend Motete was already very old. He had been born during the Gun War. His head was snow white and his eyesight by now weak, but his intellect was still so very alert that his way of articulating himself could not be matched by the young.

He stood up with his spectacles resting on his nostrils, far from his eyes, so that it seemed unlikely that they could help him to see. He was a huge man, with a voice out of harmony with his size.

"I feel privileged and greatly honoured," he squeaked, "that the King has given me a chance to say a few words on this great day. I would like to direct the words I have to this son of mine, Mosito, because for King Lekaota and I, our days are numbered. One leg is already stretching towards the grave.

"Mosito, my son, you have done a great thing. You have acted according to your father's wish and worked hard in your studies, so that you can get eyes to see. But, please note, that, although educated, you still have a lot to learn.

"Just listen to what I once heard. I was going around, visiting the sick and I got to the house of a potter. She had very, very, beautiful pots. I asked her where she got them from. She said: 'All over the world, there is clay and there are pots.' She pointed at two pots and then took a small stick and tapped them. I heard one produce a melodious sound, much like the pleasant sound of iron. The second one's sound was not as pleasant. She said to me: 'Father, the second pot does not sound like the first one, because it has not been put through the fire, but the day it has been in the fire, it will also produce a melodious sound. It is the small twigs in the clay that make its sound less clear than the other one, which has been fired.'

"I greeted her and left. Returning home, I kept thinking about those pots. The education we receive from the day we were born until we are men and women is the clay used to mould every human creation. Today, you have returned from the hands of a potter, the school that has moulded you and made you what you are. But you have not yet gone through the oven of fire to burn out the small twigs in the clay. The fire you have to go through is to love and labour for God with all your heart and all your strength. Our love of God, our works that please Him, our faith in His Son, our daily prayers throughout our lives – all these are the oven of fire that burns the twigs of sin that are with everybody. These spoil the good picture of our souls, which God wishes to see. Please note, if you forget your God, He will forsake you and all that He has given you will disappear at once. Contemporaries of Mosito, listen carefully to what I am saying, because it is also relevant to you: let God's will be the fire moulding your lives."

After the minister's short sermon, he offered up a short prayer and food was served.

2

Mosito's marriage

It had been two years since Mosito had arrived home from school in Lovedale. As his father was already very time-worn, most of the work related to government was performed by the young man on behalf of King Lekaota. Due to the help he received and his natural intelligence, Mosito performed well and learned the ways of governing quickly, which made things run smoothly – one might even suggest better than when he had been away at school.

One day, at the beginning of the third year of working with his father, the old king invited Mosito to his home. As the young man settled down opposite him, the old man introduced his discussion.

"Mosito, my son, I sent you to school and you have completed your studies well." The King smiled fondly and benevolently.

"Yes, Father, that is true, I have studied hard."

The old man was silent for some time, but his lingering smile indicated the pleasure in his whole body. After a while he spoke again. "You see, my son, I am already old and about to leave this world, which for us human beings is just a cattle-post. I am passing on to where your forefathers have gone. I wish to tell you that, now that I have taught you how to govern and you have indicated that you are man enough for it, I should complete my work by making you a true man. I should get you a wife."

"I understand, Father."

By this time Mosito was also smiling. Every young man is pleased when a parent informs him that he intends finding him a wife. That is the wish of all young men: to have a wife who will bear him children and be his companion in many things.

After a pause, the old man continued, "I am obliged to complete my duties towards you while I am still alive. When I am gone, there will be no one to get you a fitting companion who would be suitable for the position you were born for.

"Times change my son, and an intelligent person is the one who is ready to change along with them. It does not help when a person keeps on saying that during the times of Moshoeshoe things were done in this and that manner. The times of Moshoeshoe passed with him, and were buried with his bones up there on Thaba Bosiu. I compare one who clings to the past with someone who is being swept along by a full river clasping onto a small reed in the middle of strong floods. Even if he wishes to be saved, he will not be saved by clutching to such a reed. There is only one thing that awaits him – death. We, who belongto days gone by but are also fortunate enough to live in these modern times, are floating rapidly along this full river whose waves resemble the oceans, heaving us up and down – the river being civilization and seasons that are continuously changing. We therefore realise that we have nowhere to clasp and have to go along with the tides."

"I understand, Father, although I do not understand why you are saying all these things."

"Wait, don't be in a hurry. In Moshoeshoe's times I simply would have told you that I have seen the daughter of so-and-so, have spoken to her parents and have come to an agreement. But because of modern times, I want to plan it with you. The European education you received has taught you that a person has to choose his own life partner, one he feels would suit him. Is this not the case?"

13

"Yes indeed, it is like that, Ntate. You have said exactly how we as youth would prefer things to be done."

"But still, that does not mean that I will allow you to do as you please and marry a girl I find unacceptable. What I intend to do is to indicate the families I know that have girls who might be suitable, and you could go and meet those girls and choose the one you most prefer. Then you can inform me, so that I can open up the conversation to arrange the bride price. I hope we can agree on this, my son-from-the-Mokoena-clan."

"Ntate, my father, I lack the words to thank you, the words that will explain the depth of my elation. Be pleased, my father, when I say I thank you. I never thought that one day you would allow me to do what you have just said I could do."

"It is good, my son, that you are happy with this arrangement, because that will facilitate matters, and our mission will be concluded at the appropriate time."

"Now tell me, Father, where do you think I should go?" Mosito gave only a small smile, although inside he began to quiver excitedly.

"I have already said that I, personally, will not choose one for you. I shall only indicate the families I know that are appropriate. Go and select the one you fancy and tell me."

"But which families do you have in mind, Father?"

"At the moment I am thinking of the family of King Khare's senior wife, Maposholi, at Thabatseka. In that family there are two maidens, Maleshoane and Sebolelo. I think perhaps you may already know of them. You are the one to explore which of the two might be the one you love."

"Yes, I know them, Ntate, but am not sure whether we will agree that it should be one of them. I say so because although I am not highly educated, I have, one can say, a little bit of schooling. It is therefore imperative that I should have a partner who will appreciate that the times we live in have changed, and it should be someone who has also been to school. But don't be concerned, let me first go and see."

"All is well, Mokoena. I like a person who speaks as you do, one who listens to the parent's advice."

It was in the evening, around dusk, when three young men arrived at the neighbouring King Khare's place. The visitors halted their horses outside the courtyard, but they were clearly expected. Once they had alighted, some men unsaddled the animals and took the saddles to where the visitors would sleep. The horses were taken to where they would be kept and well fed. The young men, Mosito, Pokane and Khosi, entered the courtyard to offer their greetings. Their mission was the one Mosito and his father had decided upon the day they discussed his marriage. After they had introduced themselves to King Khare, food was served and then they were taken to a house where they would spend the night. As they were tired, they quickly went to bed. They had been informed that they would meet the young women the following morning.

Before they fell asleep, Pokane asked Mosito whether those they were about to meet had been to school and how far they had studied.

"I have no idea," said Mosito, "but I am told that these two, those we have to choose from, did attend school. What I do not know is what standard they passed. I think that is what I should find out to select the right one."

"That is correct, Homeboy," said Khosi.

Although Mosito was the son of a king, he was not brought up in a way that made him regard himself as a king. Neither did his contemporaries regard him as such, yet. They used to call each other *Wa hae*, meaning Homeboy. Mosito liked the name a lot.

"That's a fact, Homeboy," said Khosi, again. "To marry an uneducated woman is like inspanning a horse and a cow to the same horse cart. When one pulls this way, the other one pulls that way, and the cart will not move. Eventually it will break and injure the riders. Just imagine, explaining to an uneducated woman the news you have read in a newspaper and she is unable to understand what is going on."

"That's the gospel truth, Homeboy," said Pokane. "Man, it's pathetic to see an educated person who has married an uneducated wife. When the husband's friends visit and they start discussing educational matters or talking about world news, the wife will remain in the kitchen as soon as she realises she cannot understand what is being discussed. At times when she forces herself, poor creature, to be where the men are – for fear that they might regard her as aloof or inhospitable – it will become obvious that she is in a deep panic. She will be uncomfortable as if she is not in her own home. When people laugh, she will just grin along with them, without knowing why everybody is laughing. Even when the discussion is in Sesotho, she will be ice-cold, as cold as frost in June.

"Last year, I saw a king, whose name has just escaped me, at Qacha to meet the Deputy Commissioner. As his wife was sickly, she had come with her husband to Qacha to see a doctor. When this king met the Deputy Commissioner, he introduced his wife. 'Oh, what a wonderful opportunity,' said the Deputy Commissioner, unexpectedly. 'Seeing that I have just arrived from England in Lesotho, I have not yet had an opportunity to visit the kings in this district with their wives. I shall therefore be delighted to have lunch with the two of you at our home. My wife will also be thrilled to meet your wife, so that they can talk about matters related to their affairs. Will that be in order, our king?'

"The king accepted the invitation. The Deputy Commissioner phoned his wife and informed her that he would be coming with the king and queen for lunch and she must prepare for them.

"At lunchtime, the Deputy Commissioner took the royal couple to his house. The king had had some schooling and sufficient command of English, so he didn't need an interpreter. But his wife was an ordinary Mosotho woman who had attended school, but before she had finished standard two, before she could write Sesotho properly, she decided to leave and said she saw no need to continue schooling as she could read and write. So English was completely foreign to her.

"At lunchtime the king and his wife were happily welcomed by the Deputy Commissioner's wife. The table was prepared and they settled down to eat. Now, the poor queen was in trouble. She found there were too many forks and knives and she did not know which one to start with. Actually, she had never used a fork and knife in her life. However, she tried her best, although at times she used her hands. While the men were conversing, the Deputy Commissioner's wife tried to discuss something with her, but she quickly discovered that there was no way they could understand one other: the queen did not have even a smattering of English, just as the hostess did not have the foggiest knowledge of Sesotho. The king had to stop his conversation with the Deputy Commissioner and interpret for the wife. It was clear that the queen also had another problem. Where have you ever seen a person sitting at table wearing a lefitori?"

"Goodness, why did she not take off the blanket?" Khosi asked.

"How could she? How could she sit there with a vest, without a blouse or something? You must be joking!"

The three of them burst out laughing.

"Indeed the poor king had a big problem, Homeboy."

Laughingly Mosito responded, "This is the reason I want to find out exactly how far these young women have gone in education, and hopefully they did not stop schooling in standard two, like that queen."

After a long discussion and feeling tired, they snuffed the candles, said a prayer thanking the One who had protected them on their journey, and fell asleep.

The following morning, they were given water to wash and then it was time for breakfast. Afterwards, they were led to the big royal house, where they found some women already waiting. According to Sesotho custom, not only Maleshoane and Sebolelo were present; all the young women of the village had been invited to keep the King's daughters company.

The young men introduced themselves. Maleshoane and Sebolelo, the King's daughters between whom Mosito had to choose a wife, were both remarkably beautiful. Maleshoane was of medium build, had a glowing brown complexion, and a small gap between her two upper front teeth. When she smiled, she had lovely dimples. Sebolelo's skin was the colour of a lion and her teeth as white as drops of milk. She was a tall, striking woman who had the bearing of a queen.

When Mosito was introduced to them, he was immediately drawn to Sebolelo and decided to speak to her.

When young men paid young women a visit in those days, the women did not sit on chairs like modern people. They spread grass mats on the floor to sit on, while the young men sat on chairs. After the introduction, each young man would choose the woman he fancied and talk to her. Then the young man would leave his chair to sit opposite her on the grass mat, squarely facing the one of his choice. If there were only a few young men, so that some women were left without conversation partners, the women would leave, one by one, to prepare meals and to give the others a chance; although at times they would prefer to stay on, making it look as if the young men were cowards because they had failed to talk to them. On that day, the girls who had no one to talk to left, until only Maleshoane, Sebolelo and a third one, Lineo, remained. The young men left their chairs and sat on the mats. Mosito sat with Sebolelo, Khosi with Maleshoane and Pokane with Lineo. The conversation began.

Mosito had spent quite a long time away from home in the Cape, as he had gone there already in standard three, so he was not familiar with the latest games young Basotho men and women were playing. He was not aware of the fun young women made of men, when they exhibited an interest in them. So, when Mosito had introduced his feelings, he was taken aback when Sebolelo said, "I hear you say you love me, now show it!"

First Mosito was tongue-tied, then embarrassed.

"What do you mean: show me?" asked Mosito. "I have already said that I love you. What else are you expecting from me? Is there something better than this?"

"Yes, I hear what you are saying, but what should *I* do next?"

This playful dialogue continued and the bewildered Mosito began wondering whether he was dealing with an irrational and clueless girl. But, as always, a man devises means when someone interests him, and in the end Mosito managed to hook the foal that was refusing to be caught, and so saved the conversation. When the main visitor succeeds, those accompanying him also find the going to be smooth. That was how things worked.

Then it was lunchtime. After the meal, tea was brought. The cups, overfull, with their saucers placed on top, covering the tea, were put on a table that had been laid with a white tablecloth. Poor Mosito and his friends did not know anything about this next lighthearted trick of the Basotho women. The young men took off the saucers, but when they tried to put the cups back on the saucers, the tea splashed and stained the white tablecloth. They frantically looked at each other, but decided to leave it like that. However, they knew that a person who spilt tea was regarded as ridiculous by young women, who would say, "You know, the friends of so-and-so are real pumpkins."

After tea, water was brought to rinse their mouths. They were surprised when they tasted that it was nicely sugared water! Yes, that was what the Basotho woman could do!

But none of these things discouraged the young men. They simply assumed that things were done that way by the girls who were serving them, and soon forgot about it. Toward sunset, the young men were in high spirits and all was well in their company with the young women.

Then it was time to leave. But when they started going down into the valley, they found the young women clandestinely waiting to take them halfway. They alighted and each young woman led her prospective lover's horse, chatting happily amid vivid smiles.

After some kissing, the guests left on horseback.

The young men reached home after sunset, where the herd boys unsaddled the horses. In the courtyard, they were welcomed home by the King, but they didn't even need to say anything – their glowing, exited faces said it all.

The following day, towards midday, King Lekaota called Mosito and they went to the royal guest house. When they had settled down, the King asked, "How did you fare, Mosito?"

"We had a very pleasant journey, Ntate. Indeed very pleasant."

"You saw the young women at the royal place? Between the two, whom do you favour?"

"I saw them Ntate, but was almost in a fix about what to do."

"Why? How can a man be in a fix when he is with a young woman? What is wrong with today's young men!"

When the King said that, he chuckled, as he was reminded of the time when he was still a young man like Mosito.

"But eventually, I chose Sebolelo."

The old man smiled, indicating that he was suspecting that. He knew those girls well.

"Sebolelo, yes. That is fine, my son. It is clear that you are good at choosing. I also had her in mind, although Maleshoane is a very beautiful person as well, fit for you."

"That is true, she is a beautiful girl, and though I ended up choosing Sebolelo, initially I did experience a bit of conflict."

"But are you satisfied now? Do you understand fully, Mosito, that I do not force you to choose from that family, and you are under no obligation if you do not love her because you are afraid of hurting me if you don't? If that is the case, I have another place I can refer you to for a suitable wife."

"I understand you very well, Father. But Sebolelo is the one. My conscience tells me she is a suitable wife, created just for me."

"But you should bear in mind that marriage is not an easy affair, especially these days. It is very difficult as children no longer take after their parents. If these were the olden days, I would be saying you have chosen a wife for yourself. I know what kind of family that girl belongs to. But today's children are difficult."

They paused for a while, then King Lekaota said, "Now, concerning education, how far has she studied? Please remember that I am not an expert on these issues around books. What standard has she reached?"

Now Mosito was hesitant, but he had to tell his father the truth.

"She has gone as far as standard four."

Mosito was looking down as he said it, because he did not want to meet his father's eyes – what if his father was not satisfied with such a low standard of education?

"She reached standard four only? And you, what standard have you attained?"

"Standard ten, Ntate."

"That means you are six standards *above* her? No my son, do you think you will pull well together? If she had at least reached standard seven or eight... I mean, after all, the man is the head of the family, and must be above the woman educationally. But, if the wife is that much less educated, I think it is improper. You must understand, Mosito, even if I am not educated, or even a Christian, and though I am a polygamist, I regard marriage according to how you Christians view it. The Church teaches you to marry one wife, and that I support wholeheartedly because polygamy creates a lot of tension. So, if you choose a wife, then marry her; and know that you have tied yourself with a thong that will be untied by death only. If you are a true Christian, you know you cannot divorce the woman you have chosen yourself.

"To select one wife for such a long relationship is therefore a very difficult task and a person has to be very careful. If you really feel that Sebolelo is the woman of your choice, then that is fine. If you feel that you will live happily together, despite the fact that you are not equal in education, I say all is well, I shall go to pay bohadi for you. But you have to understand clearly that the choice was yours and if things do not work out according to plan, I will not be to blame. You may go."

Mosito left the house a very happy man. The golden complexion of Sebolelo, her moist bright eyes, her sparkling white teeth, her smile full of love, her regal, gracious walk – all these presented themselves with full force in his feelings and woke an uncontrollable whirlwind of love in him that had been unimaginable before. He accepted fully that a woman, a wife, was indeed a man's rib. Sebolelo was such a rib. She was the flesh of his flesh and blood of his blood.

The bohadi process was undertaken. After a few weeks, when finalised by his family, the festivities and ceremonies began at the bride's home, from where she was escorted to her in-laws. Sebolelo was welcomed in the traditional way by slaughtering a goat to initiate her into married life with a big feast. The village people celebrated and welcomed their new Mother Queen.

3

The death of King Lekaota

Mosito had been married to Sebolelo for three years. Their first born, a boy, Thabo, was already running around and speaking all kinds of phrases. The lives of Mosito and Sebolelo – who was also called Mmathabo, mother of Thabo – were bound together thoroughly.

No longer addressed by her maiden name, not even by her husband, 'Mathabo radiated so much happiness and kindness that people flocked to her home. No one who arrived there left without having had something to eat. The disabled who were usually found at the King's premises were treated fairly, like everyone else. Daily, 'Mathabo reminded Mosito that a king was a king because of people, so everybody deserved to be fed so that they could willingly perform important work, such as ploughing the royal fields. 'Mathabo saw to it that beer was brewed and food cooked, and people worked happily, knowing that they would return to their homes with food in their stomachs.

'Mathabo's friendly and sensitive provisions made the community love Mosito even more. They felt that they would not be lost if the old King were to die. Mosito had married a caring person, from a good home. What the wife resembled, was what the husband was.

But happiness cannot continue forever without something bad happening – all things have an end.

It was a Tuesday afternoon and people were returning from hoeing weeds in the King's fields. People arrived home, men were served beer and they began singing songs. King Lekaota mounted his horse and went back to the fields to check on the work that had been done that day. But that evening, just after dusk, he suddenly stood up, looked at Mosito and the men enjoying their beer and said that he felt a bit tired and wished to rest. He went to his room and slept while the men continued with their entertainment for the night.

The following morning, the King did not emerge from his sleeping quarters. Mosito went to see him, and found him in pain. The son was concerned.

"Don't worry, son, I will be fine. Why do you look so scared? I have to die some or other time," the King said.

"I know, Father," Mosito said, miserably.

"When I die," continued the King, "I shall die in peace. I have sent you to school, found a wife for you, and I have even seen my grandchild. Why would you cry for me? Are you not aware that I am old and I have to go to my ancestors? If I had not done all of these things, I would die reluctantly."

"Ntate, death is something nobody can get used to, although it was created long ago. So if someone you love is taken away by death, it is terrible because you know you will never see that person again. That is why you see me so wretched when you are ill."

The old man's face brightened as if he were in no pain at all, although the pain continued uninterrupted.

"You surprise me, now, Mosito. You say you have been to school and on top of it you are also a Christian: does the Church teach people to fear death?"

"No, it does not."

"The way I see things, according to my illiteracy, death is something that everybody should accept willingly. Death is the key that enables a person to gain the riches he has been working for, since the day he or she was born. To me, death is the Master – in front of him we tremble like slaves. We serve him faithfully for many years, but are promised freedom after a certain period.

"When that day dawns and the slave stands before the Master, he will shiver when he sees the Master putting his hand in his pocket, taking out a key and handing it to the slave, saying: go to my riches and take out the money you need; go and live your free life after death as you wish. Once that has happened, the slave will stop all trembling. With the key in hand, he will enjoy the fruits that he has not known since birth.

"I am also such a slave, my son, because, since I was born I have been serving the Master faithfully, keeping in mind the rewards he promised me. Now, when he calls me, do I not deserve the key that will enable me to get the everlasting reward? And you, Mosito, should you not rejoice with me because of the good fortune I shall receive and the riches I shall have? If you love me, you have to, you simply *have* to, rejoice with me."

"When you put your argument this way, Father, I do understand it, but we human beings, because of our lack of faith, we never view things quite like this. To us, death is like a scarecrow frightening children, and we do not want to hear people talk about death, we shun it, even though we know that it is awaiting us all."

"But bear in mind, son, when a person has served his Creator faithfully, he cannot fear death, his deeds will not make him afraid to appear before Him and speak about what he has done during his lifetime. Shame and fear are the companions of wicked work."

Lekaota spoke with his son for such a long time that Mosito almost forgot that the old man was gravely ill. As it was shearing time, he left after a while to see how the sale of wool was progressing. The old man assured him that the pains were subsiding, so he left him to rest.

That evening, when Mosito returned from the shop, he immediately went to see how his father was. He found him resting in the same way he had left him that morning. In tones that spoke of respect and deep attachment the two continued their conversation.

That evening, after the evening prayer, Mosito decided to sleep in his father's room. In the middle of the night, Mosito was awoken by his father's groans. He quickly lit the lamp and found him sweating profusely, like someone who had been running.

"What's the matter, Ntate?" Mosito was frightened. He could see clearly that his father's condition was alarming, but asked out of common habit.

"The pains are getting worse, son."

Mosito, distressed, did not know what to do. Doctors were miles away and there was no possibility of getting help quickly.

"Tomorrow morning I will rush you to a doctor, Ntate."

"If I am still alive tomorrow morning, we can do so, but the way I feel now, it will be through the mercy of the Almighty. I can feel that I am about to pass beyond the earth."

Mosito loved his father so much that he did not know how to respond to a remark like that. Both of them were quiet for some time. Distraught, like every child who knows the good things a father does for his children, Mosito frantically tried to think what he would do if his father passed on...but then fervently began to console himself with the hope that God would not be so unkind to take the King away while he was still teaching his son how to rule his people.

For a while, the old man's pains subsided and he fell asleep. Mosito remained awake, anxiously thinking. Suddenly he jumped up, terrified that the old man was gone. He rushed to the bed and put his hand on the old man's mouth. Feeling warm air from his father's nostrils, Mosito calmed down with a sigh of relief. He returned to his bed quietly, so as not to awake him, and, after a few minutes, fell into an uneasy asleep.

When the first cock crowed, Mosito felt as if someone was calling to him in his deep and muddled sleep from very far away. He heard the voice calling again, and surfaced. It was his father, and he could hear from his voice that he was in great discomfort. Mosito left his bed and knelt next to his father's.

"What's the matter, Ntate?"

"Just put on the light."

Quickly Mosito lit the candle and went back to his father's bed. Kneeling, he looked at the King's face and realised it had changed considerably. It was evident that he was in great pain.

"What's the matter?" Mosito repeated anxiously. Lekaota was quiet for a while, but then indicated that his son should pull a chair to the bed. Shivering, Mosito fetched it and put it close to the head of the bed and sat down. Desperately, he looked at his father, and was filled with a great pity.

"Mosito, things are shortening. I am on my way. That is why I woke you up from your sleep."

Mosito was tongue-tied and could not utter a word. He breathed heavily. After some time, he frantically asked his father why he was saying he was on his way. Where was he going to?

"How can you ask me...knowing full well the place where all the people go? Where are your grandfathers, your grandmothers, some of your brothers and sisters? The road I am following leads me to where they have gone."

"Oh, Father, is that how it is?"

The old man smiled a bit, like someone who felt good; then was quiet for a moment.

"Yes, that is how it is. It's a fact," he said. "As it is, if my own father had not turned me back just now, saying that I should not leave stealthily, I would already have arrived where I was going. The road leading there is very short, you cannot believe it."

Mosito was confused and speechless. He saw clearly that his father was correct when he said he was on his way. When he looked at the King, he found his face calm and clear, indicating a kind of peace. He was puzzled: the change had occurred so suddenly.

"Now that my grandfather has sent you back, where are you going?"

"No, he did not send me back for good. He simply said I should not go away without your knowledge. That is why I returned. Now that you are awake, I shall go. Now I am healed. For you to see that I no longer belong to this world, please just touch my bedding and feel what it is that I'm sleeping on."

Mosito touched and found the normal everyday bedding.

"You are sleeping on your mattress, Ntate."

King Lekaota laughed a bit, and said, "You say I am on the mattress because you still belong to this world. Where I am sleeping, I am already on soft wool, the kind you will not see in this world. And don't you understand? I say I am healed. All the pain has vanished!"

This stunned Mosito, who began to suspect that the King's illness had affected his brain. But he was only to be startled even further.

"For you to see that I am well, and my brain sharper than before, I am telling you that your aunt, Senate, will soon arrive."

Reeling with all this information, Mosito became even more convinced that senility had touched his father. Suddenly, there was the sound of what seemed to be horses outside. He opened the door, saw two horses being unsaddled, and, when he walked towards them, found that his aunt, Senate, had just arrived.

He took her to where Lekaota was sleeping.

"Oh! Is my mother's child still alive?" she asked, entering. "The day before yesterday I had such a bad dream, so I came. Dreams of this nature usually tell me the truth." She knelt at her brother's bed. Looking at him, she at once started crying loudly.

Mosito reprimanded her, asking her not to cause trouble, as people would be frightened. She listened and was quiet, but tears continued rolling down her cheeks. King Lekaota raised his head slightly and asked to be supported by pillows. Then he ordered Mosito to call his mother, because, since he was now on his way, he did not wish to leave her without her being aware of it.

Mosito hurried and returned with his mother. When they had arrived, the old man spoke.

"My children, as you see me now, I am on my way. I am with these people I can see."

They looked around in the house, but there was nobody.

"Yes, I think it slipped my mind that you won't see them, because you are still with those of flesh and blood. Here is my mother on my left. She is with my grandfather and grandmother, and all our forefathers who left this world long ago. My children who left us are also here. There is Lireko standing next to Mamosito, and there is Mojela standing behind my father. They are all very contented, they have come to fetch me so that I can join them in the pleasure they revel in, in the everlasting glory. But my journey is very short. They tell me it is just like opening a door and stepping outside."

No one knew what to say. Everybody was quiet, observing the patient and then looking at each other. But when they looked at him, they found him well. Clearly the pains that had tortured him were gone. He seemed normal and healthy.

"I have called you to bid you farewell and to recommend Mosito, who will succeed me; recommend him to you while you are looking on so that you will be witnesses of this endorsement."

The queen, 'Mamosito, wept silently and not like an unbeliever. She believed that people do not die; they merely sleep, and wake up to another world of happiness.

"Mosito, today you are a man," said the old man. "I have got you a wife; you have your own home. When I lay my head down, you will remain and will have to rule our people with justice. After I am gone, I would like your rule to bring easiness and not frustration. The community should be at peace as they have been during my reign. The time has come for me to leave you. I wish to finish my life by advising you: be a man and be not deceived by other people; listen to your conscience and do what it tells you to do; reject what it tells you *not* to do. It does not matter whom you are advised by. When your conscience doesn't agree with that advice, do not follow it. Your conscience is your real guide. It is a person's real and sincere friend, and if you obey it, you will also, when your day comes, be like me. Those who are here today, but whom you do not yet see, have been sent to call me home. They will come again, and on that day I shall be among them as well.

"But if you reject your conscience, and waver and allow yourself to be misled by others, doing what is against justice and humanity, know that my face, together with those who are here with me today, will never be seen by you. Even if you do see them, you will not see them as happy as they are today. They will be deeply unhappy, and the very happiness that they are leading me to now, you will never see. I have advised you and that's enough. If you have not heard me by now, you will never hear me."

Then he asked 'Mamosito to pray. After the prayer, he said, "Although I am not a confessing Christian, I have lived a life that is without any blemishes and my weaknesses were those of any human being. I, therefore, yearn to be welcomed into the glory of the ancestors. I allowed you to be Christians and my advice is that you should continue praying, morning, noon and night, because prayer is the key that unlocks the doors of God."

His grandson, Thabo, and Thabo's mother, 'Mathabo, together with other junior wives and their children were called, and when they had all entered, he greeted them one by one with a word of encouragement. Then he concluded, "When I have departed, do not mourn me, because your mourning will distress me. I shall not be able to rest in peace. I am not going far. I am going very near, where I will always be able to see you, any time of day and night – although I will not be able to talk to you, and you will not be able to see me with your eyes."

When they heard the old man's words, they were consoled. The mourning ended in their hearts so that they should not hurt him.

"Yes, I have talked too much and now I am tired. I wish to rest a bit. Do not disturb me."

After he said that, he put his hands on his chest, closed his eyes and that was the end.

4

The installation of Mosito

It was a full year since Lekaota had been in the grave and Mosito had completed the mourning rituals. He was conducting the affairs of the community in the same way he always had while his father was still alive. He had been in charge then, anyway, as his father had been very old when he died, and, while he was preparing him, the King had seen to it that Mosito acted on his behalf. The educated young man was working with his school friends, Pokane and Khosi. They harboured great dreams for the community, but kept them warm, like a broody hen's eggs, until the chicks would be ready to peck the shells and appear. They were waiting for the new king to be formally installed before putting their plans for the good of the community into action.

The day signalling the start of the hatching of their ideas was announced. On the twelfth of March, at ten o'clock in the morning, the Deputy District Commissioner would install Mosito in the place that his father had so carefully prepared for him. His contemporaries were excited, because the various things they had studied in the Cape schools for such a long period could at last be put into practice, and the pleasant fruits be appreciated by the nation.

The people joyfully assembled in the gateway of prosperity, because they were already under the guidance of Mosito and had no misgivings about the abilities of this young new Pharaoh.

Everyone was in a jovial mood because they had seen the manner in which Mosito was conducting their affairs. At the appropriate time, a car was seen approaching from Qacha, heading for the bridge near Mpiti's shop. Three other cars followed, carrying the police. They also crossed the bridge and passed the area where cattle were usually dipped. When the convoy appeared at the royal place, applause and ululating rang out. People shouted "khotso" for peace, "pula" for rain and "nala" for abundance and prosperity.

Those living up in the mountains spilled down and settled in the village, at the royal place, everywhere. The gathering resembled swarms of locusts. There were multitudes of people, multitudes of horses and multitudes of ululations from various directions, even from the road leading to Rooijane.

The Deputy District Commissioner got out of his car and the police escorted him to the podium from where the proceedings would be run. Mosito and his advisors applauded happily. When he got out of the car, this slender one, he was dressed in a snow-white uniform, carrying a shining sword in a black sheath. Even the hat, a hard helmet, was white. Somebody in the crowd remarked: "Indeed, this one is a real Englishman from overseas, from grandmother Victoria's place – definitely not one of these commoners we usually see who claim that they are from overseas! Look at that complexion! You can swear that he washes with milk in the morning and evening!"

Once more, the Basotho applauded. It was as if they were supporting the remarks of the one who had just expressed his opinion. The sound of the ovation crossed the rocks, resounded in the caves and moved up against the rising cliffs that echoed their applause a thousand times.

Everybody sat down. When everything was quiet, the Deputy District Commissioner stood up. All eyes were on him. In the hearts of some a fear was nagging that he might say Mosito could not be installed to succeed his father.

"Children of Moshoeshoe, I greet you. I am very glad that today I have the opportunity to meet all of you here. As you know, this is the second year that I am with you, coming from overseas, from England, where I was born and where I grew up. Ever since I arrived, I have been wishing for this day, the day that I could be part of the district of Qacha ruled by King Mosito.

"Through God's grace, I have been preserved until this day, and that is the reason why I am happy. The mission of the day is to install Mosito as a king to succeed his father, the late King Lekaota, but, before I conclude that mission, I wish to look back to where we have passed. The nation of the Basotho is well known. Although very small when compared with other groups, its fame has spread over the whole world because of its remarkable king, the wondrous King Moshoeshoe, renowned for his wisdom and kindness. It is through him that I am here today. If it was not for his foresight, things would not have developed as they did during those times. Had he not acted, the Basotho nation would have perished as so many others did, scattered by wars and famine.

"To us, the British, it is a great honour to regard the descendants of this great king as part of the British Protectorate. You have a saying in Sesotho, 'otwana la rremoholo sele, le leng sele', meaning: here is the footstep of our forefather, and there is the other one – which means to try your best to rule the people according to Moshoeshoe's wisdom. This I learned when I was still a young man, not realising that one day I would be standing in the very midst of the Basotho, as is the case today. When I arrived in your country, King Lekaota was still alive, and although I met him when his health was already faltering, I got to know him rapidly and discovered that he was one of the Basotho kings still following Moshoeshoe's example.

"Today, I have come to install his son as king. I hope he will follow the route of his father. To you, King Mosito, I wish to quote your Sesotho wisdom: 'morena ke morena ka batho'– a king is a king through his people – because it is important. If you wish for your rule to stand firm, you should rule those under your care with kindness and mercy. You should know that the king is a servant of God to lead people towards righteousness. If you harass your people, they will desert you. You will remain alone, ruling the ruined. Your rule will perish forever. But if you rule well, they will love you and serve you with open hearts. Also, if you rule righteously, you will attract neighbouring communities who will regard this place as their Canaan, and come in great numbers to be under your rule, and your kingship will grow.

"I know that among many African nations there is a belief that one's rule is strengthened by medicinal herbs. And for a king to be loved by his people, he must be treated with horns full of all these very strong herbs of herbalists. But you are educated. I do not need to waste time by telling you that none of this is true. You know, as well as I know, that the greatest medicine for a king, the kind that gives the king dignity and strength, is the love of his people; his kindness, and not things dug from the ground, is decisive. I have been working with you for a reasonably long period, and am inclined to think that you have that kindness. I advise you to keep it up; stay with it. Follow in the footsteps of your great-grandfather, Moshoeshoe, and your rule will progress well.

"Let me conclude: with the power vested in me by the governor and the commissioner, I declare openly amid this congregation that today, in the place of your late father, I install you as king in the district of Qacha, and wish you a long and prosperous rule that will glorify the name of the Basotho."

When he had finished and sat down, the cliffs once more resounded with applause. Then the messenger of the Paramount

King of Lesotho rose and delivered a strong, kind message encouraging Mosito to rule according to how his father had taught him. Applause and ululations followed. Then a young man, remembering the late King Lekaota, felt inspired and began praising him, going back to the Basothos' famous War of the Guns:

Here I praise my bird, Letloepe,
The grey one of Lechesa of Rasenate,
The young man who jumped into a wildfire,
Burning fiercely, smoke reaching high,
Boys scorching their young moustaches,
Scrapers who smell like black pig.

Son of a white man, why are you sleeping in the dark,
While our friends are in wildfires, the hills are coals?
We were honoured with bee sting when we were young,
And here it is today – your neck jerks;
It jolts and lurches, the crow gashes blood
The parents and girlfriends will miss you!

The ghost at Moli's area is very angry!
And speaks a language of overseas,
It demands: swear by the Major Warden of Bloemfontein,
Here at Thesele I will not walk much,
Guns blazing like the stings of bees,
I throw away my gun and run!

When he praised what was on his heart, he pranced. He leapt forward, walked with pretended menace while scratching the ground, raising dust and parading in front of the Deputy District Commissioner, pointing to and fro with his assegai. The crowds cheered. Then he stabbed at the ground with his assegai, going this way and that way, humbling himself, and those who did not know better imagined he was insane.

After the people shouted "khotso, pula, nala", it was the end of the day's official activities and people were served food, school choirs sang, young men danced, young women displayed their art and everybody was happy.

A few days after this, two men, Khati and Sebotsa, came to see Mosito. They were councillors of the late King Lekaota. Khati was an old man, but an absolute giant. Although he had aged much, it was evident that during his prime he was so strong that he could wrestle and pin down a bull so that it stood still. His bloodshot eyes made it very hard to face him, to look for a long time directly into his eyes. There was something in them that was impossible to endure. His contorted face was horrible and had various bumps of different colours. The bridge of his nose had a dent, as if someone had hit him with a fist while the bones were still soft.

The other councillor, Sebotsa, was an old, short man with small shrew-like eyes. Facing him, one would find that he blinked his eyes habitually in a kind of nervous twitching movement, so that some people nicknamed him Ntutubatsane – to close one's eyes. On his face he had a scar in the form of a horse shoe. Those who knew him said that he had been kicked by a horse when he was young and had nearly died.

The two old men found Mosito with his close friends, Khosi and Pokane. The three of them were always together. The two were Mosito's advisers: Khosi the secretary and Pokane the chairman of the council. He was in charge of all the cases that were heard. They worked most harmoniously together and it was clear that great things were in store for the community.

When the old men arrived, they greeted the King and sat down. After exchanging the usual formalities, Khati said, "Your worship, we would like to have a meeting with you, child-of-my-master." When he said that, he looked at Sebotsa, and looked down. Sebotsa looked at Mosito, looked at Khosi and Pokane, and blinked repeatedly.

"I am listening, old man," said Mosito. "You came at the right time because you find me with these two gentlemen who assist me."

He pointed at Khosi and Pokane.

"You may introduce the idea you wish to discuss with us."

"Well, our king, the news we would like to discuss is intended for you alone, and we would appreciate it highly if the two gentlemen could excuse us by leaving the room. That will give us an opportunity to discuss freely, with nothing to fear," said Sebotsa, blinking slowly as if painfully.

"Sebotsa stated the case clearly enough," said Khati. "This is a case that you should know of, now that you are king; a case that should be known to the king only."

"What case is it that Khosi and Pokane should not know about? I hope you are aware that Khosi and Pokane and I are inseparable. We are one ear, one eye, one mouth – in other words, we are one body. I would appreciate it highly if you would be kind enough to state the case so that they can also listen and advise me accordingly, if, indeed, what you have in mind is something that needs advice."

"Please, our king, listen to us and do as we request you. We are old people as you see us, and we know what we are talking about," said Sebotsa.

"If a case cannot be presented where two of my advisors are present, listening, I will have failed."

As Mosito said this, he stood up and went to stand at the court door. The two old men did not move. He came back and looked at them and repeated, "I say, if your case cannot be heard by my two advisors, it will be useless to me. You may leave with it. It won't matter."

He sat down again, looked at Khosi and Pokane, shook his head slightly, and then looked at the old men.

There was silence, and then Khati said, "Dear King, as you see us in front of you, grey-headed, bald here and there, do you think we came here to be a joke? Please just listen to us, let us talk to you and then we will leave you with your friends."

This time the two young men looked at each other and Khosi said, "Our dear king, maybe the old men know something that might be useful to you. Allow us to give you a chance, so that they can feel free to talk and tell you what is on their minds."

"I agree with him, my lord," said Pokane, getting up to leave the court hut.

"No, do not go out," said Mosito, "do not go out. If it is you two who decide to give them a chance, then I accept that, but I want everybody here to know that nothing can separate you from me. We grew up together. We herded cattle together, attended school together, and I do not see what should separate us now that we are adult men. I, however, shall pretend, today only – but that will be the first and the last time that I will do it. Please remain here. We shall go to another house where there will be no disturbance."

He went out, followed by Khati and Sebotsa. Pokane and Khosi remained in the court hut, asking themselves what it was that these two old men wanted to discuss with Mosito.

"He will see now, our Homeboy, how the problems begin, now that he is king," said Pokane. "But you must remember that to these older people, being a councillor is a great honour. Maybe they are advising him to stop working with us, because they think we will mislead him. To them, we know very little, all we do is to talk English, and that, for them, is precisely what misleads us." Pokane laughed, while shaking his head.

"You know," said Khosi, "what you are saying is true. I also think that they are going to discuss precisely this issue. But if Mosito allows himself to be duped by these two old men, he would be a fool."

"No, he cannot allow that, even if they threaten him."

Mosito walked to the house, where he could talk undisturbed with Khati and Sebotsa. After they had settled down, Khati insisted that the door be closed, as he did not wish anyone to hear what they were about to discuss. Mosito agreed, and suddenly was intrigued.

"The talks have started," said Khati.

"That is exactly what I want," Mosito said, crossing his legs to listen.

"Our dear king, we are aware that because of your education, you do not regard us as people who could guide you: we, who wear blankets day in and day out. However, clinging to those who wear small jackets, like you, won't help. We deem it our duty to come and meet with you, because we are the men who served the late King Lekaota. He instructed us to remain loyal, to advise you, and to look after you. That is why we have come to see you today. Yes, this is just an introduction. The matter we wish to discuss with you, you will hear from Sebotsa."

Mosito said, "I understand when you say that my father said you should look after me, and I am glad that you have obeyed his word. But I want you to know and understand very well that my father did not say that, in advising me, you should separate me from my contemporaries. I started working with Pokane and Khosi while my father was still alive, and on no occasion did I hear him say that he was unhappy that I work with them.

What I do remember is that he specifically said I should stick to these two young men, as they would help me to become a better human being. And the manner in which they conduct themselves towards me convinces me that, indeed, I am dealing with real men, men who will be with me through thick and thin. Now, I heard you say that they are men with 'small jackets'! I have to inform you, I detest such remarks. I do not think them funny; they are disgraceful. The word 'libakana' – small jackets – is derogatory and belittling, and the one who belittles or disparages these two men belittles me, because they and I are one. I have given you a hearing."

"Well, you should not take us amiss, son of my master. Leleme le nne le tshwepohe ka nako e nngwe – there are times when the tongue goes astray," said Sebotsa, blinking several times in succession.

"But let me start with the matter that has brought us here," continued Sebotsa. "It is our Sesotho tradition that, when a person is installed as king, he should not stay where his father lived. He should move to another place nearby, and settle there."

"That I know, old man, I need not be told that. I do not see the need to move. Here where I live currently, I will be able to rule without having to build a new house. Is that all you wanted to talk to me about?"

"Well, then, why are you in such a hurry? I am arriving at the main case that brought us here," said Sebotsa.

"Pardon me, I *am* in a hurry. I thought that if you were finished, I should be going, because there are letters to be written to the Deputy District Commissioner and the Paramount King, and when you came in just now, I was discussing that with Khosi and Pokane. Because of you I have already delayed them."

Undaunted, Sebotsa continued, "When a king builds a new home, he must strengthen and peg it with a strong charm. In the old days, such a horn was easy to fill because there were many wars, and the potions were always available, but today, as there are no more wars, such potions are more and more difficult to get."

"What kind of potions can only be procured during a war?"

Sebotsa closed his eyes interminably. It was evidently difficult for him to speak openly and state what was on his mind. Then Khati took over.

"My dear king, I am aware that Sebotsa is hesitant. Let me call a spade a spade. The potion needed is the liver of a man, and that is why he said it is difficult to get, because there are no longer any wars. The liver could still be obtained easily if you exhumed a dead person at the cemetery, but for the medicine to work really well and properly such a liver should be of a person who has just been killed. So, the liver of a person who died of natural causes would not suffice. You have to find a victim so that you can use his liver."

"Goodness me! Now look here, the two of you, do not force me to lose my respect for you as old people and disgrace your grey hair. What you have said just now should never ever be repeated, never! Let us presume it was a slip of the tongue. If you were not such old men, I would have ordered your removal for a very good lashing, so that you can stop with these terrible habits. Can you imagine? Villages fortified by means of human livers! Your old age means absolutely nothing to you! I have a good mind to call the police to arrest you! To how many people do you teach such evil deeds?"

"My lord, you say that out of ignorance. You are still young," said Khati, his eyes more bloodshot than usual, and the dent on the bridge of his nose looking deeper. "You see how old we are. I lived with your father, so why would we want to lead you astray?"

"Don't you dare mention my father! He never did such a thing!"

"I do not say that he did something like this; I know very well he didn't, but I am trying to give you a true way of dealing with facts. If you wish your rule to be strong and real, I beg you to listen to us, my lord, and heed our advice."

Sebotsa was quiet because Khati had taken over. All he did was blink repeatedly. It was probably clear to him that this case did not augur well for them and he was at a loss as to how to overcome the King's stinging remarks.

"I have answered you and I have finished," said Mosito. "I shall never do what you suggest, no matter what. There is no village or home that will be fortified by the use of human liver. And that is finished!"

The way he spoke made it clear that this was the end of the discussion and he was not waiting for a response from them. He went out and Sebotsa and Khati followed. They left with swollen lips, their noses being as huge as the Souru Mountain!

5

The minimising of the courts

The month of June in the year 1944 had just begun. As the Second World War was still in progress, wherever men gathered there was only one subject: when the war would end so that the Basotho soldiers could return home.

One Monday, Mosito was sitting conversing with his councillors. His friends, Pokane and Khosi were present, because wherever he was, they were also there. Apart from them, Khati and Sebotsa and many other men were also present. The court hut was almost full. A big fire warmed the place.

Next to the fire was a pot of beer, and Sebotsa was stirring it. The men were drinking and all was well. The work in the fields, the reaping, thrashing and transporting of mealies – all were done and it was pleasant to enjoy what was in their homes.

"You who read newspapers, what do they say, when will the war end?" Sebotsa, as he asked this question, was holding a calabash. He stirred the beer with it, then drew and drank. As he swallowed, he closed his eyes a bit, licked his moustache and it was clear that he was drinking something he deeply enjoyed. He looked at Pokane. "I am asking – what do they say, when will it end? So that our children can come home."

"We don't know, but I suppose it is about to end. Last year the Italians surrendered and on the thirteenth of October they joined the English and the Allies to fight the Germans. It is also said that their commander, Mussolini, has been captured."

Khati moved slightly and scratched his back, contorting his face into many folds, so that, with his eyes and bumps he resembled a bull ready to fight after a mighty bellow. "Does that mean that Hitler is now fighting alone?'

"Yes, and it appears that he is in real trouble, because on the sixth of June the English and the Allies attacked Germany from all sides. That means the war is now being fought in Germany, at home, and, as you know, once the fight has reached home, it is very bad because the children might also be hit by the bullets. As I see things, the Germans will surrender even before Christmas because they have been so severely weakened."

"That cannot happen," said the old man, Khati. "You previously informed us, you who read newspapers, that that young man, Hitler, whose moustache resembles a brown-haired caterpillar, thinks that the English will never overpower him, that he is a complete wizard! It looks to me that they will eventually have to leave him as he is."

"You know, you who always have such a lot to say about Sesotho witchcraft," – this came from Khosi – "why don't any of you arrest him, using the medicinal abilities you claim to possess? Go and get hold of him, arrest him and hand him over to the British general, Montgomery. You can earn thousands of pounds as a reward from the Kingdom of Your Royal Highness, the Queen. On the other hand, if someone indeed manages to capture Hitler, and bring him to Lesotho, I doubt that the amount of money spoken about would ever be paid."

"But the truth is, King Mosito, our children continue to die overseas, what will we, the Basotho, get as compensation for our blood that is spilled daily, and will continue to be spilled as the war rages on? Only last year you said a ship sank with six hundred and twenty-four Basotho, and that means orphans and widows in their hundreds. Who will look after those children? Who will support those widows?" As Khati said that, it was his turn to take the drinking calabash, dip it into the beer pot, draw, and drink.

"The government will give compensation money that will help the children until they reach maturity," answered King Mosito.

"But, my morena, I, personally, do not believe this compensation story."

"Why, old man?" asked Pokane.

"I say I do not believe it because the money they receive will be too little. If you look at a widow with four or five children, and a pound or two: is that the kind of money that can maintain her under such difficulties? I doubt it!"

"If you always view matters in such a way," said Pokane, "you would have been the appropriate man to represent us, indeed. I agree wholeheartedly that the money they promised to pay a soldier cannot support even one person. But what can we do if the money does not belong to us? Despite being the money from the taxes we pay, it is in the hands of the Europeans!"

At that moment, a boy arrived who had been sent to Mpiti's shop to collect post. He gave the letters to Khosi and left. Khosi looked at them, and then opened and read them, passing them over to Mosito to look at them himself.

Among those letters was a greyish booklet with the picture of a crocodile on it and the words: 'Printed in Lesotho'. After King Mosito had looked at it for some time, he gave it back to Khosi, asking him to read what was written in it so that he could relate the message to everybody. Khosi paged through, reading here and there, checking the captions, suddenly grunting.

"What's happening, Khosi? Why don't you read so that we may hear," demanded Khati.

"It's nothing."

"Why then are you making these sounds?"

"It was only because of a paragraph."

"I said: read it to us. We do not know, but we have to know," said Khati.

"It will be best if you get the news the day the King has a meeting."

"Do we need a whole panel of councillors before we can get news from people from faraway places?"

"Just read it to him, Khosi, so that he can leave you alone. You know that nothing else will be discussed except this booklet," joked King Mosito.

"Well, then, since the King instructs me, let me read. This booklet is from our Paramount King, to notify everybody about what is happening with the creation of a fund for the monies of the nation. He wishes us to inspect all these suggestions, and render our views in full and openly, without any fear. When the nation has expressed its views, the Paramount King will take note, and then formulate his considered views on the whole issue, to be read to the Council of the Nation, 'Mantsebo Seeiso, signed by our Paramount King, on 23 June 1944."

"Is it this that caused you to make all that funny noise?" asked the old man, Sebotsa, blinking furiously as usual.

"No, it's not that, but, as I said, I was reading the *letter* that informs us about the booklet."

"Well, we have heard that, so now tell us, we're listening."

Khosi reopened the book and read: "With regard to the courts, the committee has discovered that the Basotho have 1,340 courts that review cases at present. This is far too many, and the number has to be reduced to 117, which is the appropriate number to administer justice cases, according to the needs of the nation..."

Sebotsa's eyes twitched torturously. "Is it said that the number of courts should be reduced? That there are too many?"

"Yes, it says the number should be reduced, if I have read properly. There are too many."

All the men were quiet for a long time and it was clear that each one was trying to digest the information, to assess how the position of King Mosito would be affected. After some silence, King Mosito said, "It does not say how many courts will remain here in Qacha?"

Khosi paged through the booklet again. "There must be an explanation somewhere." He checked the pages carefully and saw that Qacha district should only have ten courts.

"Fellow-men, this is a tragedy," said Khati.

"What kind of tragedy?" asked Pokane.

"You ask what *kind* of tragedy? Don't you realise that we shall be deprived of our court?"

"How can we be deprived of it?"

"We shall be deprived of it because it is written here that we are near Ratšoleli's place and our cases will be heard there."

Sebotsa closed his eyes. "Do you see why I condemn the British rule? Our children have died and they are still dying. They continue to die while the war simply goes on; dying for the so-called justice it's alleged that they are fighting for. But is this justice, what they are now doing to our kings?"

"But at present we are unable to explain convincingly whether it is justice or not, because we have not yet examined this booklet thoroughly; and you should also remember that this booklet is not yet the law. It is merely talking about what was produced by the committee that was chosen, which the nation may accept or reject. That is why the Paramount King says that the nation should digest these proposals and if the nation does not go along with them, they have the power to reject them," Khosi explained.

"That is typical of the Europeans," said Khati, "when they wish to introduce something. They normally say people must come up with ideas, and when that has been done, they don't regard these as in line with their own ideas. Tell me, who will be for this idea? But the government will act as it wishes, whether we oppose it or not."

"Well, I say that we should give Khosi a chance to read this booklet carefully," said King Mosito. "He should examine all its corners and explain to us how the Paramount King wants to implement things. When we have heard the outcome, we will be able to analyse our views, so that the day we are called to Ratšoleli's place we will know exactly what in this booklet we want and what we do not want."

"You are correct, my lord," said Pokane. "Maybe, once we have examined it properly, we will discover that the suggestions of the committee are in fact good enough, and perhaps the first step leading to where we all eventually want to arrive at, namely, independence. I agree wholeheartedly that we should not rush to conclusions."

After this intervention, the issue of reducing the number of courts was no longer raised and people only talked about other matters, until the time of closing the meeting, so that everybody could go home to sleep.

Khosi and Pokane stayed awake for a long time that evening, examining the suggestions contained in the booklet, so that they could explain the gist and details to members of the council, and carefully guide them. They knew that changes of this nature were not always easily accepted, as many people still wanted things to run according to the old ways.

The following day, the men arrived punctually at the court hut. Because they had dispersed the previous night without any further talk about reducing the number of courts, most of them had spent the greater part of the night restlessly brooding over it. They were, therefore, eager to listen to Khosi, who was to enlighten them properly about the suggestions related by the Paramount King.

When all had settled in the court hut, Sebotsa introduced the discussion by asking whether Khosi had examined the committee's booklet thoroughly.

"Yes, I have gone through it well, and it contains significant news. The ideas are very important."

"Now, quench our thirst," ordered Sebotsa.

Khosi produced a small piece of paper, examined it again and then said, "The suggestions in the booklet are too numerous. So, on this piece of paper I have jotted down only the main points, the important ones I would like to put before you."

There was absolute silence, every man asking himself what could be these points?

Khosi continued. "The first point is that the payment to the courts will no longer go to the kings, but should be deposited in the community's saving fund. I think the main reason why this has been done is because many kings exploit their subjects. They give people excessive fines for any wrongdoing, because they know that the money will be theirs."

Sebotsa cleared his throat, blinked his eyes and said, "Now, if the fines will be collected for the national fund, how will the kings live?"

"Your question leads me to the second point. Seeing that the kings will no longer be able to feed themselves from the payment of court fines, they will be paid a salary according to their rank and responsibilities, in terms of the work they are doing for the people."

"I'm still meditating; continue," said Khati.

"The third point – and remember, at this stage these are mere suggestions – relates to lost properties where the owners do not show up. These lost properties should no longer be taken by the kings, but should rather be sold and the money deposited into the national fund."

"But that's unreasonable!" said Sebotsa, with Khati concurring. "It becomes very clear that our kings will simply be young cattle herders for that fund."

"How will a king become a herding boy, as he is, anyway, the person who looks after these lost properties?" countered Pokane.

"Please, people, payment is made because the king looks after this lost property," argued Sebotsa. "It is payment for the trouble the king takes, looking after it. He does this on behalf of the people."

"Looking after lost property is part of the work a king has to perform, it is part of his governing, and will be included in his salary," Khosi explained.

"Wait a bit, there; just explain to me in simple terms, Khosi – now that the kings will be paid, how much will they receive?"

"It doesn't say in this booklet, because all the kings are not included here, only the senior kings and their deputies are mentioned. The kings will be paid according to the taxes their subjects pay. That means if a king has many taxpayers, he has more work and his salary will also be higher. But where there are fewer taxpayers, his salary will probably be less.

"On page fifty of the booklet, it indicates that in the Leribe district there are 43,000 taxpayers; therefore the committee specifies that the king is entitled to the salary of £1,680 per annum. While the king of the Qacha district has 13,262 taxpayers, and therefore the committee should pay him £1,296 per annum. Now, I hope things are a bit clearer?"

"I understand when you speak," said Sebotsa, "but I—"

"Steady, Sebotsa, let me enter here," said Khati. "So, where does King Mosito feature in these conditions? If there is justice in this proposal, he would be indicated, but I do not hear you say anything about him."

"Yes, of course, in this pamphlet he is not mentioned, but seeing that these are just suggestions, there should be nothing to be concerned about. Because on the same page fifty, where the remuneration of the kings is given, there is something in section two below, where it says: 'People indicated in this section are those the committee found to be known as the kings of the districts. If there is a king omitted from this list, who thinks he should be included as the king of a district, he is free to report his case to the Paramount King.'"

"How many kings does the booklet name in the Qacha district?" asked Khati once more.

"Only one."

"No second one?"

"No, only one."

"We have to sit down on this. If a king such as Mosito can be left out, and we don't vehemently object, we are throttling the child of our king. Isn't that so, Sebotsa?"

"I agree, absolutely. If there is still a chance to lodge a complaint, we must do so."

Throughout the discussion, King Mosito kept quiet, as though it had nothing to do with him, until Sebotsa asked him directly whether the suggestions of the committee were in order for him or not.

"As far as I am concerned," responded Mosito, "there is nothing wrong with them. What I appreciate most of all in the suggestions is that even the widows of the senior kings of Lesotho will receive a remuneration. That will be great mercy to them, because, until now, they have been simply abandoned, with no one caring for them. With these new conditions, they might earn something, which is preferable to being simply overlooked. Giving the widows a little share will reduce the burden the Paramount King has been shouldering for years. These recommendations also make me realise again that people are not happy about unjust cases, based on unjust laws, used by kings to benefit personally from fines."

Khati tightly screwed up his face, his eyes even smaller than usual. His behaviour indicated total opposition to what King Mosito was saying, but he kept quiet.

"Once, I visited another king, whose name I cannot recall at this moment," continued Mosito. "And I discovered that he was holding somebody's sheep that had been found in the grazing area reserved for the king. By the time the owner found them, they had been in captivity for two days. But now, that king had his eye on a hamel among them, and so demanded to be paid a shilling per day for each sheep. This meant a pound for the two days! The owner simply didn't have that kind of money, so the king told him to pay with the hamel.

"What else could the poor man do? He parted with that animal, but the moment he left with his other sheep, it was slaughtered immediately. What kind of justice was that? Therefore, I really feel that if these recommendations could be accepted, cases of blatant unfairness would cease. When a person pays, he will get a receipt to indicate his payment for the case, while in the council book a copy of that will remain, so that when the books are audited, everything will be reflected.

"Seeing that payments will no longer go to the king, he will begin to charge a person a normal fee and the payment itself will benefit the community. Even if the king raises a hundred pounds a day on fines, that money will not increase his remuneration. He will be paid a normal amount. And equally, if he raises one shilling for that day, nothing will alter in his salary. I find these changes very fair indeed. If things were to go according to my thinking, these recommendations should be accepted immediately so that next year they are put in place and justice and fairness for the communities could begin."

Everybody looked at one another and nobody said anything. King Mosito had shut their mouths completely. He was in harmony with all the things they were making a noise about.

6

The fruit of disharmony

Towards the end of 1945, the case of a national fund for the community had been discussed and endorsed by the National Council in Maseru. Everywhere in Lesotho people were talking about this new step sanctioned by the people, and everybody was anticipating its implementation. Soon afterwards, the government selected young men to be taken to Maseru and trained on how to handle the money, in order to oversee the funds of the various branches to be introduced to all areas in Lesotho.

Although the news was welcomed by many, in some quarters there were a few who said that these changes would undermine kingship among the Basotho. Every district had its discontented, and at Qacha we could name Sebotsa and Khati, and a few others.

After the question of the fund was settled, it was realised that King Mosito, being near Ratšoleli's, would lose his council, so that people could go straight to Ratšoleli's. Many people were happy about this, because they thought that justice would prevail sooner than in the past, when they had to go through many channels before ending up at Ratšoleli's court. The consequent delay in finalising their cases used to frustrate many people.

Khati and Sebotsa and those siding with them were greatly opposed to these new arrangements. They wanted King Mosito to object, so that he could retain his council. They were also very unhappy that Mosito's remuneration would not be substantial, because, by removing his council, he would have less work and responsibility. Khati and Sebotsa decided to urge Mosito to lodge a protest. The Basotho have a saying: 'ngwana ya sa lleng o shwela tharing' – a baby who does not cry, dies in the cradle-skin. A few individuals – Khati, Sebotsa, Maime and three other men – approached the King. They found Mosito alone; Khosi had gone to see Ratšoleli, and Pokane had gone to Qacha.

After a few minutes, Khati introduced the news. "Our lord, we have come to see you in connection with grave matters. We ask and beg you to listen prudently, because these matters concern you."

"I am listening, old man."

Khati took out his snuff, emptied some in his hand and put it in his mouth. After spitting twice, he began. "Our king, our mission is a single one. Son of my master, you must meet with the Paramount King to review your case carefully. You should have your rights attended to, so that you have your own council, and you should be recognised as the king of your area. According to how Khosi explained to us, we noted that in all the districts of Lesotho the only areas where there is only one king were our area, Quthing and Mokhotlong. In some districts there are kings who qualify to be called area kings, whereas in our opinion they are not nearly as recognisable as you are."

"Old man," said Mosito, "I hear your case but I don't under-stand it. I can only say I hear what you say because you are speaking Sesotho. But I don't understand because I do not have the facts yet to support my own argument."

"Our king," said Sebotsa, "I understand when you say that. And at the moment I also don't have evidence to support our case. But, even so, I agree with Khati that we should not leave this matter unattended. We shall supply the reasons for our plea, if you allow us to speak. There is nothing that can beat men when they stand together. At the moment, I want to point out one thing: there are kings who kept their areas, but they are not nearly as educated as you are. We feel that the government should help you to get the areas that match your qualification – the details can be sorted out later."

Among these men was one called Maime. He was a middle-aged man, tall and strong, with a resonant, strong voice. When he spoke, the sound thundered through the air. He was the caretaker of reserved grazing, and when the boys talked about him, they called him Poko-Poko, because he used to lash them at the cattle posts. Today, he was quiet while Khati and Sebotsa talked. When they had finished, he came up with his story.

"My lord, you know, I am not a talkative person, but today I deem it necessary to speak. The way in which you have been treated by those from Maseru does not satisfy me in the least. I worked many times with the late King Lekaota when you were still a child, and I know everything. Every year, the amount raised from lost sheep went through my hands. When sold according to the selling price of those times, before the Second World War, they yielded more than two hundred pounds. Together with the fines from the courts, the amount would come to roughly five hundred pounds. In addition to what King Lekaota earned, the full sum was about seven hundred pounds per annum. But, according to how I see things now, your annual salary would amount to one or two hundred pounds at most. Actually, it would be less: about one hundred and twenty pounds per year. So, taking everything into account, being deprived of the council and fines for lost property, your annual salary would be less than six hundred pounds. This is outrageous! A king of your calibre carrying such a heavy load won't cope under such circumstances."

Khati, Sebotsa and the other men nodded their agreement constantly and often looked at King Mosito to see how he reacted to what Maime was saying.

"It is true: the money from the fund will pay widows," Maime continued, "but those will be the widows of the senior kings only, starting with the wives of King Letsie. Nothing is said about the wives of other kings. At present you are able to support King Lekaota's ten wives because you still get money from the council and the fines from lost property, but, as of next year, I do not see how you will manage that load, because the source that has produced money has been diverted into another direction and your river of money is running dry."

At this, Khati nodded his head emphatically. "You have spoken very well indeed, Maime, and the King should note that very well."

King Mosito sat quietly and it was evident that, despite everything that had been said, he was unmoved.

Maime continued, his voice rumbling like heavy thunder. "I know that, due to your education, you will not allow yourself to be convinced by illiterate people like us. But if you think carefully, you will realise that if you do not rise and protest now, you will be regarded a big fool! Wake up, our dear king, and protest like a man, otherwise, what you are will be steadily throttled, while we are looking on!"

"I hear you – Maime, Khati and Sebotsa. What you are saying is logical. In reality, I will be unable to perform my duties. This is how it is: my right hand has been chopped off. I cannot work. So, I shall consider this case carefully, and, when I have reached the place where I cannot go further, I shall inform you on how I intend to forge ahead."

When a king has spoken like this, the meeting usually closes and nothing further is said. The men filed out and left Mosito alone to digest matters.

That evening, King Mosito met his friends, Pokane and Khosi, and related all that had been discussed with the old men earlier in the day.

"Now, dear friends, I want you to advise me carefully on what I should do when matters are at an uphill, like this. Personally, I am in a fix." After that, he kept quiet.

They all seemed to be thinking about what they should say next. Eventually, Pokane said, "Chief, this matter is really very serious and you have not acted wisely. I think we should at least do some research and find out what other kings think, who have also been stripped of their power. How big were their losses, if any, if their salaries were taken into account? One should remember that even when a salary is reduced, it may not affect a person too harshly. However, if we are not clear about the way things are done, your loss could indeed be considerable, my lord."

"But what should I do? When you tell me about my loss, you tell me something I know very well! So, how does that help me? What I want to know is, what I can do to compensate for these losses I will suffer? And bear in mind that when the fund plan is implemented, I will be carrying the heavy load of my father's widows on my shoulders."

"But I detest this kind of protest," said Pokane.

"Oh! So you want me to persevere in carrying my burden, even when I have been saddled with a heavy bag, put on an oozing wound?"

"That will depend on you, my lord. I am saying: leave things as they are. What I do not like are the expenses attached to challenging the matter in court. The way I see it, your protest will not end up at Matsieng. If it comes to the worst, it could move up to the Lesotho High Court. There, you will have to get an advocate to represent you, and truly, their fees are very high. We do not know what such a man may charge, but I've heard up to one hundred pounds... And after paying that amount, you may still lose the case! On top of that, you have to pay all the other legal costs, which apparently simply keep rising. That is why, in the end, one realises that one should have left things as they were. But, of course, by then it is too late."

"And you, Khosi, what do you think?"

"My lord, I really support Pokane. These disputes about the areas of kings usually create problems and fierce animosities, and if a person wishes to live in peace with others, the best thing to do is to put them aside, ignore them if possible. Such cases are a source of many other things, bad things, for the people. Maybe, my lord, you suspect that we say these things because they do not really concern us, and we do not feel the pain as you do.

"But, my lord, I want you to remember that, while we were growing up together, our fervent wish, the three of us, was always that one day we would see the whole Basotho nation independent, ruling itself as one and managing its own affairs. To enter into a dispute such as this one places a big stone on the path of progress for Lesotho and the Basotho; and by so doing, you yourself shift backwards on the road of progress.

"You are educated, my lord, and you know that one person may save a nation; a person who understands that he has to sacrifice himself so that, even if he dies, his people and his children can live in freedom.

"In my mind, I feel that you, because of your education, have been chosen to sacrifice yourself so that the Basotho nation may live. You are not the only king who has been left aside, who feels that he should have been included among those who get good salaries. If all those kings protest, will that not derail this big, wonderful scheme? For me, this fund is a stepping stone towards independence and if we can remove this obstacle of smaller areas, we shall be where we have all desired to be. Accept the challenge, my lord, and the Almighty will bless you a thousand times.

"I also want to add that our late King Lekaota left you great wealth, so that you will be in a position to live and help the orphans who are under your care. Can you, therefore, cry over the five or six hundred that you will lose, knowing full well that every year you get one thousand pounds or more from the wool of your sheep? This is a small matter and small things occupy small minds, but you, because you are educated, should not worry about such a minor issue. Sit down, our king, and work, and we will help you. I say that your protest should be the good work you do, while you are silent. The Paramount King and the government are not blind. When they see your good work performed in silence, they will arrange things for you. Your silence will be supported by the good deeds performed silently."

"I understand your advice and see your approach," said King Mosito. "I welcome it and feel strengthened. During the day, when you were away I was very frustrated, so much so that I did not know what to think or do. To be honest, I had already decided, aggravated by the words of Maime and company, to protest. But you know; now you've given me courage and I feel brave enough to sacrifice myself, as you put it, so that my father's people may live. I thank you for consoling me during my state of weakness. Now I am in a position to face Khati squarely."

The following day, King Mosito summoned Khati and his friends. When they settled down, he challenged them at once. "Yesterday I said I was going to digest your case. Today I have, and I have come to a conclusion. Let me sum up the matter you brought here: I wish to thank you for your advice, but regret to say that I am bound to differ and object. The reasons that compel me to differ are many and need not be stated. There is to be no argument. I wish you to accept, without any disagreement, that I am not going to dispute anything. I drop all claims and am satisfied with my position. By ruling this way, I am not *disputing* your advice; I simply find it beyond my ability! But, in future, please continue raising your opinions without fear. Remember that you are always welcome here, and whenever I find your opinions appropriate or useful, I will accept them. But this particular one was not tolerable to me."

That was the end of the meeting. The old men left the King alone, their hearts saddened, not knowing what the next step should be now that he had opted not to change his mind.

7

The Queen speaks out

Khati, Sebotsa and Maime were not satisfied that King Mosito refused to heed their advice. Whenever the three of them met, their discussion was about what could be done to make Mosito listen to them, because they were convinced that Mosito had a case that could be put to a court of law. Their reason for sticking so stubbornly to their idea could only be grasped by someone who grew up with the Basotho, who knew how they reasoned when dealing with their kings.

One evening Khati invited Sebotsa and Maime to his house. His first words were, "My fellow men, we should really fear the tie-wearers!"

"What do you mean by this?" asked Maime.

"I say so because of Pokane and Khosi – these boys mislead the King very badly. They keep him under their armpits so that some of us no longer know what our standing is. During the time of King Lekaota we were important men. But these days I feel greatly disturbed."

Sebotsa blinked and twitched as usual. "If we could find a way of getting him out of the grip of these boys, we could turn him into a man, but now he is in trouble, he does not want to hear anything said against them. If you talk about them disparagingly, he may even challenge you physically. Education has harmed us and contaminated our king. He is sucking up to those boys and refuses to go against them by going to court. It is clear to me that he could win his case."

"So what are you saying?" asked Maime. "Do you suggest that we leave him like that, even when we notice that he goes astray out of youthful ignorance? But will that be the right thing to do? *We* are the ones to advise him because *we* were his father's advisors."

Khati said, "This is the reason I called you. We have to discuss this matter, and see what can be done."

Sebotsa, carried on, "We are duty-bound. We are destined to advise him, but if somebody ignores your advice, there is no way you can force it on him."

Maime said, "Well, maybe we have not failed yet. If we think carefully, we have a big weapon we haven't used up until now. The day we fire it and still lose, then we can surrender, admit our loss and let things go their own way."

"A weapon? What are you talking about, Maime?" Khati and Sebotsa spoke simultaneously. Surprise could be read on their faces, as they had not expected something like this.

"Think with me. In the Holy Scriptures, when Satan saw that he could not persuade Adam to do something, he kicked him in the stomach by turning to Eve. Each time you struggle to catch an animal, you simply catch its young, walk away and the mother will follow you. You put the young where you want the mother to go and leave. After you have left, the mother will go in and you can now close the entrance. The animal will be captured and that's its end.

"With human beings, it's the same. When a man does not listen, kick him in the stomach by going to his wife. If you manage to convince her, the husband is like clay in your hands; you can mould him to your heart's delight. Our final weapon is Queen 'Mathabo. We have to test her feelings. I think, because she is a Mosotho woman, she will catch on quickly to what we want. If she agrees to assist us, we shall catch Mosito through her help."

"Now you are really talking, Maime!" Sebotsa was highly pleased. "You are right! This trap never fails. You know, I somehow knew when I didn't see you these past few days that you were trying to find a solution. People often want to know why I love you. They don't realise: I love you because of your sharp intellect!"

Sebotsa, however had a qualm. "Who will talk to the Queen? You know that he loves her very much, so I don't believe that he will oppose her. But what I fear most of all is that, after we have spoken to her, she will go and tell Mosito that we are trying to persuade her to help us. That could spoil matters even further."

Then it became clear: no one was prepared to speak to the Queen. What Sebotsa was saying was true. No one really knows how matters stand between a husband and wife. It was dawning on them that the pros and cons of their approach hadn't been fully weighed.

"How about you going, Sebotsa?" said Khati.

Sebotsa repeatedly blinked, twitched and distorted his neck and face. Although he did not say anything, his body's actions made it clear that he was unwilling to go but had difficulty expressing it.

Maime broke the long silence. "Evidently no one is willing. So I shall force myself to meet her. Although I am nervous, I shall try like a man, and if I fail, fail like a man." He thundered that last sentence loudly enough to crack the wall of the house they were sitting in.

"You have spoken like a man," said Khati. "And I hope that you will succeed in your honourable mission."

So they continued talking until it was time for bed, and the visitors left.

The following day was a Tuesday. In the early morning, Mosito and a few men, among them Khosi and Pokane, left for the kampong at Qacha. Khati and company met again and continued to discuss the matter at the court hut, planning when to go to meet the Queen so that she could understand the seriousness of the matter.

"Are you ready, Sebotsa?"

Although still hesitant, when Sebotsa heard Khati speaking, he said yes, everything was in order and they should go. Arriving at the Queen's home, they found her happy, as usual – her kindness left nothing to be desired. They had come to the place where, in the time of King Lekaota, they had been waited on and served many times.

"Our queen," said Maime after they had settled down and begun to relax, "we are here today about an important issue we wish to discuss with you and for which we need some assistance from you."

"What could that be," she asked, laughing. "What could be the news you wish to bring to me, good people?"

The three men looked at each other. Although they did not say anything, it was evident that they were relieved about the way the Queen answered them. They felt suddenly that yes, things might turn out well.

"We need your help, our queen," said Maime, "because our king doesn't want to give us an ear when we try to advise him about things that concern him greatly; things touching the lives of his children – in other words, also Thabo's future."

Suddenly the Queen looked alarmed. It was clear that when they mentioned Thabo, they touched a very tender spot.

"What kind of things?"

Her desire to hear the news had been aroused, and there was no way she could hide it any more, even if she wished to.

"We hope you have heard already that the government wishes to minimise the number of courts that are run by the kings, and to take away the fines claimed by kings from lost properties?'

"I did hear something about that, yes, but we women are not always keen to know what goes on in the affairs of men. Besides, no one even attempts to inform us properly. The little I know is from crumbs I pick up here and there."

"I accept that, our dear queen, this is exactly how things are. The courts have been reduced, and according to the new plan the council of King Mosito ends this year. Next year we will have to go to the court of King Mosuoe."

"Oh no, don't say that, please!"

"This is a fact, our queen, but that is not the end of the story. The reduction of the councils is tied up with the issuing and gathering of fines by the kings. All of this has been abolished. From now on, all payments will go to a community fund. The fines from lost properties are no longer administered by the kings, but belong to the people."

"Now, how do you want me, a woman, to help you with such a big issue that belongs in the affairs of men?"

"You could help us in this way, dear Queen. King Mosito has not only lost his council, but his name does not even appear on the list of the kings of this district of Qacha. This means that he will not be paid a salary. All the kings will receive a monthly salary in an effort to compensate for the loss they suffer under all these changes. We tried to advise him to lodge a complaint, so that his name could be included in the final list and he can get a salary as well as the rights reserved for kings. But he disputed our advice, and we have become mere spectators. The main thing is he would not have defied us, had it not been for those two young men who are his friends and advisors, Pokane and Khosi."

At this stage, the three men felt completely relaxed; their blood ran smoothly. They could see that the Queen accepted their story favourably. At this moment Sebotsa took over from Maime.

"You will realise, our queen, that if he does not lodge some protest now, demanding back his position as a king in the Qacha district, your son, Thabo, will never see kingship in his lifetime. He will become the slave of Khosi and Pokane and their children. What will you then say you have raised him for – to turn him into a slave for his father's friends and their children? The Basotho say, 'mmangwana o tshwara thipa ka bohaleng' – the child's mother holds a knife at the sharp end. There's no one else who will fight for your son except you, his mother. Our plea this morning is, therefore, that you should pity your child by talking to his father and advising him to lodge a complaint; because if he does not do so, he will be taking a rope, thrusting it over Thabo's neck and throttling him while you look on, not even raising a finger to help him!"

When you want to wake a woman from her sleep, start with her child, the one she delivered in pain. And suddenly, a woman who has always been as tame as a lamb, never bothering anybody, will become wilder than a lioness, to protect her young ones. For Queen 'Mathabo, it was exactly like that. Maime's utterances made her so angry that she was short of breath and unable to speak.

"This is difficult and painful," she said when her voice finally allowed her to speak. "How shall I tackle it? Besides, the King will want to know where I've learned about it."

Maime smiled like a young man who has realised that a young woman is about to yield to his proposal of love, although she is still looking to and fro and unable to say: yes, I accept your proposal.

"That's a simple matter. Tell the King that you heard women discussing it, and ask him whether it is true. If you ask him that way, he will have no suspicion. He will tell you everything; maybe even that he dismissed our advice. If he tells you *that*, things will be very easy, because we are convinced that if you harass him a bit, he will agree to follow our advice. On the other hand, if he does not talk about our advice, it would be up to you, our queen, to devise ways for bringing him where you want him to be. But my guess is that you would have no problems."

Khati spoke up. "Bear with me, Madam. My advice is that you should never say you were with us and that we discussed this matter. It may spoil everything for good. Rather speak like someone who has heard a rumour. Be someone who wishes to get to the crux of the matter, so as to have proper knowledge and no misgivings. If you succeed and can help, you will have fought for and saved Thabo."

"Well, I understand you," said the Queen, "and I shall try, although the King is someone I fear and respect very much. But I will try to the best of my ability as a woman. And if I fail, I will accept it as one of those things which did not go according to plan.

"We shall be so grateful if you assist us, Madam," said Maime. "You should really beg him, and point out to him that if he does not fight for his rights, he will be burying Thabo alive. When Thabo reaches the stage of taking over as king, he will realise that his kingship ended a long time ago. You should also make the King aware that he will be unable to support the orphans and widows under his care, because the food that fed them has been taken away. I hope he will listen to you because you are his wife. Us, he has pushed aside completely. But please keep our visit a secret."

"I understand and shall do everything in my power to assist you."

The men went out and left her alone to think about ways to approach her husband. Their hearts were contented – things had gone according to their desire, and they were convinced that the war for their way of life was still on. They were happy because they had armed someone with a bomb that never fails to explode; like that big one that beat the Germans and stopped the war immediately. They spent the rest of the day happy and proud, waiting for the King to return from Qacha so that they could hear how the bomb detonated.

In the late afternoon, King Mosito arrived back with those with whom he had travelled. They found everything as they had left it in the morning. It was not evident that big things had been planned during their absence; things the King could not have guessed, because there are no deeper waters than the human being. You may travel with a person, talk to him, drink with him, and not know that he is a murderer, has just killed someone and buried him in a shallow grave.

Shadows stretched and the sun went down. Everything came to rest. People put their bones down on their beds to be peaceful. Like everyone else, Mosito also went home to rest, but when he lay down, he collided with news he did not expect.

"Good evening, Thabo's father. You know, during the day when we were down at the stream, some women talked about something that I heard for the first time. Did you know that the number of councils and kings were being reduced? Do you know anything about it? I was so surprised, because I've never even heard about such a thing!"

"Oh! Do you want to know about that? It's nothing but women talk! Why on earth would they wish to meddle in men's affairs? Anyway, yes, there are discussions about that but nothing is finalised. It's still being debated."

Mosito tried to answer in a way that was supposed to suggest that it was a small issue; something even that he, himself did not take seriously, but in the process he failed to see how important it was to 'Mathabo. She found the way he responded demeaning, as if he wanted to belittle her so that she should stop discussing the issue. Yet, she tried again: "I am surprised you think it's such a small matter, since the women thought it was a very serious matter when they discussed it. Please, tell me more about it. Do you find it fitting that I, as your wife, should get the news from women whose husbands are not affected by it? Shouldn't I have been the first to know? Just tell me what is going on, so that I know the truth and don't pick up crumbs from other people."

"I repeat; you women are fiddling in places you do not belong to. Can you imagine how that case will affect you if you allow it to go to such great lengths that it is discussed in all the valleys?"

When he said that, he couldn't help smiling a bit as he was actually enjoying talking to his darling in that manner. He then told her all the things that we already know, mocking them, so that if 'Mathabo had not already been schooled on the matter, she would not have bothered to dig deeper. But Maime had sharpened her. She probed the King and so he told her all he knew. When he had finished, she sighed, "Oh my goodness! What bad news this is!"

"It's totally irrelevant."

"But what are you going to do?

"About what?"

"About all of this. You are the one who says that your name is not included on the list of kings. Yes, and so? What do you say about it? Don't you even want to know why you were left out?"

"Even if I knew, what would that help?"

"If I knew, and the reasons did not sound convincing, and my name was left out without a good reason, I would go to court."

"To court?"

"You absolutely have to go to court because you are fighting for your rights. You must remember our late father left with his government intact. You were ushered into it, intact. It is your responsibility that, on the day *you* depart from this earth, your government should be left as you found it: intact. You should leave it for Thabo, and he should preserve it for his son, and this should continue forever.

"If you don't protest, it is obvious that when you die, you will leave nothing for this eldest child of mine. He will become a wanderer and a beggar. Why do you want our children to curse your grave? Today, every Mosotho who goes to Moshoeshoe's grave feels proud, and does not leave before honouring his bones. Because he, that old man, saved his nation, his children, the country of Lesotho and the Kingdom of Lesotho, those structures are all still standing. You, what will you leave behind for your children that they can remember you by?"

At this point 'Mathabo's feelings were greatly disturbed. She was no longer merely talking because of Maime's request. She was keenly aware that Thabo's bread was being taken away and divided among strangers, and that he could be left with nothing.

"I repeat, do you think that if you don't protest, your kingship will remain? Do you think Thabo will pay homage at your grave like people do at that of King Moshoeshoe? Do you rather want him, when he has failed in life, to pass your grave every day, and instead of paying homage, spit on it? He will spit a ball of sputum and say: 'Today, I am a vagabond because of the fool who lies here.' That he will say, heaving up a big stone and throwing it on your grave as if you should feel the pain. Surely, if you do not decide to protest, you will be doing a foolish, unbearable thing!"

Houses appear to be beautiful from the outside, but people do not know what happens inside. So we must leave King

Mosito and his wife 'Mathabo in the secret of their home. What they discuss in there is not for us, but only belongs to them; it is a personal matter between the two of them. Besides, we have already erred by going half way, hearing a few things which in actual fact were meant for only the two of them.

What they talked about was a matter between a man and a wife. We can only speculate, and, if we fail, try to read the King's plans for the future from his deeds.

That same week, a man known as Selone arrived. He was a herbalist and an evident expert, carrying a large number of bags and ornaments. It was rumoured that nobody could ever uproot pegs planted by him. He had long hair with knots dangling from the sides of his head.

It was common practice that, when a visitor arrived at a place where he was unknown, he had to introduce himself at the royal place, so that the King could know that there was a visitor. Selone arrived just after dawn, and found men seated at the heart of the court. After greeting, he asked to be accommodated and his request was granted. He put down his bags and moved towards the fire to warm himself.

"Where do you come from, brother?" Khati asked after Selone had sat down.

"I am from Makhaleng, Ntate. I go about treating the sick."

"We understand. Where are you on your way to?"

"Oh my lord, does it ever happen that a doctor can say where he is going? I have come here because there might be people who are not well and whom I might be able to help. But my aim is to treat the sick and then move on to King Lekorana, where I have a few head of cattle from people I treated last year when I was there."

"Well, that is understandable."

Then Selone was asked the usual questions that are asked when a visitor arrives at a village of the Basotho. He was also questioned about agriculture and the harvest and spoke without hiding anything.

When they had finished, Sebotsa's eyes began to twitch like that of somebody with a nervous disorder, though those who knew him no longer even noticed.

"The case of reducing the number of councils is keeping us on our toes here. How do people view this matter where you come from?" He blinked a final time and then looked questioningly to the guest.

Selone was quiet for a moment. He was thinking about how to answer. After a few minutes, he said, "Sebotsa, my lord, we are also worried. Everywhere I go nothing else is being discussed but this. I do not believe that any right-thinking Mosotho man would agree to the councils being reduced. Many people do not accept it, but it seems we are losing the battle, because these small wise men whom we have chosen as representatives at the National Council maintain that all is well. They have already agreed with the Europeans that the national fund is something very good, and should be established. But the way I look at it, it seems a tactic to kill our kings and what remains of the Sesotho kingship."

"You view things like I do, my lord," said Maime. "If we do not stay on our toes, this thing could reach a stage where there would be no more royal kings. The king will be chosen by the government without any regard for who he is, who his father was, and from which house amongst the royal family he comes. That would be complete domination over our traditions. And I realise that there is nothing we can do about it, because the National Council has already agreed."

"This fund will produce a lot of disputes, bringing problems and hatred. Just the other day, one of the kings at home, King

Sekate, found that he has been left out of the list of the kings of the region, and his council has been dismissed. If you want my opinion, he will become someone living from hand to mouth. And as I travel around, I see that he is not the only one treated like this. There are many kings like him who have lost their rights. Everywhere in this country, Lesotho, you hear the laments of kings!"

"Indeed, we shall perish badly!" said Khati.

"But the king at my place is not a boy," said Selone.

He spoke as if to suggest that his king was somebody with unsurpassed intelligence, but one should remember that it was a habit among the Basotho to speak well of their kings in front of visitors.

"Right now, as I speak, my king's case is already at Matsieng before the Paramount King. He demands to know why he was left out of the list."

All the men listened to Selone, and continued speaking to each other with their eyes only, reminding themselves that their king had made a big fool of himself by refusing to protest. Selone, as a student of human nature, noticed fear among the men in the audience and began to surmise what was happening in the court where he found himself.

Emphasising the words as he spoke, he repeated: "I say he's already in court, as we speak. He is not a fool who will allow himself to be killed, while he is looking on. Only fools could be thus cheated. One cannot allow one's king to be made a slave of a fund, when one has no idea about its origin. My king is a born king and we won't accept the madness of the Europeans!"

Selone's words penetrated the hearts of especially those three men who had attempted to advise King Mosito, and pierced sharply so that each man thought that it would have been better if they were ruled by King Sekake, who refused to have his eyes gorged out while he was looking on. While other matters were discussed, the men's hearts were no longer in them. Their thoughts were with Mosito, whose refusal was like that of a madman. In the end, they dispersed and all went to rest. The guest was shown a house especially reserved for visitors. Although the others went to sleep with heavy hearts, Selone slept at once. He was fatigued because he had travelled a lot that day.

8

The decision to dispute

It was a Saturday. The sky was clear, but the ground still grey with frost. The sun rose and the frost melted quickly. It became hot so quickly that many felt winter had passed and was giving the young one, spring, a chance to move in and reign.

As the harvest season was over, in all the villages people were enjoying the beer brewed to entertain them. On that day at Mphahama's there was an abundance of beer and many people rushed there quite early to arrive while the beer pots were still full. Both men and women spent the whole day enjoying beer and singing. That evening, they went home in a jovial mood, tongues chatting, relating stories non-stop that continued throughout the night. King Mosito stayed at home with Pokane and Khosi, while Khati and his group joined the multitudes to Mphahama's.

The King was unhappy the whole day. His friends tried to distract him by telling stories he usually enjoyed, but on that day he did not show an interest in anything. He spent the greater part of the day not talking, and his face showed that something was amiss. Pokane and Khosi noticed that immediately – when you have grown up with someone you realise quickly when something is amiss.

"What is the problem, King Mosito, you look so unhappy today?" asked Pokane while they were basking in the sun. "You seem to be ill."

"Nothing is wrong. I am well."

"But you are not as we know you," Khosi insisted.

Mosito did not answer but looked far into the distance beyond the mountain pass at Rooijane's, where it disappeared towards King Hlapalimane's. While he was still staring there he sighed; sighed like a baby who had cried a lot. Khosi became concerned and asked again what the problem was.

"Khosi, I do not know how to answer you. I am very unhappy, I—"

Pokane interrupted in a disturbed manner: "Why, my lord? Please tell us so that we can help you?"

"To tell the truth, I am disturbed by the reduction of the number of councils; especially the fact that my name has been omitted from the list of the district kings. When I first heard about it, I took it lightly and thought it didn't matter. But when reconsidering it later when I was alone, I discovered that it actually meant that I was ruined. My main source of income will be taken away and there is no way I will get it back. All the prospects of progress I had in mind have miscarried. I will be stripped of my kingship; I will be made a peasant. I will receive instructions from seniors, instead of issuing instructions myself.

Mosito was so disturbed that, were he not a man, he would have shed tears. But because a man is like a sheep, he does not shed tears, but only cries inwardly.

"My lord," said Pokane after a few minutes, "I think you may think that we do not sympathise with you because we also tried to view this matter lightly – just like you did when you first heard it. But that is not the case, my lord. All the matters that affect you also affect us. Everything that makes you happy makes us happy, as well. All that makes you unhappy makes us unhappy. What has been done to you has made us terribly sad. We tried t o look into all the possiblities, to see whether there was any way to avoid this matter, but we haven't yet found a path to pursue.

"But the way I see things, there will be a way out soon. King Ratšoleli loves you very much and he knows your good work. He will look after your case. So I want to tell you to be brave, son of my master, and not lose faith."

"I hear what you say, Pokane, but you should remember that my kingship was not thrust on me, artificially and by appointment only. My father was born a king. I was born to be a king. That is why, today, I deeply resent being treated as if I had been just *given* a position that can be taken away at will. It becomes clear that, if I have to beg to be a king, sail on my belly all my life until the day it is convenient to the masters, the day *they* feel satisfied that I have sailed long enough, they can say to me: 'Accept, here are the remnants, just have a taste.' And when would that be? In ten years?"

"Well then, my lord, what do you think should be done?" asked Khosi, feeling very concerned.

"I think I should go and raise it at Matsieng."

"At Matsieng, my lord?"

"At Matsieng. That is where I shall try. If possible, even overseas, England, is where I should take it."

"If you were not an educated king, I would say it is because of ignorance that you speak as you do, but because you are an educated king, I cannot respond. If you would just listen to me, I would tell you to be patient and wait until these new changes happen and then see where the senior people will place you. I am confident that there is a big job in store for you. It is not possible that a king of your calibre, who is educated, could be just thrown to the side like somebody who had never been to school.

"I want to remind you of the words of the late King Lekaota. Do you remember when we were still at school, he used to say to us: 'Today's times have changed, and we have to change and move forward with them. The nation should be alerted and the kings should be alerted, because if they are blind, they will be unable to lead and guide those who can see a little bit.'

"He also used to say: 'Royal kingship is no longer relevant. The kings who want to be in a position to rule well will have to be educated.' Those words sounded like a prophecy, because what is happening today looks exactly like what he was predicting. You, my lord, are educated and you have to use your education in such a way that the government and the Paramount King will realise that you are special and put you in the right place. The notion of challenging the processes makes me uncomfortable. In most instances disputes create hostility and problems. I say all these things because of my love for you. I do not wish to see the problems created by disputes. Your name will become associated with muddy issues caused by quarrels that are irrelevant. The National Council has already acknowledged the changes and this very council has advised the Paramount King accordingly. The Paramount King will never refute what he has already sanctioned. If he does, he will appear unreliable to the people and the government. I may even add," said Khosi, "and I say this as an educated person, you know very well that the National Council has been elected by the people. Whatever they do, they do in the interest of the nation, and now that the changes have already been sanctioned, they have been sanctioned by the nation.

"If you protest, you will be protesting against the nation, you will be disputing the feelings of the nation. You know the saying in Sesotho, 'morena ke morena ka batho' – a king is a king because of his subjects. That means if there were no people, there would be no kings. Therefore, if a king wishes to remain a king in his rightful place, his rule should be in line with the wishes of the people, because once he begins to rule according to his own wishes and does not listen to the nation, the results will be oppression and unrest.

"You know very well how the French people went against their king and his councillors and even killed some of them because they were no longer governing the nation in the just and fair manner the people wished to be governed in. The life of a poor person in France was the same as that of an insect. Even in the British government, as you know all too well, there was a time when the nation revolted against their king, and he was also killed, because he denied that the poor were oppressed. These things you know; educated people know them. I am merely reminding you of the Sesotho saying that a king is a king through his people. What the people decided upon through the members of parliament cannot be dismantled if they were done according to the law and well known. Do not get involved in disputes, my lord, and work through us, your servants and you will see what kind of privileges you'll get. What is the use of disputes?"

After a pause, Pokane added: "When somebody goes up the ladder, he must go step-by-step, because if he takes two or three at a time he might miss a rung and tumble down horribly. We understand, my lord, that together with other kings who are not on the list, you have been put at the bottom of the ladder, but there is a saying that you can ascend at your own will until you are where you wish to be. Take your steps one-by-one, until you get to where your heart desires. Do not be deceived by illiterates who say you should protest. They mislead you. Listen to us, who love you, who wish you the best, and are eager to help you in all your endeavours."

"People, do you remember that there were a lot of kings we learned about at school, but we just learned their names to pass exams, not believing they were once real. But when we look at the conditions we now find ourselves in, we realise that they also had to struggle. You refer to the Sesotho proverb that supports your argument, but then again, the Basotho also say, 'ngwana sa lleng o shwela tharing' – a baby who does not cry, dies in the cradle-skin. The French and British people – if they had not woken up, they would still be under that yoke of oppression today. But because they raised their grievances, complained, uttered their outcries and let their quivers fall on lances, the yoke of subjugation broke into pieces, and soon their emancipation was achieved." The King was now animated. "I should also complain, though not by quivering. I have to use the current ways available to me to sound an alarm and only consider myself defeated if I have tried and then failed. What does it help to keep on moaning while doing nothing? How will that ease the bruises in my heart?"

They continued arguing for a very long time, with Khosi and Pokane trying to advise the King not to take up any protest, but he seemed absolutely determined. When they parted, his idea was still standing, and he showed no sign of changing his mind.

Towards midnight, when people usually go into their houses, King Mosito sat alone in the royal house to meditate. After a while, he went out and spent a longer time outside. After about twenty minutes, he returned to the house and a few seconds later, in came Khati, Sebotsa and Maime. These men had just returned from drinking, where they had been since dawn, and they arrived properly soaked in beer.

"We have heard about your meeting, our king. How can we help you, Sir?" Sebotsa threw himself on a chair, abandoning the shyness he usually displayed before the King. The other men also sprawled on two chairs. They too were lacking the restraint they normally displayed.

"I have called you to seek advice."

Then the King kept quiet. The men were also quiet, waiting to be told why he had called them. When they saw him not saying anything, Sebotsa blinked slowly.

"Our advice you will definitely get when you are ready to ask for it, my lord. That is, when you have told us what you want, what has baffled you."

"Fellow citizens, the case of reducing councils makes me uncomfortable. At first I regarded it as something that was inevitable, but as I continue to digest it, I realised that the situation is weighty and serious. I also want to tell you a big secret, which must not leave this house."

"My lord, I have been telling you that this issue of reducing the number of councillors is big," said Khati, "and I am happy that you also see it that way."

"The cases of councillors need to be tackled seriously, my lord, because these new suggestions strangle our kings," said Maime, delighted, as he realised that the Queen had acted precisely as they had requested of her, although the King could not say this to them.

Sebotsa closed his eyes, opened them, blinked. "Is there a secret that you want to tell us, my lord, which you do not want to be discussed?"

"No, I'm sorry. If one wants to keep a secret, you have to keep it in your chest alone. One cannot expect that those it does not belong to, should keep it. I therefore beg to apologise."

No man wants people to know that each time his wife speaks to him, he changes his mind. After his wife had talked to him, Mosito had planned to inform these men that the Queen did not give him any rest. She insisted that he should protest. But the fact that she was behind it came to his thoughts, unprepared. So, before he could voice anything, he quickly changed his mind: he could not tell these men that he had discussed this matter with his wife. Telling them might invite their scorn and make them think he was someone who did not know the difference between his own mind and that of his wife. So he quickly apologised and nobody could blame him, but his guests knew, then, for certain that his wife had changed his mind.

"Well then," said Mosito, "I would like to know – since the day we adjourned the meeting, has your opinion changed?"

Now Sebotsa's face became alive: he blinked, he contorted his face like a gorilla. "Our lord, I presume to speak also on behalf of these two when I say that, when we stated our case, we did so comprehensively. We hold the same opinion we held that day. There is only one thing to do: fight for your kingship. Nobody has ever been killed for protesting on sound grounds. In short, I'm saying, continue with your protest, my lord, we will support you with all our might." He ended up with closed eyes.

Maime's voice reverberated through the roof of the house as if a tornado was on its way. "My lord, I wish to support Sebotsa's words fully. From the outset, we told you that there is only one solution to this case. Our happiness is overflowing because today you realise the importance of the words we spoke to you. This indicates that we are not ordinary people. All the young kings like you are advised by honest men who, like us, are mature, know their affairs, and also know the traditions. I have never heard of a king who is advised by boys who know nothing. Now that you acknowledge who we are, you are following your father's route and we will do what we mastered under your father's command, and guide you by teaching you the Sesotho rites. Is that not true, Khati, when I say this?"

"Nothing is more true than what you have just said, Maime! You formulated the truth well. This case is the one that will give King Mosito prominence in the eyes of the Paramount King and the people. They will know: at Qacha there is a king."

Mosito digested this for a while. At the same time, his feelings gathered around what Khosi and Pokane had said to him during the day, convincing him that a dispute did not befit his status and was only appropriate for foolish kings. He found that most of the time he accepted wholeheartedly that the only correct advice came from Khosi and Pokane, but then, he thought of his wife and what her reaction would be if she heard that he had changed his mind, again... He really did not wish to protest. The poor king was in two minds. One had to pity him.

In the end, he said, "I thank you very much because *you* have not changed your mind, and agreeing with me that I should protest gives me courage. I can now move on my intention knowing that there are men who will support me. I thank you!"

"A peasant does not deserve to be thanked by a king," said Sebotsa, "because the peasant is merely performing his duty and privilege when he advises the king. Why do you think God created kings and subjects? He did that so that the king may give orders and the subjects will do as instructed without expecting any pay or thanks."

"Now, these are my intentions," said Mosito. "This case is supposed to be in the hands of the Paramount King, but as I see things, there is a possibility I might lose it, and if I lose, I will go to Lesotho High Court."

"That is a perfect strategy, my lord," said Khati. "You have decided wisely, because this cannot be abandoned midway. We should push it until it ends up overseas, at the British Council. Only if we lose there, will we accept our fate. But I won't consider it a failure until we've reached that stage. It is likely to end up at Matsieng only."

"But you interrupted me; I hadn't finished," said Mosito.

"Pardon me, my lord. I think it was because of the joy that you are now on the right track. Continue, Sir!"

"Now, the clever commander, when attacking with his soldiers, has to plan ahead about what to do if the war becomes too heavy, to ensure that his army does not scatter like the young of the quailfinch. I have decided to prepare myself for what to do should I lose the case. I will consult lawyers in Matatiele on Monday, to check if there are any loopholes, so that if I lose at Matsieng, I will know what to do in the government courts. I will need bold-headed advocates, who clash with arguments, while we look on from a distance. This is what I intend doing. What is your opinion?"

Khati stood up and went out without speaking. He left and returned. When he sat down, he said: "I'm sure you are surprised, my lord, that I just went out without saying anything. I heard some noise outside and went to check whether somebody was listening to our conversation. Well, I found Maime's dog, looking for its owner. We have to be careful, because there are many wicked people. There may be people who try to befriend you, but deep in their hearts are terrible enemies; people who are next to you with the aim of killing you at the earliest opportunity and when you least expect it. The Basotho are right when they say white teeth are deceitful."

"I hear what you are saying, but what's your response to what I intend to do on Monday?" saying this, Mosito could not hide his agitation.

"It is true that when people are in a happy mood, they take their time discussing their own matters and never hurry over the real issues in any meeting. They also love to indulge in transgression," said Khati. "That is where I am coming to, my lord. I was just introducing your idea of wanting to consult lawyers. You are wasting your time. We have our own lawyers, Basotho lawyers. The European ones will drain your pocket without making any progress. These lawyers are big crooks."

"Who are the Basotho lawyers, Khati?"

"Patience my lord, I am getting to that point. As an old veteran, although I am an illiterate, I know exactly how a lawyer works. Just for advice, he will charge you a lot of money because he has to work through all the Sesotho laws, especially those dealing with kings, to get to a point to hold on to. That work takes a long time because he has to go through all the pages, and for just doing that, he will charge you a lot of money."

"But you have not answered my question. I'm asking: the Basotho lawyers you are talking about, who are they?"

"They are here in our village, my lord."

Mosito realised that Khati was not answering his question, but, as the old man was tipsy, he dropped the question and said, "You are saying I should not consult lawyers for advice."

"You heard very well, my lord. I am saying exactly that."

"But if we lose the case at Matsieng, an advocate will be needed when we have to go to the government court. Is that not so?"

"If it has to go there, an advocate will be needed, but I am saying that it will not have to go there at all. It will end up at Matsieng, where your rights will be restored."

"I repeat: when a general goes to war, he does not think of winning only, because he does not know the strength of the enemy. He thinks about the possibility of losing the battle as well – how he will retreat, without seeing his soldiers scattered in all directions."

"Now why do you not listen to *me* who knows? We will win the case before it reaches Matsieng. I am the one who knows the tricks of the Sesotho courts."

"You speak in riddles, old man. I can't follow, and I don't see how we can win the case before we even *get* to Matsieng."

"I'm telling you: we have Basotho lawyers. They are the ones who win the case for you. Why do you think that God made all the herbs and allowed them to grow for people? He gave them to be used in matters such as these. Cases are fought by means of herbs and not the tongue. The herbs are the lawyers among the Basotho."

Here Sebotsa took over. He realised that he had been closing and opening his eyes continuously for a long time, and was not getting a word in: and just now Khati was talking about a thing that lay deep in his feelings; that he believed in with his whole heart.

"You are one hundred percent correct, Khati," he interjected. "Cases have been won ever since creation by means of herbs. These villages that you see, my lord, were fortressed by means of herbs in the past. When your case commences, all the divining bones should have been arranged already to mislead the witnesses, so that their evidence tallies with your case. If you say you are going to a European lawyer, you will be wasting time and money. The Basotho lawyers are the herbs."

"Old men, you are leading me now onto a small road I do not know, a road that I was not brought up on, and on this we shall never agree. I have never heard of herbs that have won a case. Never! A case is won by means of reasons that support it, and through the intelligence and fluency of the person who defends it. This idea of yours that herbs are lawyers, I don't accept."

Maime was working himself into a frenzy. "Now is the time you should learn the wisdom of the Basotho. You grew up down in the Cape, staying with Europeans only. You were taught the wisdom of Europeans. Sesotho wisdom you do not know, and today you will know it. The Basotho have a wonderful gift, which the Europeans do not have, which they will never have! It is the gift of herbs. When we introduce this topic, we are educating you the Basotho way. Trust Sesotho science, medicines and potions made with complete knowledge from the ancestors. If you follow the ways of European education, with British lawyers, you will never succeed here in Lesotho. Khati and Sebotsa are old men; they know the Sesotho culture deeply. They will never desert you! Those who mislead are the ones who say you should go to European lawyers, who would milk you without showing any progress."

He smiled slightly and looked at Khati and Sebotsa to indicate that now he had concluded the deal and there was no loophole for Mosito.

"My ideas do not change like a chameleon," said the King. "I have told you what I have in mind and that suffices, I shall not shift a bit."

"You asked for advice from us and we have given it to you, and if you refuse to accept it, that's your decision, my lord." With those words, Khati stood up and left. The other two followed him and Mosito was left alone in his house.

Khati and Maime got to Sebotsa's place and had another discussion.

"Are we hitting against a mountain again, Sebotsa?" asked Khati.

"You mean when the King says he does not believe in our medicine?"

"Yes."

"I also see it that way. It is clear that he is not going to shift on this issue. If we keep on pushing, he will drive us out with our small blankets flying in the air just as he once did before, you will recall, Khati."

"I do not believe that he will stand up against us and beat us for good," said Maime, the man who never accepted that some things could beat him.

"Where do you get such courage?" asked Khati.

"If you cut with a knife once and discover that it is sharp, you have to continue cutting with it. You have to continue to cut anything that needs cutting with this knife, until it is blunt or breaks, and then buy a new one. We have a sharp knife, one we once cut with, and it convinced us that it is sharp. Why not use it to cut deeply again?"

"You mean the Queen?" asked Khati.

"You heard me loudly and clearly. Did you notice how effectively she dismantled the King's ideas around fighting for his rights to kingship? There was a moment that he nearly said that the Queen made him look at it differently. I am convinced that this change was caused by what the Queen said to him. We must go back to her again to help us, because we are stuck again."

"You are right, we should go," said Sebotsa, "but I doubt that she will have the guts again. Still, that is the only solution. If we fail, it'll be the end of our journey."

While King Mosito had been discussing with Khati and company, Khosi and Pokane were at Pokane's house, arguing like orphans left all by themselves, not knowing that when things have reached this stage there is little to be done. They had tried all day to convince the King of the pointlessness and time-wasting exercise of pursuing the case. But in the end they discovered that they were tilling a piece of field that is difficult to cultivate.

It is extremely painful to see a person who has two good eyes refusing to go along with people who see issues in the same way. Choosing to be led by the blind is to opt to walk clumsily, not seeing where one is going, falling off cliffs and into dongas. The sad thing is to see the person who is supposed to see clearly falling in with the blind, holding their hands, and then *they* become the ones who lead him, taking the rein.

It is also a known fact that whatever the blind hang on to, they never let go, they hold on tightly for good. Although not completely similar, one can compare Mosito's friends with angels who have to guard somebody and then feel ashamed when the man discards advice leading him towards everlasting life, but listens to the devil's counsel. It is terrible to see such a person clinging to such advice, when one knows the ending will be death. If we can imagine how such an angel feels, we will have understood the situation.

Khosi and Pokane were just like that when they saw their friend, their king, siding with the blind, and they had no way of getting him out of the blind people's claws. They cracked their skulls to come up with something to make Mosito listen to them and to enable him to turn back on the dangerous journey he had embarked on, but they could not find anything at all. Eventually they parted and went to sleep, seeing only darkness before them, with no visible way out.

9

Mosito stands firm

It was already midnight when Khati and company left Mosito and he fervently hoped that the Queen was asleep. He entered the house quietly, so as not to wake her up and perhaps disturb a warm winter sleep. He undressed quickly and slid into bed. The bedding was ice-cold as if it were disciplining him: stop having secret meetings of which your friends have no knowledge! Just about to snuff out the candle, he heard 'Mathabo next to him: "Why do you arrive at this time, when everybody is fast asleep? What were you doing all this time?"

"Well, I had to discuss something with Khati and the other men."

"Lately you've had a lot of discussions with Khati and his companions. What's going on? You usually work with Khosi and Pokane; aren't they your friends?" She emphasised the last two words.

"With Pokane and Khosi we discuss different issues altogether. In the discussion we had tonight I did not need their advice."

"May I know the purpose of this meeting?"

"You may know if you want to, but it's already late into the night. Let me not spoil your good sleep."

"You know that I am not governed by sleep. But these days sleep and I are no longer friends."

"What's wrong?"

"How can I make friends with sleep when my child is faced with death wanting to swallow him?"

"What do you mean by that?"

"I mean that since the time you told me about the reduction of the number of councils, I have had no peace. My thoughts are stuck on Thabo, who will become poor as a dog." 'Mathabo sighed.

"If that's caused you sleepless nights, you can sleep in peace now. After you spoke to me, I decided to follow your advice. I will protest."

"When did you decide to do that?"

"The same day you spoke to me. What you said gave me no peace, and eventually I realised that you have a point when you say you want me to protest, because if I didn't do that, I would be killing Thabo, as the kingship would be forfeited."

"So why do you discuss this with Khati and his friends, and not with your daily advisors, Khosi and Pokane?"

"I discussed it with Khati and them because they were the ones who initiated the idea. Pokane and Khosi want me *not* to protest – they believe matters will eventually sort themselves out."

"Oh, well, if that is the case, then you are correct in casting them aside. But you must remember that you are also someone who doesn't want to be advised. If you were listening to any advice, you would have walked away from them long ago. Those two tell everybody that they are educated and we see them acting according to this so-called 'civilization' of yours. So, what did Khati and his friends say?"

"We agreed and disagreed. We agreed that my kingship, and that of Thabo, should be defended. We disagreed when it came to how the protest should be conducted. I say the protest should be conducted through lawyers, the legal people."

"And what did they say?"

When she said that, she rose from her bed and supported herself with a pillow so that she could hear clearly what Mosito was saying. She wanted not only to hear, but also to see the face of the one who spoke. By just looking at a face while speaking, one can often learn more of the things the person does not wish to mention.

"They wanted me to work according to the Sesotho approach."

"The Sesotho approach? How?"

"They said talking to lawyers is a waste of money. What I *should* do is get a herbalist who would straighten matters in my favour by means of medicine."

'Mathabo was a Mosotho child, and suckled Sesotho culture from her mother. All the customs of the Basotho, all the things the Basotho believed in, were packed inside her. She viewed life according to the wisdom of the Basotho. Mosito, on the other hand, viewed life according to the wisdom of the Europeans because he had learned their logic. So what amazed 'Mathabo was Mosito's confession of an inner struggle.

"So what did you disagree on?"

"We disagreed when they said I should look for a doctor who will use medicines to make my case go smoothly."

"But don't you know that these doctors are exactly the ones who spoil or correct things?"

"Look, 'Mathabo, I was brought up by a person who did not believe in these things. My father believed in Basotho doctors who could heal bodily sicknesses and other natural ailments, but he never even mentioned these mysterious doctors who are said to influence things by means of various potions. I think I am correct in saying he did not believe in them. So, therefore, I do not see how I can submit to such things at this stage of my life; especially since my father, who taught me all that he deemed necessary for the kingship that I hold today, did *not* teach me about them."

"Your ignorance is really unfortunate. There are many things that one could learn on one's own, that nobody needs to teach you. Saying this, is it not possible that he meant to teach you about healers and herbs as one of the things you ought to know, but in the end it just escaped his mind? Maybe he was unaware that you needed guidance in a basic thing like this."

"I hear you, my wife, but, I repeat, my father taught me all that he knew and believed in, knowing that I would need this knowledge when my time came to rule. He definitely did not teach me the things he neither used nor believed in. I must walk the path he put me on and shouldn't deviate from it. If I depart from it and roam about, trying to follow various short cuts, I will soon find myself lost in a wilderness."

'Mathabo looked at her husband for a long time. Her gaze was filled with pity for him, being so unaware of a big matter he should have known about.

"Just tell me," she said, "what does a woman have to be for her husband? Is the bearing of children her only duty? Is that all?"

"No, that's not her only duty."

"What are the others?"

"She advises her husband when he needs advice, because by marriage they have been made one person."

"What you say is what I also believe. Therefore, I, as your advisor and your partner, tell you that the advice of Khati and the others is the right advice. As a Mosotho child who was brought up in the Sesotho way, I identify with it, it speaks to me. How do you think names such as Maime, Molomomonate, Phonyoha, and many others came into being? It was because they were important herbs that were used in our courts. While such a person talks, all the listeners will hear Molomomonate's sweet tongue and his words will land well in their ears. They will simply agree to everything he says."

"I know these names you are quoting, but what I do not believe is that those dry herbs have the ability to change the feelings of a person who is a total stranger to you. That I will not accept, until the day I die."

"Even if you do not believe, listen to me, your advisor, who has true knowledge. Do you think I would force you to believe in something I know would be useless to you?"

"I usually listen to you, but this time I will not. I will start with the wrong foot if I start with what my father did not teach me. If I am to step forward in order to win this case, I will win it without the use of a single herb. If I lose this case, a herb wouldn't have mattered anyway. I will try, but I won't be the first to lose a case, nor will I be the last. Many people have lost in the past."

"Well, seeing that I do not have the power to force you to do what your heart rejects, I give up. I tried to be helpful as your loving wife. But you should bear in mind that, by rejecting advice from Khati and friends, with whom I agree wholeheartedly, you neglect a problem that does not concern *you* so much as your son. You dismiss Thabo's kingship, so that he will turn into a slave, a person who owns nothing. I am deeply aware that you are deluded by your young friends, Pokane and Khosi, who, because they are educated, say you should do away with the Sesotho ways. They are misleading you and you will be sorry, but by then it will be too late!"

She covered her head with her blankets and sobbed quietly.

Mosito took a long time to digest this argument, but he could not arrive at the point of understanding how it would help him if he accommodated the advice of his wife, Khati and the others. He recalled his father's advice: "It doesn't matter who advises you, when your conscience does not accept that advice, do not follow it. Your conscience is the true shepherd, the true friend to man, the true advisor..."

These words rang in his ears vibrantly, like a bell. It was as if his father were talking to him right there.

He began to feel sleepy, but then saw his father's face, which looked just like it did on the day he had spoken those words to him – on his death bed, ready to depart. His father's face, as clear as it was in the last few minutes of his life, appeared vividly to him and he felt an enormous happiness flowing into his heart. He heard a faint voice, happy, kind, saying to him: "You should fight this war like a man. Follow the tracks your father left, and everything will be fine."

He did not know where the voice came from. It felt like he was daydreaming – dreaming while awake – but it threw a shadow on the approaching sleep. He again thought of his father's life, but could not find a single example that convinced him that the old king believed in the kind of stories he was hearing from his wife and Khati and his friends.

Eventually, sleep that consoles those in distress moved forward and took him in its broad soft arms. When he woke up, it was dawn. He jumped out of bed; going to church was routine for him. After the service he returned home and spent the whole day until sunset with Khosi and Pokane, though his distress remained visible. Queen 'Mathabo spent the day alone, and it was clear that she was heartbroken. She spoke only when asked a question and was obviously not in the mood for talking.

On Monday, King Mosito went to Matatiele to consult lawyers and came back in the afternoon. He was noticeably more disturbed than when he had left that morning, though he continued to converse normally when necessary. In the evening, he went to sleep quite early, as he was exhausted.

"How did you travel, my brother?" 'Mathabo asked when they were in the privacy of their room.

"I travelled well."

He gave short answers and kept quiet once he had spoken, showing that he was not open to having a conversation.

"And how did the lawyers advise you?"

'Mathabo asked this, though she could see her husband was not in the mood to talk. But, being a woman, she pressed on.

"They advised me not to protest, because they don't see how I could win the case."

"So, what is your next step?"

Although Mosito did not wish to talk, he ultimately spoke to her. To be faced by a woman who is taking up the defence of her son is unbearable.

"I do not change colours like a chameleon," he said. "I have decided to go to Matsieng, and that is what I will do."

"Do they have no hope at all for the case?"

"No, but they advised me that if I do want to continue, I should go the Paramount King in Matsieng, and find out how to proceed. If I fail there, I could still go to the government's court, but the lawyers can't intervene at Matsieng, because it is a traditional Sesotho court."

"Are you still prepared to listen to my advice?"

"If you don't wish us to clash, you should stop talking to me about that! I told you that I would do such a thing only when I am dead, not while I am a living person. I refuse to be deceived by advice that is obviously utterly useless!"

That was the end of the conversation.

At the beginning of September, King Mosito went to Matsieng where he had to present his case to the Paramount King. He went along with Khosi as his secretary. It was only the two of them, as Pokane remained behind to look after the affairs of home, overseeing the council, as usual. Mosito and Khosi boarded a train at Matatiele on Tuesday and arrived at Matsieng on Thursday.

On the long journey, Khosi spoke again to Mosito about the case, because he had noticed that at home, the King avoided being alone with him and Pokane. He had been evading them because they continuously discussed the issue.

"My lord," said Khosi as they travelled, "although we are on our way to Matsieng, I am concerned. You refused to listen to our opinion, which was sincere."

"Khosi, I am created in a way different from many people. When I decide to do a thing, and my feelings about it are settled, I do it. All the reasons you and Pokane advanced to dissuade me, I acknowledge, and do not dispute them. I am convinced that they are genuine, but my conscience has persuaded me that, if I do not protest and appeal to the Paramount King, I shall be turning myself into a fool not fit to rule. Every precious thing that one gets in life, one gets after going through great difficulties. If I sit down and fold my arms, saying nothing about it, who will come carrying my kingship on a plate to give to me? If that is how you reason, you are dreaming of miracles indeed! At school we've learned the history of many nations on this planet, and we know that not a single one got its freedom by its people folding their arms. How do you propose I get my rights if I do not fight for them?"

"Well, I never said that there is such a nation. But I argue that your rightful place in this changing world would be determined by your good work."

"That is exactly what I refuse to accept. Can't you see that today's conditions are difficult? Everybody is looking after his own life and that of his children. Who on earth will bother to attend to Mosito's affairs, if Mosito himself is not doing anything about them? Do you remember the Sesotho proverb, 'pela e ne hloke mohatla ka ho romeletsa!' – a rock rabbit has no tail because it depended on others. If I sit down, doing nothing on my own about my own affairs, I will soon reach a stage where I will not be able to do anything! The time we have now is the time we have to use, because these changes are still at infancy stage. We may still be able to change our fortunes. Just be patient and we will see what happens at Matsieng. But after Matsieng, if we fail, we should accept our fate and I will be satisfied. But if I had not tried, I would keep on saying that, maybe, if I had made an attempt, I could have been successful."

"I understand you, my lord. I am your subject, and I will always care for your wishes and serve you with honesty."

Khosi realised that it was useless to press the debate further with Mosito, because it would only lead to an exchange of unpleasant words that would spoil their journey. For a long time neither man said anything and Khosi decided to make peace and wait to see how they fared in Matsieng.

On Thursday at midday they arrived by bus at Matsieng and were well received. Mosito had to see the Paramount King on Friday and spent the night working hard to organise his arguments so that he could put them systematically to the King. At dawn he was up and walked up the mountain to view Matsieng from the top. Looking towards Makhoarane, he fed his eyes on the beauty of the country and breathed fresh, cool mountain air. Then he went down to the village for breakfast, before he went to the place where the council meeting would start and where he wanted to spew the poison that he had carried all the way from Letloepe. At nine o'clock the meeting commenced and he was the first to be called. How he put his case, how the questions were put, what the council asked so that they could forward everything to the Paramount King, would take a long time to discuss. Therefore, we shall only tell the readers how his case was concluded.

After King Mosito had declared his dispute, he pointed out the number of taxpayers, which, he felt, was large enough to earn him the salary of a district king; he also explained how it was his birthright to be on the list of district kings. The council closed the meeting and referred the case to the Paramount King.

After lunch, the council met again and gave the reasons why he had been omitted from the list. The first reason given was that he had few taxpayers. There were only seven hundred, therefore, according to the committee's decision, he did not make it on to the list. It had been decided that for a king to qualify for a district, he had to have at least eight hundred taxpayers. As the responsibility of the work was not big enough, he could not be put on the list.

The second reason given was that he did not qualify by birthright, either. There were other kings in the Qacha district who were, by birth, more senior than he was, but who also did not make the list. His dispute was, therefore, unfounded and could not be accepted.

The council then concluded by reminding him that, although his name did not appear on the list of district kings, according to section 4(b) in the Lesotho booklet, this did not mean that he would not receive any salary, because that section stipulated: 'The sub-chiefs and headmen whose taxpayers were more than 350 had enough responsibilities to give orders and rule so that they could deserve remuneration. The amount would be determined by the work and their responsibility, of which the number of taxpayers would be a good yardstick.'

His remuneration would be determined by his seven hundred taxpayers, as was the case with the district kings, and also by the recommendation of his good work by the district kings of Qacha and the Deputy Commissioner. Therefore, this case was one of those that would have to be examined individually when remuneration was to be determined.

The council relayed the Paramount King's message and concluded that Mosito was instructed to work enthusiastically in his rule, following in the footsteps of his late father. That was the end of his case. The following day he was on his way back home.

"Do you see now, my king?" Khosi said when they sat down in the train. "If you had listened to us, you would have spared yourself all this trouble that brought you to Matsieng."

"Yes, I agree that indeed you had a point."

"Look, my king, we would never mislead you. This Lesotho booklet we read together carefully, including this very act relating to you, which the council now threw at you. But you followed your own mind. Bringing your protest before the Paramount King made you look like a big fool – to me. You should understand that by now, my king."

Khosi continued speaking: "As an educated young Mosotho man talking to his friend and contemporary, do not think I look down on you when I say that I am saddened that you have allowed yourself to be deceived by the blind, by people who cannot read and see changes for what they are. By so doing you have given those who speak badly about education the power to scorn it; and they will say that education is useless. Because here you are, an educated king, but you went as far as Matsieng to protest against a process, which you were told, and knew yourself, was unstoppable and authorised by the government. Khati and his group wanted to lead you into trouble because their understanding of life is soaked in the red ochre of paganism. You know that your late father warned you not to get into the habit of sitting around the same fire as these men, for they will lead you astray. I hope that what happened today convinced you that we wish you only the best at all times, and that we should remain supportive of each other."

"I will do my best, Homeboy. I have been obstinate of late, but shall try to listen to you from now on."

10

The fame of Selone

Since the first day Selone had arrived at King Mosito's place, people had turned up daily in large numbers to consult him. Traditional healing was highly respected and loved amongst the Basotho. Every time a new traditional healer arrived in a village, people would flock so enthusiastically that nobody would blame you if you concluded that it was the first time they had seen a traditional healer.

While King Mosito was in Matsieng, Selone was in Qacha, treating people as these doctors usually do: diagnosing by throwing divining bones, preparing herbs to drink for medication, making incisions, nailing wooden pegs around the village in order to protect it against evils – doing everything a Mosotho doctor habitually did. Khati and his friends, Maime and Sebotsa were the first to engage with Selone, asking to be strengthened so that the King might like them, since it had become obvious to everybody that because of Khosi and Pokane, they were no longer recognised as the advisors of the old days of King Lekaota.

Selone had a strange habit, a tendency people were not aware of and one that people were also not familiar with. At the time when most people retired to their beds, he would pretend to be retiring too, only to wait until everybody was fast asleep. When all was quiet, he would get up and secretly visit a few houses within the village, a practice which made his name very popular. He became so famous that people only needed to hear his name and they would flock to him in big numbers. His intentions at these houses were not those the Basotho were used to, namely, some sort of witchcraft. No, his intentions, which he used everywhere he visited, were known to him, alone. It was during these times at night that he would prepare his craft in the way only he knew – a craft which we shall see more of in this story of ours.

Furthermore, it helped him a great deal when people would throw the divining bones themselves, so that he could explain to them what the position of the bones actually meant, which was not exactly how other healers did it.

Two weeks after Selone's arrival, Khati went to see him to consult the divining bones. He did what is usually done to them and cast them on the floor. Selone praised the bones the way he knew how to do it; and then said to Khati: "Man, your situation is extremely bad, it is so bad that it is a miracle that you are still alive and can still put one foot in front of the other."

Khati became irritated. "What is it that you see; do you wish to scare me?" he asked, since he believed everything healers said and would follow them blindly.

"I say so because I see there is a person who is seriously opposing you. This person is a man, and he is still a young person."

Selone may have been simply guessing, or perhaps he knew because he was fond of sniffing around – because diviners are hunting dogs. Why he said what he said, we do not know; what we *do* know, though, is that his words dropped into Khati's heart and mind like water falling on dry soil.

"I hear you, doctor, but I still do not understand well; you have not yet explained as clearly as I would like."

"I thought you were a grown-up person and would understand," said Selone, thinking he was well on the track Khati wanted him to follow. "You see, Sir", Selone continued, "I am a visitor here, I have just arrived, and do not want to cause trouble in the people's villages; it is for that reason that I am still careful with this case."

"When I came to you it was because I wanted to know clearly why I am in the condition I find myself in, and I want you to explain fully, not shying away from anything."

"Well, if you want that, there is no problem, I shall investigate freely, for I am a healer, and you will pay me." When he said that, he again inspected the divining bones intently.

"Yes, go ahead, tell me openly."

"Man, the thing I wish to tell you is that, if you had not met some men in the past, you would not be alive at this moment. I can see that some years ago you were treated by men who knew this art."

"Now you are talking; you are right. I think it is about five years ago now since I was treated by a Mopeli diviner. He left long ago, promising me that he would return to complete the treatment, but I have not seen him since, and the medicines he left for me are long finished."

"I am aware that you were not treated with medicine from this area, because here in Lesotho there are no herbs that can prevent what I am seeing here; you were helped by your resistance."

"I agree that there is a plot against me: my reasons being that there are times when my body just becomes numb along the whole left side; and what puzzles me more is the fact that I am always on the move – I seldom sit down for long periods that could cause the numbness, and that disturbs me, indeed. You are telling me everything I have already seen."

At that moment, Selone smiled a little bit, and continued: "These people have realised that they failed to bundle you into something, and they now plan to destroy you completely." Selone cleared his throat and looked at Khati sympathetically. "But your gods love you and you must thank them for the protection they have given you. For you to believe everything I am saying, I am going to give you one indication, just one illustration."

Having said that, he retrieved a little horn in which there was a potion of meat and ointments. He took a bit with his finger and said, "Come closer and kneel in front of me."

Khati did as ordered. Selone pulled out a razor and made one incision on Khati's forehead where the hairline ends; he cut deeply, so that the blood trickled profusely, almost as if Khati were having a nosebleed. Then Selone rubbed some medicine into the wound and the pain was unbearable; it ran down Khati's body, and he felt like screaming but held it back out of fear that it would weaken the medication.

"The medicine I have used on you," said Selone, "is very strong. It's the medicine reserved for kings. Now that I have used it on you it will open your eyes, and you are going to see things that, without it, would be impossible to see. But here's a warning: you must be very brave, because if you fear, the fear will work against it. This is merely a demonstration. Now stand up, go to your home and go straight to the peach tree in whose shade you usually lie. Look up and see if there is anything strange."

Khati was a bit hesitant, but Selone urged him, because otherwise he would weaken his medicine. Khati got up and went straight to his backyard. Less than five minutes after Khati had left Selone, he dashed back, breathing heavily, terrified, his heart beating so loudly that he could hear it. His eyes were fierce and he kept looking over his shoulders, maddened by the touch of his own pants and trying to tear them off. The blanket he had thrown away as soon as he saw what he had seen in the tree.

"What have you seen?" asked Selone. ·

The fright that overwhelmed Khati nearly stopped his breathing; he could not speak, he just kept making signs with his hands, like a dumb person. Selone stopped questioning and waited for him to calm down. "What did you see that made you throw your blanket away?" he asked, smiling like somebody enjoying himself.

"Oho! Since I was born I have never seen..."

But before he could finish, he was shuddering again, his body quivering all over, his hair standing on end, while Selone laughed out loud.

When Khati saw that, he gathered some courage, "I have never seen such a monstrous snake in my whole life."

That night, the moon was brighter than usual. It was the kind of moon that the Basotho people believed exposed witches. Everywhere, everything was eerily visible and clear. Khati explained that, when he reached the place where he usually lay under the tree, he looked up and there, above him, was the biggest and most horrific snake he had ever seen, hovering above him, and it was clear that it was about to attack him; he did not look at it a second time, since it was already flaring its throat. While relating this, he trembled all over again. Yes, then his survival instinct kicked in. He knew that to survive, he had to dash, sprint and run, shedding everything on the run. As the words of his ordeal left his tongue, he shivered with a frightening intensity and was clearly finding it difficult to endure anything near his body.

"I told you," said Selone, "this is just to demonstrate what I can do, so that you believe me. You were able to see the snake because of the power of this medicine that I have used on your forehead. The snake was planted there by someone to destroy you, as I have told you."

"Now doctor, how will it be killed? How am I going to get home? I'm sure it's on my doorstep, already."

"No. It won't harm you at all, because it's dead. Let's go and collect it!" said Selone.

"No, I am definitely not going there!"

"I have to get it; I will mix some medicine to work on it to haunt and destroy those witches who wanted to destroy your life."

"I've told you I'm not leaving this place to tamper with a snake where it may be lying. The person who should go is you, you are the doctor."

"Now, if you behave in this manner you are disturbing my medicine. When I provide my services to a person, I want him to witness everything to satisfy him completely. Now you refuse to go with me; tomorrow you will tell people that the snake was mine! Perhaps there was no snake; it was just a fallen branch of that tree! So, we have to be together, because it was you who saw it and you should point it out to me."

In the end Khati yielded and they left, but all the way he kept a safe following distance and refused to walk next to Selone, who was in front. When they reached the tree, Khati stood a little bit further away, pointed at the snake and then immediately retreated backward. If the snake was to strike, it should strike Selone and not him. He suggested that Selone should go closer if he truly was not scared of it. Selone moved closer and yes, he saw the monstrous snake that frightened Khati so much.

When he had shown Selone the snake, Khati retreated, so that he could run away easily should the snake decide to attack. But Khati saw Selone pick up the snake without any fear, bringing it down from the tree and simply carrying it to his place. When they got home, where there was light, Selone showed Khati that the snake was dead. Khati came closer and inspected it.

"Are you familiar with this type of snake?" asked Selone.

Khati looked on, trying very hard to be calm. Finally he was able to hold and inspect it. After a long time, he said he had never seen that kind of snake before.

"Have you ever heard of a mamba?" asked Selone.

"I have heard the name quiet often," replied Khati.

"If you've heard the name before, well, today you have seen it, although it is dead already."

"I have heard that it is only found in the forests of Natal. How would it end up here in Lesotho? I have heard that it is found in areas that are warm throughout the year," remarked Khati.

"My brother, today you will learn that these people are not some kind of cow dung one can make fire with; they don't like to be played with. This snake was sent to kill you. Fortunately for us, it was still young. Look at its length; it comes up to my waist. It's very small. When it is fully grown, its length is awesome."

"Was it sent to kill me?"

"That's correct! But you became too heavy for it because of the medicines I used on you and it died instantly. Now remember, since it's a man-made snake, you could not have seen it without my medicine. If you inspect it carefully, you'll notice that it died a while ago. You would therefore appreciate it when I say there are people out there who would like to smash your head. This snake is most poisonous and dangerous. If it bites someone, that person will die before he reaches the shop over there. Had it bitten you, you would be dead by now," Selone explained.

At that moment, Khati was paralysed with fear, when realising the danger he had escaped unknowingly. According to Sesotho custom, he then asked Selone to treat him, fortify his household and return the snake to its owner.

"Sending it back is something I will gladly do. However, I need a type of potion which I do not have presently. It is a potion which is not easily attainable. The people who have it are the Masaroa but they live far away. There is a Mopedi doctor I know in Pretoria who could have the potion. When I leave from here I should be going there. When I come back your wish will be granted. As for the protection of your property, I shall do my best to make sure that no one intrudes."

Selone had demonstrated his abilities and Khati was, without doubt, convinced. Often in life, when someone discovers a fountain with cool water, he is keen to tell his friends about it so that they can also enjoy drinking from it. Similarly, the following day, Khati told Sebotsa and Maime about the mysterious acts performed by Selone, and their esteem increased. Subsequently, they also felt the need to know this visitor. They visited him individually, and returned completely happy, and related his expertise to those who cared to listen. So the doctor's fame spread. Many villagers confided in Selone about their closely guarded secrets, secrets they had kept alone and silently. Each person returned satisfied, after Selone indicated that he would deal with their adversaries.

Mosito returned from Matsieng and found conditions just as we have described. On his arrival, he found almost everybody eagerly waiting to hear about his experiences. He informed them about the journey, the presentation of the case, how he lost and why. Everybody in the village sympathised with him, because by now his subjects were beginning to like him and were getting used to his style of leadership. Out of everyone, those who were hurting the most were Khati, Sebotsa, Maime and Queen 'Mathabo. What distressed them was that the King had ignored their advice to consult one of the greatest and most experienced diviners, to make it easier for him to speak well and convincingly at Matsieng.

Although they were unhappy, on the other hand, they were happy. The King losing his case this time might help him in future to heed their advice.

The second evening after Mosito returned from Matsieng, there was a pitso. We call it a pitso, because there was a purpose. Although the pitso was not intended for all the King's subjects, we, however, can still call it a meeting – mainly because there was an agenda. Four people gathered and nobody knew about it except those involved. The convenor was Khati. He brought Sebotsa and Maime, together with a new face who was the fourth person: Selone, the one who had the power to talk to the gods and the ability to uncover people's secrets and to anticipate an evil force before it reared its ugly head.

"Fellows, the job that we have to undertake is big and heavy," said Khati when everyone was seated. "Our king is in great trouble, and while being in trouble he wants to avoid us. I say this because he has spent the whole of today going with Pokane and Khosi. We were aware, however, just before he left for Matsieng, that he was avoiding *them* at all costs and leaning towards us. I have called you because I know you love the King. I want us to share our thoughts on how he could be helped to retain the rights and authority he has been stripped of. I, therefore, humbly ask you to open up and tell me how this could be achieved. Let me conclude by saying I have also invited our new friend Selone, who, according to my humble thinking, came to our village as an interventionist from the ancestors to assist the son of our former king, who is being misled by those who hate him. By now, I believe everybody knows Selone and his marvellous works and I believe that you won't object to his presence here today at this special gathering."

"I entirely support his presence at this gathering," Sebotsa said. "I have seen him and am convinced by his works. He is the man who has the ability and skills to help us in our endeavour."

"I have no other words except to say I totally agree with you all," said Maime.

"So what should happen now that the King has lost his case at Matsieng?" asked Khati.

"I am overjoyed that he has lost at Matsieng. Losing the case will teach him to humble himself and learn to listen. When a calf is being tamed and the person who tries to ride it for the first time refuses to use the taming rope – in the belief that the rope has no purpose – and the young boys leave him to his own fate as well, he relies on his cleverness to stay on the calf with his legs only; the calf will throw him off and he will fall on the ground, senseless. When he gets up and wants to try again, the first thing he will do is to look for a rope. The King also refused to ride his calf with a rope, but today, now that he has been thrown off, he will be wise enough to use it. By saying that I suggest we go back to him to show him the folly of refusing to consult a traditional doctor before he went to court. I am certain that we will find him unresisting and soft as lambskin."

"You have just expressed in full how I feel," said Sebotsa, blinking as usual.

"I have not finished yet."

"Sorry, my brother, excitement got the better of me. Your words washed my gut. I do not have any objections to your observations. Continue and finish your point!"

"This would be my last comment. Our king is in the middle of two groups who differ greatly when it comes to reasoning. I mean us and the boys to whom he is closely attached. Because we do not know what it is that they are feeding him right now, let us assist him in a manner that would benefit him. We have a friend whose powers have already helped us. When there is a cave nearby, and it once saved your life during a stormy season, every time you encounter difficulties you will run to that cave for protection. In this debacle our cave is our queen. She once helped us and I don't see why we shouldn't go back to her for assistance to stop everything that Pokane and company are trying to teach him. I am done."

"I hear what you are saying," said Khati. "Now, when we go and see the Queen, what do we want from her? What is it that we want the King to do to get back his rights? We have to get our facts right before we come up with a trick."

Sebotsa closed his eyes and when he opened them, said, "I'm sure I have heard Maime properly, and if I have, what he suggests is that we should find a traditional doctor, and that the doctor should provide the King with the type of service we recommended earlier and which he refused. And when all we have suggested has been done, the case should be started all over again. Is that not what you are saying?"

"You heard me as clearly as if you had been in my mind all the time."

"Right, your intentions are the same as mine. There is no way we differ in this."

When Khati had said that, he turned and looked at Selone. "My master, I hope you have heard the intentions of the three of us who work together. We have already figured out what kind of assistance we need. We don't want to assume that you are a professional in that specific field. Because, you see, we may conclude that you are an expert in all traditional fields, only to find that you specialise in one particular part of that field and so may not be able to assist us. Have you ever worked on something like this? I mean the medicine that would help win a case, the medicine that would give the plaintiff a favourable outcome in the courts?"

Selone cleared his throat and faced the three men. "I do not believe in self-praising; it is always better for a person to be praised by others. However, because I am not known here, there is no one to proclaim my expertise, so please allow me to say: that is something that I have tried before but only when the gods permitted me to do so."

"I hear you. You speak as traditional healers typically do."

As he said that, Khati smiled to show that he clearly understood exactly what Selone was saying: he meant that he usually provided this kind of service and that their specific request was in his area of expertise.

"So let me discuss this with you, doctor," said Khati, and he continued. "Our king is very stubborn. He does not listen to anyone when it comes to matters regarding traditional healing. He has dismissed suggestions in this direction a number of times, so I have no idea how to even begin reintroducing this topic to him. I know you heard Maime talking about getting help from the Queen. She tried and failed to persuade Mosito to consult a traditional healer before. I don't know how she would respond to our request to engage him yet again."

Selone said, "I know all about those kind of things. Some horses need to be confronted head on while others need to be approached indirectly. First, you get close to it and you start by stroking it, making it relax, and then you begin to saddle it gently. It is also like that with human beings. If there is anything that you want them to do, you need to study them first, know their likes and dislikes, and when you have studied them properly, you come up with a plan about how to handle them and then that plan should work easily. I haven't studied your king that well, but at this stage, I feel I can take the risk and say: maybe I have already figured out how to convert him into believing what we say."

"If you feel confident that you can assist us in solving this problem, I will try and arrange a meeting with the King tomorrow evening for all of us to have a conversation." Khati said. "However, I have to warn you, I cannot promise a one-on-one session with him, because these days it is clear he finds us unworthy of his time. We are useless. We are people who want to derail his style of leadership; and this he is being taught by Pokane and Khosi. Even as we speak, that school is in session. And indeed, people, the world is turning like the wheel of a vehicle!"

11

Falling into the trap

It was early in the morning and the sun touched the mountains. A messenger arrived at King Mosito's royal place with a letter from the royal place of Ratšoleli, inviting King Mosito to a meeting – an urgent case needed his presence that day.

Khosi read the letter and informed the King. Horses were collected and saddled and all the men left with King Mosito, except Maime, who reported that he had spent a sleepless night due to an upset stomach. Although he had taken some medicine in the morning, it kept him on his toes and made him run. Please, could the King allow him to remain home? He bent forward while pleading, grimacing to show that his stomach was in a serious upheaval. It was as if somebody was cutting his stomach with a sharp knife!

As King Mosito was a sympathetic person, he allowed Maime to stay home. Before they left, the men saw Maime running several times to the hillocks. Some even began to wonder whether they would not find him gone to the ancestors when they returned!

Riding with his people, the King was on his grey horse. Next to him were Khati and Sebotsa and others could see that they were little stars, next to the moon. The hooves clattered across the Sejabatho rivulet, and sounded until they disappeared behind

Rooijane's fields. When the party approached Baterefala, people came out of their homes and stood in small groups, watching the stately procession with its grey horse in front, gracefully showing off how swiftly it placed its hooves. The other horses moved faster to catch up, but they were already sweating, their mouths white with foam, while Mosito's grey horse looked as fresh as ever. They passed Baterefala, crossed the river and went straight to the fields of King Moshoeshoe.

When they pass old man Lesenyeho's fields, we will stop relating the journey and turn back home to see what was happening to someone who was on the verge of death!

At dawn, the women and girls scattered; some went to collect dry dung at the fields, while others went towards the river to collect wood. The village lay in peaceful silence. When all was quiet, Maime came out from the hillocks, walking slowly until he reached home. Looking around to make sure no one was watching him, he sauntered into the King's place. He found the Queen at home, seated and sewing, because, although she was a queen, she did not fear doing any kind of handwork.

"Good morning, Madam!"

He sat down on a little box nearby, and was quiet, waiting for a response to his greeting.

"Good morning Mr Maime. How are you feeling? I was informed that you could not go to the meeting with the King because of an upset stomach?"

Maime laughed so hard that one could see his molars.

"Why are you laughing about my concern?" She was surprised because Maime's laughter did not indicate a sick person.

"What upset stomach?"

"What are you saying?"

"I'm saying what I'm saying."

When he laughed uproariously again, the Queen became annoyed.

"Surely, I will tell the King that you were not sick, you were just lazy. Why did you stay when all the men have left?"

She took her hands from the machine she was sewing on, and looked at Maime, surprised.

"You do not know me, Madam. My name is Maime. Maime and Maimane – Deceiver and Liar – are one and the same thing. As you know, the Sesotho proverb says, 'bitsolebe ke seromo' – a bad name is a blot."

"All the same, please tell me why you remained behind?"

"Madam, I remained behind due to my love for the King."

"That is a strange love that separates you from the person you love. I have never heard of such love."

"If I had accompanied him, I would not be able to serve him as well as I am doing now, having remained at home."

"Indeed, you are a real Maimane!"

She turned back to her machine and continued sewing for quite a long time, as if there was no one in the house except herself. After a while, Maime spoke again.

"Madam, if I have to tell you the truth, there is nothing wrong with me. I just wanted a chance to stay behind so that I could talk to you."

Now, the Queen pulled a face.

"What is it that you want to discuss with me, Maime? Please don't cause trouble. What can I discuss with you in the absence of other people? Mosito will find out when he returns, so you can just as well stop now!"

"If you tell him, you do not love him. If you tell him, you will fail me in the work I am doing for his sake. Do not make a mistake,

Madam, I haven't come to say things that will disgrace you. No, I'm here to discuss with you the loss at Matsieng."

'Mathabo's face brightened up at once in the peaceful way that she was known for. She even smiled a bit, "Now I understand, but I can't see how I can be of help. You talk about a case that concerns men."

"You can help enormously. You once helped us, and I hope that you will be kind enough to help us again."

"How did I help you?"

"When the King had dismissed us, refusing to dispute his case, you helped us. After you spoke to him, he agreed, although he did not tackle the matter according to our wishes."

"Now, I understand."

"But here is the point, Madam: he refused to consult a doctor as we suggested, and said he had never heard of a case that was won through this kind of help. We then left him to handle it the way he thought best, and yes, there it was, he lost the case."

"Now that he has lost, what kind of help can I offer?"

"Having lost the case is a big help to us, because now his ears will give us a hearing, if you agree to help."

"But you said you failed. How will you succeed now?"

"Madam, there is only one person who has the power to control the heart of a man – his wife. I am sure that if you decide to talk to him seriously and show him the foolishness of refusing to use Sesotho herbs, he will listen to you, so that by the time we talk to him, he will be ready and willing to listen. Madam, I am appealing to you with my whole heart that you be kind enough to help us in this. Bear in mind that we are fighting for your son, for the day he takes over as king. He has to find that there is still something to fall back on, to live on and provide for his own children."

"Well, I shall try, but the way I know my husband, I can't promise much."

"But I have great hope. The main help I request from you is that you suggest to the King that he should be careful about the young men he has befriended. You are a Mosotho child, and while growing up you saw how national affairs were conducted. The advisers of the King were adults who knew Sesotho law and customs, and were not these boys who were brought up by a school and have never even sat at court. The King would not be difficult if he was advised by those of us who know Sesotho culture. Please advise him to push these boys aside and listen to our advice. He should listen to what older people tell him, because we know how affairs should be run. If you can do that, you will see what we can do for the King. You will be so surprised."

"Please, you may go, now. I will try in every way possible to help you, but if I fail, do not regard me as unkind and unreliable."

Maime thanked her and left a very happy man. When he came out of the enclosure, he bent forward again, walking slowly until he reached his yard, where he lay down and fell asleep.

It was late afternoon when King Mosito returned. As usual, when the horses appeared at the fields of Rooijane, ululations resounded from everywhere. The village was in a jovial mood. As the procession reached home the jubilation grew, because if the Basotho loved and respected anything, it was their kings. This was one thing that did not die out in any Mosotho. He could be anywhere, but the love of his king was planted in his heart; its veins ran through his body.

King Mosito arrived in good humour, indicative of his successful visit. We can mention that the senior king had invited him to discuss what he had in store for Mosito around the latest developments, and how this would enhance his position and give him greater responsibility. This pleased Mosito immensely and he decided to abandon the idea of disputing, which, of course, Khosi and Pokane supported.

When they reached home, Khati took him aside and asked whether the King could spare them a few minutes in the evening for a meeting to discuss a few things with him. Although he was tired, Mosito agreed to meet them because of his happiness. Khati thanked him.

In the evening, Khati and his friends arrived at their normal meeting place for discussing private issues. They found Mosito already waiting. While he was willing to meet them, he frowned when he saw them enter with Selone.

"I thought only the three of you were coming."

His frown remained etched. It was clear he did not approve of what was happening.

"My lord, we thought that because this visitor has travelled extensively, and knows a lot, you would perhaps appreciate his presence. He might be of great help to us." Khati spoke humbly and it was evident that he had not expected this obvious irritation in the King.

"I understand, but in future you should tell me in advance. I do not want to discuss my affairs with strangers. I want to stress that Selone and I do not know each other. I only know Selone as a herbalist; but his life history I do not know, where he comes from I do not know."

What King Mosito said made the men shrink. It became apparent that they would not be able to speak freely.

"What is the news you have in mind, Khati?"

Khati was someone who did his best not to show fear when he was frightened. He believed it did not befit a real man to look frightened, so he answered quickly.

"My lord, we have come to see you in connection with the case you lost at Matsieng."

"I'm listening."

"Now, my lord, we once spoke to you before you went to Matsieng, but it was evidently not acceptable to you."

King Mosito cleared his throat as if he was about to speak, but when his throat was clean he kept quiet and looked at Khati. From his expression one could see that he was urging him to finish quickly.

"We have come again, my lord." As he was losing hope, Khati's voice was faltering. "Our plea is still the same one. We believe there is no case whatsoever that will succeed without herbs. This is the truth that you should have realised by now. If you had heeded our advice, you would have been successful at Matsieng. But there is still hope."

King Mosito cleared his throat again but remained quiet. Now they were in trouble, because they had said everything that they had to say, but he was not saying anything. For a few minutes they were all quiet, looking down at the floor. Now and then they glanced at each other, puzzled.

At last Sebotsa summoned some courage. "My lord, I do not think there is more that we can add to what Khati has already said. All he has said is what we feel should have happened. We are therefore waiting to hear what *you* have in mind on this day."

"My opinion has been made clear to you and I stand by it. I have not changed my mind. You got the answer before I went to Matsieng and until this minute, today, it has not changed."

It was clear that they had reached a dead end, and the matter would not be discussed again. From his eyes they could see that, if there was nothing different they could add to what had already been said, it was better to keep quiet.

"Maybe the King would appreciate hearing the opinion of a guest who is visiting various parts of the country," said Selone.

A harsh expression settled on Mosito's face, and it was clear that he was biting back angry words. The atmosphere became so ugly, that if Selone had seen anywhere to hide, he would have.

"So now, *you*, who has invited you to feel free to tell me what you think? When I welcomed you at my place, I thought you were a doctor who was just selling herbs and treating the sick. My hospitality does not mean that I want your advice, so you can stop interfering in my affairs immediately."

The poor fellow realised that if he said anything more, he would be ordered to leave. He mumbled, "Oh please, my lord, I beg your pardon," and shut his mouth.

Mosito was filled with fury, like an angry lioness protecting her cubs, and turned to his men.

"You, Khati, and you, Sebotsa, and you, too, Maime. I have told you that for us to be on good terms, you must stop discussing such matters with me. Do you smoke dagga? Do I look like a person who smokes dagga? I warned you once, I am warning you for the second time, but I will not warn you a third time! Do you hear me, I say, I will not warn you a third time! I told you in no uncertain terms that I am following in my father's footsteps and doing as he taught me.

"This man, who is one of yours, I do not know and I shall not follow what he stands for. Is this clear, once and for all, you silly old men!"

He stood up and the others realised that the meeting was closed and their case probably also closed for good. They stood up and went out, disgruntled. From there they went to Khati's home to revise their strategy. They were dejected. No one spoke, no one cleared a throat. Each was fighting his own feelings, with no word for one another.

"Fellows, today I am surrendering, we have lost and it does not matter. We have tried everything at our disposal, but we have been beaten." Khati spoke sadly.

"Well, today I have also lost hope," said Sebotsa. "I had hoped that losing at Matsieng would make him change his mind, but he seems to be harder now than before. Could you feel that his words were getting tougher and tougher! I think we should now drop the whole issue."

"As I see it," said Selone, "what angered him was that I spoke, but I don't think you should leave him. He does not know what he is doing; he's still a baby. I swear that if I could find a way to talk to him about this matter, and he listened to what I said, he would never escape. I am not just another boy!"

"It's evident that Khosi influenced him strongly on their trip to Matsieng," said Maime. "Ever since he returned from Matsieng he has been pushing us aside. But wait, I haven't told you yet! I worked hard when you went to a meeting at Ratšoleli's. I left no stone unturned. But, if that also fails us, we will have to surrender."

Meanwhile, Selone was fuming because the King had humiliated him in front of people who celebrated him as a demigod. As we have seen, Selone had performed miracles these men had never seen before, so they regarded him as someone deserving of great honour because of his special knowledge of the ancestors, but now Mosito had spoken to him as if he were just a boy, herding goats. His feelings were in turmoil and he did not know what to do to retain the honour the three men had for him.

Eventually he said, "Fellows, not since I was born, has anyone spoken to me in this manner. Even kings mind their words when they talk to me. But your king, who is just starting to govern, spoke to me in a very dismissive way, which angers me greatly. When people speak to me as he did, things do not end well. I feel I must teach him a lesson. I am Selone and not Mrs Selone."

The men shrank and felt chills running down their spines and bodies. They thought of the terrible mysteries he had showed them and shivered.

"I repeat, I am not Mrs Selone, I am Selone! I will teach him a lesson, and he will fear me for life!"

To the Basotho, a ngaka is feared most. When Selone said he would discipline Mosito, Khati was shaken to his roots. He thought of that enormous black snake sent to end his life. Sebotsa and Maime also thought of the things they had seen from this doctor. Each debated with himself what terrible things Selone could do to Mosito. A person who can talk to the gods in his sleep, was there anything he could not do?

"Master, he is a child and he knows nothing. Please just pardon him," said Khati, as humbly as he could.

"There is nothing I can promise now. I will attend to that tomorrow. At the moment I wish to sleep and talk to the gods because I am a messenger and can do nothing without getting my instructions from them."

He stood up and left the three men greatly alarmed, because they did not know what to do to ease Selone's anger.

After Selone left, he went straight to the hut he was sleeping in, took his bags and herbs and went out and walked around in the village, as usual. He went on like that for about an hour. Afterwards, he returned to the house and slept. He slept like a man who had no problems, who was at peace with the world, who commanded everything in the world the way he wanted.

Now, let's leave him here and go to Mosito, to see what he is doing at this moment.

After the meeting with Khati, Mosito went straight home to sleep. He felt depressed and unhappy. It was understandable: a person became angry after he repeatedly had said what he did not approve of, but people continued to bother him; trying to send him where he did not want to go. On these grounds, his anger was acceptable. When he got home, his wife had just retired, but the light was still on. The Queen realised at once that the happy face she saw when he returned from the meeting at Ratšoleli's place was gone, and she was very surprised.

"What is the problem, Ntate, that you arrive looking so sad?"

"I think I have sat too long laughing with these people."

He pulled a chair next to his bed, sat down and was quiet for a long time.

"Who are those people, Ntate?"

"It is this man they call Khati! Today he dragged into our meeting a vagabond of a so-called herbalist, whom I do not know, nor where he came from, or where he is heading to tomorrow morning. I want to tell this man that he must leave my place. I do not like a visitor interfering in the affairs of the community like he is doing."

The Queen knew and understood at once what angered her husband. She decided there and then to use her female power to become involved with this war conquering so many men. She had promised Maime she would! Again, she was a Mosotho, who believed very much in mysterious things and witchcraft, who believed that some affairs could only be successfully concluded when a person was strengthened by strong herbs. She would demolish this wall of rebellion that her husband had built; she would not be done until she had crushed it to its foundation stones!

"What have Khati and his friends said to you that you decided to chase Selone away?"

"They are over-eager and tell me I should look for a doctor to strengthen me. After I told them that herbs were not part of my belief, they started all over again with the case I lost at Matsieng. It was then that this non-entity called Selone had a say. That was something that annoyed me to the extreme: that a person will try to say something about affairs totally unknown to him, and, uncalled for, suddenly want to have a word! Have I ever called him to be my advisor?"

The Queen rose from her bed. Seated, she looked her husband squarely in the face: "I don't think you are right to be angry. To me a doctor is a contemplater. Wherever he goes, he listens, wishing to hear where his services might be needed so that he can get some remuneration and then move on to another place. It's clear to me that Selone wanted to say something because he is a doctor, and he was thinking that maybe you will give him a chance. Perhaps he was hoping that if you accept the advice of those elderly men, you would possibly ask him to help you. For I believe that Khati and his friends have already told you about his work in this village. But before I continue, here's another question."

"I am listening."

"How did Selone know that you were going to speak to Khati and his friends?"

"How could he have known if not told by Khati?"

"You see, Selone is innocent. The fault lies with whoever invited him to join you in your private affairs. You are also at fault, because if you did not want him to hear your secrets, you should have ordered him to leave before the meeting started. By allowing him to stay and listen to what you and Khati had to discuss, you indicated that his advice would be welcomed. I would have also done the same if I were him. That's why he probably did not hesitate to say something where he thought it appropriate."

Mosito paused for a while, as if digesting what his wife had said. Eventually he spoke. "Well, I can see how you look at it. Maybe you are correct when you say that I am at fault with Selone: the misunderstanding was not his fault, but Khati's."

"Khati's as well as yours," the Queen added. "Now, how did you answer them?"

"I told them their herbs were irrelevant to me. Besides, the case is closed and buried, and I will not reopen it. You too know very well that from the outset I was not in the mood to tackle the case. Actually, *you* were the one who wanted me to dispute; Khati and his group I had already dismissed."

The Queen was quiet, digesting the words lying in her heart, and realised that they were deep, and to pull them out into the open would be very difficult.

"But are you satisfied that the case has ended where it has?"

"Yes, that is my opinion, and I shall not change it."

"Ntate, you and I have not been brought up the same way. You were brought up the European way, and all that pertains to Sesotho culture you were not taught because you spent your time at school in the Cape, where you were taught European wisdom only. I grew up at home; I grew up the Sesotho way, and was taught all the Sesotho customs. Therefore what I know is Sesotho custom, which you do not know. So it is with me too: what you know is European, which I do not know. I have been deceiving myself by thinking after our marriage that your choice to marry a woman who was brought up differently to you – one who could help you when Sesotho affairs were at crossroads – was a good one, because it was evident that your knowledge was wanting. But now I realise that is not the case, because in the Sesotho affairs, which I understand well, you do not wish to listen to my advice."

"When did you ever advise me that I refused to listen?"

"There are many things, but let me point out one or two. On several occasions I suggested that you put up your own new home, a home of your kingship. Because according to the Sesotho customs a new king never builds his house at the old ruins of his father. And what have you done with that advice of mine?"

"I have done nothing, because I do not deem it necessary. There are many jobs that carry higher priority. I will not waste my time building unnecessary new houses when my father left me with so many already. If that is the Sesotho custom, it is one of those I have to abandon. I see no need for it, and if we all follow it we will have a country full of ruins!"

The Queen ignored that. "The second suggestion, which you also rejected, is that at the beginning of the New Year, in spring, all the children should get incisions against lightning. But you were just as adamant and now Thabo is already grown up but has never seen a razor blade."

"What has gone wrong, due to my refusal?"

"Well we haven't seen anything yet, but you must remember that sometimes something delays showing its nose and only when it does, do you realise that you have erred. But then it's too late to correct anything. I have to tell you, what really pains me deeply is that you refuse blindly when I ask you to seek the horn of your kingship, and to get a crocodile stone that is used by the senior kings. Your refusal is already bearing fruits: you lack dignity, you come across as a lightweight and that is why your affairs fail so much. It is the right of every king to have a crocodile stone that will clothe him in dignity and make him as fierce as a crocodile. I repeat: a king must have a horn for his kingship, mixed by an expert, by a true doctor. That horn encompasses many things: it makes the king command dignity, it makes him successful in many affairs, it makes people fear and respect him, and it compels senior kings to reserve his seat, to respect his standing in the eyes of the community. Can you boast and praise yourself that you possess all these things I have enumerated? If you are honest with yourself, you will admit that you don't. If you had the horn for kingship, you would be respected a lot more, even the Deputy Commissioner would reserve space for you.

But, because of your stubborn attitude, nobody knows who you are or where your council is. Next year, you will be removed, you will regret it, but the question is: where is your name among the senior kings of Lesotho? It is not there. Where is your salary that is meant for the one who calls himself a king? It's non-existent. It will never exist, even in the future!"

Here she sighed heavily. She waited for a while to regain her composure. Mosito was quiet, with elbows on his thighs, his head between his hands, deep in thought.

'Mathabo became calm and continued: "Because of your stubbornness, you have been stripped of all that belongs to you by birth, your name is being mocked, and next year, when the new changes are introduced, you will not have a chance to stay at home like the other kings, you will always be on the road, carrying out instructions and messages. But you, you will never issue an instruction again. You say you are relying on your education, it is the one thing that has clout in the eyes of your seniors, but if you examine the situation properly you will discover that this is by far not the case – if it were, then why are you not a member of the council? If things were to be swayed by education, you should have been the first to be considered for the council of Qacha district, but just look at the blind men now sitting on it! Those elected by the community are like merino sheep that can hardly see because of the wool hanging over their eyes, falling into dangers in broad daylight. Imagine a person like Selepe elected to represent the community? Do you ever ask yourself what he has that surpasses your ability? By birth, he is far, far below you. He is a peasant in education, but there it is, *he* is the one representing *you*, Mosito, you who tell youself that you are educated, who call yourself a king! Oh! Indeed.

"I am sorry, but here you are. You do not want to listen to your wife whom you married and love; whom you chose without anybody forcing you. If you do not want to listen to my advice, to whom will you listen, then? You want to listen to Khosi and Pokane? If they were the ones you married, then there's no problem, you will tell me. But to my mind, those are the people who have misled you badly. But you should remember that they do not see things as you do. I'm told that they are cautiously guarding their own interests. Maybe you think that you love them because you grew up together, attended school together, but if you listened to those who overheard them talking, you would realise that they have long since undermined you. They were just biding their time until you became king. I shall be convinced that you really love me, and regard me as your wife who loves you, the day you withdraw yourself from Pokane and Khosi and listen to my advice, listen to the advice of Khati and his friends – old men who know Sesotho customs well, who worked with our father until he went down to the cold ground. If you don't, I shall take my boy and return to the home of my father, because I do not want to die like a dog because of your stubbornness and ignorance."

Then she returned to her bed, pulling the blankets over her head so that she did not need to look at the face of the man who exasperated her so much.

Mosito spent a long time sitting in the manner we described earlier, meditating, examining the harsh, unforgiving words his wife had left him with. While he was digesting them, a moment dawned when he felt prone to believing what she had said.

"But, this is really strange," he thought to himself. "If these things are really true, why did my father neglect to inform me about them? It's true that I often hear people talking about the crocodile stone, talking about the horn of kingship, but I never once heard my father talking about such things. Not once! So, if that is true, the real truth, how could my father have been so terribly neglectful, when he loved me so much? Besides, where are *his* horn and crocodile stone? Where are they? Where did he keep them, when up to this day I have not seen them! He died in my arms, as it were!"

His mind simply refused. His father had repeatedly suggested that he had taught him what a king ought to know, and he had never mentioned things like this. Even on his death bed, he had not uttered a single word about it. The things he had told Mosito in the end, he had also told him earlier. He had said that he was deliberately repeating things so that they could find a resting place in his son's heart. Those were the last things his father had said with his heart; the last things he had said with his own tongue.

"But 'Mathabo is my wife, who was loved by my father, whom I also love without being forced to do so. Would she really lead me astray, and drive me into a ditch? For what reason? She has always been a loving person to me. Although she is not educated, she has a natural intelligence, and there are many things that she knows. The things she predicts often turn out to be true. Could such a person deceive me, betray me, lead me into danger? What would she reap from such action? If I was a polygamist I would say maybe she's jealous, and wants to destroy me so that I can stop, but polygamy is something I do not desire. I have never even once spoken about it.

"So why would she want to lead me astray? Although I do not believe what Khati and his friends tell me, I feel drawn to believe her. Would I be going *against* my father's instructions, if I accept her advice, and even go to the lengths of acquiring the horn for my kingship? But I should not deceive myself. I lack stature, because if I had it, the things that have happened to me would not have happened. When I went to meet the Deputy Commissioner, he did not accept me with the enthusiasm I expected. He regards me as an ordinary headman. Again, because of my education, he was supposed to trust and love me more than all the kings in this district, but that is not the case. He considers me a light-weight, yet my father he respected very much. He never failed to mention that he was just a commoner and my father's servant because the country belonged to my father. Today things have changed. He is no longer a commoner. I am now the commoner and the owner of the country is no longer me, but him. Really, there are still many things I have to learn before I can settle down in my chair, be respected and be known."

He spent a long time thinking deeply, asking himself questions and answering them, trying to assess the reasons his wife presented. These remarks refused to disappear. They were firm and pointed at the truth.

After a long time, he stood up and prepared to sleep. After he had undressed and put on his pyjamas, he noticed that the window next to him was still open, and wanted to close it, but, just when he was about to turn around, he suddenly jumped and spoke to himself.

"Oh, what mysterious thing did I see?"

He struck a match to light the lamp because he had already snuffed it. He took a kierie and hit at the window. The noise woke his wife.

"What is it? What are you doing?"

"You ask me? Don't you see this mysterious thing?"

"What thing," his wife asked, terrified. "What do you see which makes you frighten me so?"

"When I wanted to close the window, I found a snake twisted on it."

He bent down and from under the bed pulled an extremely large cobra.

"Do you see?"

He raised the snake into the air. His wife jumped on her bed, shook herself and shouted loudly with a piercing voice like a person who was about to faint. Mosito put the snake down, rushed to her and told her to stop panicking as he had killed the snake.

When she settled down, Mosito inspected the snake again. It was, indeed, a cobra – a big one. The stomach was swollen, as though it was pregnant. When he examined it closer, he discovered that the snake had died some time ago because its skin was no longer moving. A snake takes a long time to die and its skin moves constantly. When a snake's head has been crushed, the body carries on moving and twisting because only the head is dead. The body is still alive.

What surprised him more was when he realised that he had hit it towards the tail. He considered that perhaps the snake was not dead, just cold, and that, when it warmed up again, it would create havoc. So he put the snake in a tin and closed it tightly, so that even if it woke up, it could not get out.

When he had done that, he slept. He slept badly because each time the blanket touched him, his body shrank.

12

The plot thickens

Mosito spent a terrible night. Every time he was about to fall asleep, he dreamt of a snake biting him and he jumped up. This fitful and restless sleep lasted until dawn. He woke up and went to the kraal as usual, to inspect the cattle before they left for the fields. The boys were milking. But all the time, while looking at the cattle, his feelings were not with them; he was simply looking at them. Those who saw him thought that he was appreciating the beauty of his bovines, the black and white ones, and the brown ones. But his inner eyes were not where he was standing. He was digesting the things his wife had said to him the night before, agonising whether or not to accept them. When he tried pushing them from his mind, his thoughts made a turn for the worse: the snake coiling at the window. Where had that snake come from? Had the boys put it there, simply to scare him? Did the boys put it there already dead? Why was there no visible wound of a deathblow? Do snakes die like other animals? He had no answers.

He quickly moved away from the kraal and returned home. When he entered the neat enclosure of his place, he met the Queen. He called her into the bedroom. After they had entered quietly, Mosito took the tin and opened it, but carefully, thinking maybe the snake was alive and could bite him or spit into his eyes.

"Do you see, 'Mathabo? Here is the snake I was talking about last night." Mosito threw it on the floor. It didn't move. It was dead. 'Mathabo froze when she saw it, but after realising that it was dead, she went closer to inspect it.

"This is indeed a riddle that such a snake would be at the window," said 'Mathabo. "In your mind, where do you think it comes from?"

"How would I know, if I only found it at the window last night? I thought you might know. Were there any boys near the house yesterday?"

"Nobody ever comes close to our house."

"But how did this snake get here?"

"If it could speak, it would."

"It is strange that we should be visited by snakes not often seen around here."

He turned it around once more to make sure it had no other wound except the small one towards the tail where he had hit it. This piled one startling question upon the other, because a snake, until its head is crushed, will not die and can still bite. Mosito was quiet and looked at his wife for a long time.

"Why are you looking at me for such a long time?"

"Who shall I look at when I am shocked?"

"This is exactly what I was telling you yesterday, you think you can explain everything! If you were not so obstinate, I would have advised you, but, as things are, it'll be a waste of time, because you don't listen to me. If I *have* to suggest something, I will say go and talk to Khosi and Pokane – they are the ones you listen to. Maybe they can tell you how this snake landed here. They are sages and there's nothing they cannot explain. The books tell them everything, including the movement of snakes."

"I cannot talk to you when you are so...so sarcastic! Which book tells one about the movement of snakes? Any advice you are willing to give me, I will welcome."

"Like what? You just want to disturb my soul."

"Well, I am the one speaking at the moment. If you can advise me, do so."

"My advice remains the same: according to my Sesotho up-bringing, a thing such as this one is a mysterious signal, and when such a pointer has occurred, people normally ask what could have caused it. You have to talk to the ancestors to find out whether there is something they are dissatisfied about. They should say it, or, if there is imminent danger, tell us. There is only one way to talk to the ancestors, and that is by means of divining bones."

Mosito sighed deeply, like a person who had found a solution to a riddle that had tormented him for a long time.

"I understand how you explain things. But you know very well that I don't believe in these things. Nonetheless, my dear wife, because I want to please you, I will do so."

"Not to please me. If you don't believe, don't even bother going there, because when those blessed with the knowledge tell you something, you will say they are telling a lie. And of course you will tell everybody that I harrassed you to consult a doctor. I want you to know: I am out of all your affairs, because you do not regard me as your wife, as someone you could trust. You know what: your wives are Khosi and Pokane. Consult a doctor if *you* deem it necessary, but do not go to please me. You failed long ago to do that."

'Mathabo felt happy speaking like this. She could see that her husband had become clay in the hands of a boy moulding an ox. The boy takes a small quantity of clay and turns it around several times to mould an ox, and then, in the middle of it, changes his mind and says no, now I am moulding a horse. And the clay will not argue with him and will allow him to do what he likes with it.

Mosito, despite his upbringing, was deeply frightened by the mysterious snake. He felt that he or his wife faced great danger.

But 'Mathabo was happy because she knew that it was precisely this mysterious occurence that enabled her to force her husband onto the road she preferred, the one she was used to, the one of using traditional methods, as befitted kings.

"I would like to know what divining bones say in this case. But could I call Khati, for we might frighten ourselves over nothing?" he said.

"It won't be right for you to call them. If you want them to be present, call them to listen to the case. But I want the doctor to come not knowing anything, so that we can prove that he knows how to deal with divining bones."

That was the first time Mosito listened to his wife's advice without any objection. He put the snake back into the tin, hid it, and went to the court hut.

'Mathabo had bombarded her husband so much that questions and answers were dominating his mind. But something else worrying him was the thought of Khosi and Pokane. He loved them deeply, trusted their advice and adhered to it completely. But in these affairs he did not wish to involve them in any way. He knew very well that, even though out of respect they may not say it to his face, in their hearts they would despise him for believing in these things. They had isolated him and placed him in a position where he did not have the social interactions most Basotho had.

Now he was in a fix and eager to hear what the bones had to reveal, and could not wait for the consultation. What was he to do? If he called Khati and his group to his home, but not Khosi and Pokane, they would realise at once that something was out of order. After debating this matter for a long time, he decided to dismiss them from his home after a short period and then, while they were gone, have another meeting with the other group. When the first group returned they would find the meeting over.

He went to the court hut and called Khosi and Pokane, going to the stables to speak to them there.

"Gentlemen, I notice that the Thamahanyane owner has sent me an account of fifteen pounds, but he has not listed the separate items I bought. In my estimation, the items I bought do not exceed ten pounds. So I would like to know how he arrived at this amount. I want you to go and ask him to indicate the cost of each item. Please make it clear to him that I do not deny the account, I just want to be sure about the exact amount. If that European agrees, ask him to show you the journal where the transactions are recorded. I want you to scrutinise them."

Mosito knew that the account was accurate, but only wanted to send these two away to have a chance to deliberate with the other group while they were gone. The Basotho have a saying: it is never difficult to make a plan, except in the case of death. Here it is; we see it happening. Pokane and Khosi were satisfied about what the King had said, so they went away without the slightest suspicion that there was any hidden agenda or that they had been sent away with a purpose. Theirs was to carry out the instructions in a manner that would please the King. On horseback they crossed the river from the shop, passed this side of the school to join the main road and reached the Mokhachane village, where everybody saw them as they meandered along the road and passed below Monateko's.

Mosito called Khati and asked him to come for a meeting with those who had been present the previous day.

"Selone as well, Sir?"

"Don't you understand Sesotho? I said: all who were present." The King turned and left.

Khati was puzzled about what could have happened the previous night. The King had parted from them with a cold, angry face, but here he suddenly wanted to have a meeting with them!

Khati quickly called his friends and found the King waiting for them.

"Sit down!" he said.

They sat, petrified, not knowing what to expect. What would the King say? They found his face coarsely thickened as if a war was raging inside him.

"So you said you are a doctor, Selone?"

Selone froze where he was seated, but we are unable to say whether he was really frozen or whether it was mere pretence to deceive the others. He then spoke with a shaky voice, "It is true, I am a doctor."

"If that is the case, and you are a doctor, I want you to throw your divining bones this very minute, just cast them and tell me what you see!"

"Please, my lord, let me fetch my bag."

Selone left quickly and returned with an old ram's scrotum skin, shiny and dirty, as the wool had worn off long ago due to frequent use. He arrived somewhat agitated, the freezing was gone and he behaved like a doctor, with wise and piercing eyes. Khati and the others saw the change in him and began to relax a bit. They were not sure whether the King had planned to trap them unawares. Selone untied the bag, took out the bones and gave them to the King, "Just cast them, my lord, so that they can tell us what the problem is!"

Mosito took the divining bones, spat on them as was the formality and threw them on the floor. When they were spread, Selone scrutinised, and then praised them for a long time. When he was done, he looked at them again, shook his head and said, "My lord, just take them again so that I can see what they really want to say. What they show me now is only disaster."

Mosito took them again, and did as he had done before. Selone praised them again.

"Do you wish to know, Sir?"

"I wish to know, Selone."

"What I am going to say, my lord, is not from my mouth. I'm merely a spokesperson for the ancestors, the ones who are talking to you by means of these bones. So, if there's anything I say, which in your mind is untrue, just object."

"I understand."

"You wish to know, my lord, and the way I see it, you wish to know about something mysterious."

"I wish to know that."

"This is an animal mystery."

"An animal? No!"

"You should note, my lord, when I say animal, I generalise and talk about all living things that can walk, a person or a four-legged animal, or anything else that is alive. Do you want to know something about this mysterious animal?"

"According to this definition, I would say it is an animal, but – no, let me just agree – yes, I want to know about that."

"That's correct, Sir; this is your wish."

He looked at the bones again, his eyes going from bone to bone the way someone with shoes crosses a river from stone to stone, from rock to rock. He starts by jumping the first distance with his eyes to see how far it is, so that when he has to jump again, he manages to reach it and does not accidentally jump into the water.

"Although I said the mysterious event relates to an animal, it is not a four-legged animal."

"That's correct," Mosito confirmed spontaneously, and this showed how satisfied he was about what was said. "That's correct, Selone, it's not a four-legged animal."

Selone felt encouraged. He realised that the road was leading him to where they wanted to be.

"Now, this animal... Is it alive? Is it dead? Yes, it's an animal, but it seems dead. Yes, my lord, a mysterious dead animal."

Mosito confirmed quickly again, indicating that he was still satisfied.

"This animal has no legs, it glides, therefore it cannot be called an animal, but rather a sliding animal. You wish to know something about such a thing, my lord – that glider is a snake!"

Mosito's face relaxed at once, it was glowing, he even smiled. Khati and the others looked at one another in amazement. Although they already knew the work of the doctor, their amazement had just increased.

"You are correct if you say it was a glider!"

"My lord, I do not praise myself, because what I have is a gift from the ancestors. I have no reason to praise myself. But I can tell you that the ancestors agreed to talk to you and they will open great secrets for you. This thing you found was already dead, and you found it in the house, is that so?"

"Yes, it is like that, I found it in the house, dead."

Now Selone was full of energy. He knew that he had crossed the river. There were only a few stones left, which were so close to one other that it was unnecessary to jump. A stretch of the legs would reach them easily.

"I realised long ago, my lord, how conditions are. Before I proceed, let me just ask a question."

"Well, what now? I told you that *you* must tell me, and not ask questions. Tell me!" But Mosito smiled when he said that.

"No, my lord, my question is not like that, but will satisfy you that the ancestors have agreed to talk clearly to you."

"Inquire and let us hear you."

"Just tell me, my lord, the crocodile stone, which your late father used to keep with him and which he put under his pillow when he slept, where is it? Answer me freely and don't fear anything. These men are yours and I believe that you can tell your secrets in their presence."

"My father never had such a stone."

"Are you sure?"

"I can assure you, he…he…he…never had one!"

"Maybe you should have said you don't know, my lord, and not that it was never there, because, as we speak, it *is* somewhere, where you do not know… You will find that stone in the stomach of the snake. Did anybody enter the house where your father was during the last day of his illness?"

"Yes, people were entering, but I never knew that my father had a stone."

"Well, among those people who were going in and out, there was one who stole that stone. I am about to tell you about the culprit. He took that stone so that, when your father died, the one who had to succeed him would be without the stone; the dignity of kingship would not be on you because of not having that stone. That man has been keeping that stone until yesterday, when he let the snake swallow it."

"That is unreal!"

"But let me convince you, my lord. I'm proceeding because I haven't finished yet. This snake was sent to slither in among your blankets, so that when you slept, it should bite you and you would die. But the ancestors preserved your life and killed this snake before it could perform its mission. When you got home, it was already dead, but you did not know."

"What are you saying, Selone?"

"That is the position, my lord." He gathered the bones and put them in the bag. "That is the position, my lord, there is no other alternative. There are people who are fighting you."

Mosito was quiet and motionless for a long time. He was in deep thought. Eventually, he stood up, took the tin out from where he had hidden it and gave it to Selone to open. Selone took it. When he opened it, he dropped it to the ground. Everybody jumped up, except Mosito. Selone seemed quick to suppress his fear and took the snake out of the tin. When they looked at it, it had a big bulging belly.

"There is the snake the bones indicated, Selone. Cut it open and see what is inside – it could be small snakes, alive – so that we can crush their heads."

Selone took the knife and cut the belly open. Everybody was stunned. Selone took out a round, black stone; a smooth and beautiful thing, indeed, that was polished by an expert sculptor. It had a thin red line around it. When they first saw it, they thought it was a line drawn by hand, using blood, but on closer inspection they discovered that it was part of the original. Even after they took water to wash it off, they found it was a permanent red colour. They all looked at it with amazement.

"Selone," Mosito said finally, "ever since I was born I have never visited a person using divining bones. This is my first time today, but you have convinced me that a living person like me can have a secret known only by me, unravelled only in the manner you did here. You are a qualified doctor, and you should open a school where you could teach student doctors to use divining bones. If, in the use of herbs you are as good as in divining, surely I respect you!"

"Well, my lord, as I have already told you: I am just a messenger of the gods. They use me to speak to their descendants. When they're in a good mood, they point the herbs out to me and then I manage to present a gift from the gods to someone. That is the reason why one should never praise oneself, because the ancestors may decide this one is becoming too proud, and then deprive him of the gift."

"Now, in your mind, what should I do? You know that I have not dealt with these things before and now want to hear about our way forward."

"The thing is to strengthen yourself, my lord, because, according to what the bones say, the environment in this village is bad. It has become a playground for boys and girls, you know, those we call wizards. They take chances here, while the village of a king should be respected. I will take this snake with the crocodile stone. Both are important potions to be included in the horn I shall prepare for you, for a king."

"I understand and shall wait for your work, as directed by the ancestors."

"You formulate correctly, my lord, I am controlled by the ancestors. Therefore I cannot work now or tomorrow as the potions to be used will be pointed out for me by the ancestors. If you are fortunate, they might direct me tonight, but normally it takes about two days before they indicate. You have to understand, my lord, they may talk to me at night when I am asleep and even show me the leaves of the tree and roots of the medicine that I must gather or dig out, and how to use them."

"But if it is so obvious that I am in great danger, that something terrible may happen to me at any time, can't it be avoided while you wait for their instructions? Could they delay until the danger befalls me?"

Mosito was visibly afraid and not even trying to hide it. His voice was filled with remorse for his former scepticism about divining bones. At this stage, he could be compared to a raw head, a novice, who, on the day he accepts the Word of God, turns into a kind of lunatic, incessantly talking and revelling in the Word and its revelations, without fear or inhibition. Mosito became like that.

"I understand you well, my lord. I shall prepare a hut where you will shelter during the storms until I build you a real fortress."

After Selone, Khati and company had left, King Mosito remained alone, brooding. The things Selone had told him were sinking into his mind, spreading through his feelings, and he was accepting that ever since he had taken over as king, he had been foolish, deceived by school education. But something remained that he could not understand: why did his father not teach him what he learned today – especially since he taught him *everything* else that was necessary?

"If Isanusi were still alive," he said, "I would go and fetch him to come and talk to my father, as he did while working with Shaka. He helped him to talk to his father."

These were the things on his mind, but his lonely heart was disturbed by his wife. Queen 'Mathabo entered, her face radiant and smiling because her heart rejoiced as her husband had done what she most wanted. She spoke to him in a sweet voice, full of love and melodious, like a canary exulting in the forest during the summer over plentiful food.

"What did the bones say, Father?" She smiled and the dimples on her cheeks made her even more beautiful than she already was.

"The bones reveal something very frightening," he said, grimacing. Repeating, word for word, what Selone had said was not a pleasant exercise. But, to please his partner, he told her everything.

"Indeed, that is bad," she concurred. "Yes, that is really bad, and you will begin to see the reality of what I have been begging you to understand. Refusing to listen to my advice was not a good thing. I hope that from today you will take advice from older people, and not children who know nothing." She stressed the last word. "Because when older people advise they do from knowledge they have and do not talk out of ignorance."

"I understand, my sister, and I promise you: from now on I will be vigilant, act carefully, and open my ears to listen to your advice and that of the people who supported my father when I was growing up."

"I am happy about your commitment! Nonetheless, if you had listened to me from the outset, we wouldn't have had conditions deteriorating to this stage – nearly beyond remedy, filling up ditches and setting traps."

But the Queen was even happier than when she entered the room. Instinctively she felt that the warm little corner in her husband's heart – closed to her before – was now open and ready to accommodate her and she was contented that it would belong to her for as long as she lived. Which woman would not rejoice over such an occasion?

In the afternoon, Pokane and Khosi arrived back from their errand. They were lighthearted and cheerful because they had successfully carried out the instructions of their contemporary, the King, whom they, as young boys moulding clay oxen had vowed to support through thick and thin in adulthood. That vow they had already been carrying out, from the time Mosito started with community work, and it was soon evident in the eyes of the community that these men had dedicated themselves to support the King and serve him well.

"We met Thamahanyane, my lord," said Khosi when they arrived at a court hut where the King was sitting with other men.

"We checked the books carefully with him, and we are satisfied that the account is correct." He produced a piece of paper showing all the items the King had bought and their prices. He gave it to Mosito to check and satisfy himself. Mosito took the statement somewhat reluctantly, scanned it and put in his jacket pocket and said curtly, "It's fine!"

Khosi looked at Pokane, surprised, then turned to Mosito again, and found his face so hostile and averse that he could not continue talking to him. At this moment we may try to analyse Mosito's feelings to explain the complexity of this strange, sudden change Khosi and Pokane encountered in their king. When they had left that morning, he was the man they had known from childhood as contemporaries. Now, the Mosito from Lovedale in the Cape, the Mosito they had engaged with all their lives had suddenly changed dramatically.

From the time Mosito had parted with his wife that morning, he had started to analyse, from scratch, each and every word Selone had uttered. He dissected them like a scientist who wants to understand how something has been assembled: after dismantling the whole, carefully studying each piece under a microscope to see how it was formed, and what things could not be detected by the naked eye.

Among everything Selone had said, the gesture that stuck in his mind was the following: when Mosito cast the bones a second time, as ordered by Selone, he noticed that the bones formed a bunch and only two stood out and rolled to the side. Selone, when describing the dangerous situation, singled out these two and gestured by nodding his head that Mosito should watch them! Mosito took a long time reaching clarity on Selone's hint about those bones. But Selone did what most doctors do when they do not want to be blamed for sowing discontent: let the person seeking information from the divining bones interpret the bones. The gesture was left to be unravelled by Mosito with his sharp mind. He had taken a long time analysing what that nod had meant. In the first throw, the divining bones made a group suggesting all his councillors stood together at the very beginning of his reign: Khosi, Pokane, Khati and his friends. In the second throw, the two separate bones indicated Khosi and Pokane. That was Mosito's conclusion!

Were they not the ones who had advised him not to protest? Were they not the ones who continued to advise him after Khati and his friends' visit not to make a fool of himself by listening to their advice? Yes, whenever a person is influenced towards evil and suspicious thoughts, he fails to see any good in anything around him. Whatever he sees, he regards with a mistrustful eye; fails to see any good but feels haunted by a world swirling with evil intentions. The adverse feeling Mosito arrived at after digesting Selone's nod, made him forget everything Pokane and Khosi had done for him over their many years of friendship.

13

The potion is due

Five days and nights had passed since Selone had strengthened the home of King Mosito. After every daybreak, Mosito called Selone to hear whether the ancestors had pointed out the necessary herb for kingship, but each time the reply was negative.

On the sixth day, Selone came to the usual meeting place; he no longer required a messenger to call him to meet the King. He settled down. "My lord, to date nothing has been said, and I have to confess, I'm surprised. I don't know what could have gone wrong. The waiting time is unusually long, so I begin to think that the ancestors might be so unhappy that they have decided to stop talking to us."

Mosito did not answer immediately, absorbing the news by himself. "Now, what could be done to please them?" he asked after a very long time.

"When this happens, my lord, I usually tell the person with whom the ancestors are angry to slaughter a black sheep to mediate between the offender and the ancestors, so that they should pardon him. I think this is what we should do, my lord."

"I understand, Selone. Now, when should this be done?"

"To allow the process to run smoothly, it should be slaughtered very early in the morning before the sun rises, or very late in the evening, but before the sun sets and light is still visible over the mountain peaks."

"It is fine, as far as I am concerned. Shall we do it this evening?

"Yes, I had that in mind, my lord."

"I shall instruct the shepherds to bring the sheep home in time."

"That will be good, my lord, but I nearly forgot one important point: the blood of the sheep must be handled carefully so that the dogs do not lick it. That would anger the ancestors in our field of traditional healers. If the dog licks the blood immediately after the slaughter it means the dog has eaten before the gods."

When he finished explaining the process and procedure, he took a bow and left.

At that very moment, Khosi arrived at Pokane's place. He sat down and they were quiet together for a long time, exchanging looks.

Finally Khosi talked, "Homeboy, man, I cannot bear it a moment longer. What do you think?"

"Our thoughts seem to be transmitted by electrical wire. You arrived just when I was about to come to you to discuss this matter and see what we should do. We are sure about one thing: King Mosito does not wish to see even our shadows."

"I have also noticed that, Homeboy! I think we should just confront him and ask what he harbours against us. It seems he no longer wants to work with us. He must tell us so that we can decide whether to leave, to perhaps serve other kings. What I cannot stand, is to be looked at daily as though you and I have done something terrible."

Pokane did not answer. Instead, he stood up and together they walked straight to the King. They met him as he was coming out of his house, where he had met Selone. After greeting, Khosi said, "My lord, we have come here to discuss something with you that disturbs us greatly."

Mosito looked angrily at him, "What is your issue?"

"We will tell you, my lord, if you give us the opportunity to talk in private where nobody can disturb us, because the matter concerns all three of us."

Deep down, Mosito was not a cruel person and the love he had for Pokane had not diminished in his heart. But there were times, when the new sickness in him rose, that it vanished. His irritation usually showed when he saw how these two, who had turned into his enemies, enjoyed the privileges they had under him; so when he saw them now, a storm rose strongly in his chest and he felt fury in his heart. He said to Khosi, who was looking at him in exasperation, "If there are any secrets we have to discuss, *I'll* be the one to tell you. At present I do not need you. Besides, since when do you have the impertinence to look for me at my house? There is a courtyard where men congregate."

They ignored the question and Pokane said, "My lord, we are not here for an argument, because we don't like it. Our request is that you should talk to your heart and just listen to what we want to say."

This time, a tiny human flame came into Mosito's heart, and he calmed down. He turned back into the house and they followed him, not waiting to be told to do so.

"I give you five minutes to state your case, and then go to court or to your homes."

Mosito sat down, biting his upper lip which was so red it looked about to bleed.

Khosi cleared his throat twice and looked at Mosito. As they had been given five minutes only, he prepared himself to stick to headlines.

"Today, a week has passed since we noticed that you changed drastically. But we do not know what we did wrong. You are not as we knew you from the days of our youth. Your face indicates that you do not wish to see us, ever. That puzzles us because we do not know where we wronged you. We are pleading that you tell us why you resent us so."

"Please, my lord," added Pokane, "we would like you to tell us straight out without beating about the bush. Tell us whether you still need our services or that we should go, because you are tired of us at your village."

Mosito was quiet, yet fuming inside. His anger was so palpable that it could crush rocks. When he had his anger under control, he asked, "Finished?"

"Our lord," they said simultaneously.

Then Khosi continued, "From our side, everything is still in order. We wish to carry on working as usual."

"But, my lord," it was Pokane's turn to speak, "from your face we conclude that you are not as we have known you. If you are honest with yourself, you would agree. Your face does not show any happiness at all."

"My domestic affairs do not concern you. If you see me unhappy, and you are certain that you did not play any part in it, don't worry and don't involve yourselves. I am troubled by my own domestic problems and do not see why you should be involved. Again, if you really feel worried, interrogate the issue of a guilty conscience that harasses you."

"My lord, I have to confront you," said Khosi, "because we love you. You must have heard something strange that you do not want us to know about, because you think we played a part in it. Understand well, my lord, it's my opinion alone. Pokane may think differently. Come on, open up and please tell us what it is that you heard."

"Whatever Khosi is saying, is exactly how I feel too," said Pokane. "We argue with the same facts. You are hiding something from us. I want to go further than that and say you are working on a secret mission that you don't want us to know about. Is that not the case? Your eyes tell what you have locked up deep in your heart, my lord. We are aware of secret meetings held in the village and we are not being told anything about them."

Mosito stood up, looking at them with eyes blood-red with anger. "I told you: your jobs have not changed. So there is nothing more to say. But there is one thing I want you to understand very well: I am the king in this country and this village, so I am the one who decides who is to be invited to secret meetings and what is to be discussed with whom. You will not dictate to me whom I discuss my secrets with. You've heard me, and I have finished talking."

"This is acceptable, my lord, the choice is yours." Pokane stood up and went to the door. "We will continue with our work, but tomorrow you will think of us."

Khosi got up and followed Pokane. They left with whatever they had brought to the King. Mosito remained alone, in some turmoil.

When the shadows gathered, the boys collected the sheep and let them graze near the village. The sun went down, but some light remained at Souro. The sheep came home in silence with the bleating of the lambs as the only sounds.

King Mosito went to the sheep's enclosure with Selone and three additional men who lately dealt with whatever he needed. Mosito pointed at a black hamel. The boys caught it and brought it to the slaughtering place.

"There it is, Selone, a sheep for your people."

"I see it, my lord. Now take a knife. The blood must flow from your hand so that the blessings fall upon you, my lord."

Mosito took a knife from Selone, the men held the sheep, and he cut its throat. Its blood flowed into a container and he was careful to make sure as little as possible splattered on the ground.

Where a drop or two fell, the men covered them with some soil and cow dung. The sheep was skinned and the meat taken to the house.

At midnight, Selone and Mosito went to the graveyard carrying thyme mixed with blood, plus a herb Selone had dug up in the veld and crushed. When they got to the cemetery, Selone asked Mosito to point out his father's grave and then to take the potion and put it on the grave.

When that was done, Selone gathered some dry cow dung and made a fire on which, once it had burnt down, he sprinkled some powder until smoke went up. They left the graveyard and took the direction to where the Sejabatho stream and Senqu river collided, carrying the emptied out tripe. There they looked for a big stone, tied it to the tripe with a rope they brought from home, climbed onto a rock and cast everything into the river. By the time they returned home, the first cocks had just begun to crow. They got under their blankets and slept. At sunrise, they woke up feeling refreshed.

During the day, Pokane and Khosi went on with their daily routine as usual, but they were bothered. They saw there was no peace with their king even after they had spoken to him. It was only when he was in the company of Khati and the others that he looked really happy, talking freely and laughing, but as soon as Pokane or Khosi appeared, a black cloud fell on his face and the radiant smile turned into a scowl.

"We are about to get the news, Homeboy," Khosi told Pokane when they were alone. "Something strange is happening in this village. We can see Selone being called from time to time by the King, so something serious is going on."

At this stage, Mosito was no longer pretending that he and Selone were engaged in some serious official business. They were now great friends, whereas earlier, when his integrity was still intact, he would have nothing to do with people of Selone's sphere of influence. But because of the regular ridicule by his wife and Khati and his friends, Mosito was forced to break ties with his young contemporaries, and he was yielding intimately to the road his father's old friends advocated.

That evening, Selone, Khati, Sebotsa and Maime went to their usual meeting place with Mosito. They found him already waiting. His face was beaming with his happy mood. During the day Selone had hinted that the reply had come and promised to narrate everything at their usual meeting.

They all came in, basking in the joy on the king's face, and relaxed. Khati and his group happily highlighted the fact the King had finally arrived where they all wanted him to be.

"Selone, you hinted that the reply has come. What do they say?"

The rays of the sun from his face seemed to spread and light their faces, and their faces brightened.

"Yes, my lord. I got an answer and the potion has been identified."

"Was it not said why the answer was delayed?"

"No, nothing was said, my lord. In most cases, once the ancestors are happy, they forget the past. They don't dwell on anger, bitterness and revenge."

"I hear you. But please talk now; you seem to want me to dig out the information instead of just going ahead and telling it."

Khati and his group listened carefully to the message from the ancestors and Selone did not hide anything from them.

"My lord, when we returned from where we had gone to pray, I slept, and I fell into deep sleep at once. In my sleep I saw a man who told me he was the late King Lekaota. After he had greeted me, he said I should inform you he had forgiven you. He told me that he had spoken to his heart and had seen your weakness. He said he and the council of gods had decided to make you a very senior king."

"He has decided to make me a senior king!"

"He has decided to make you a very senior king, my lord! On one condition. If you want your kingship, and if indeed you want to be the senior king, you have to earn it. You have to prove to yourself and all those around you that you are worthy. However, you still have to find the relevant potion."

At this stage, everybody was so silent you could hardly hear a human breath. Everybody had their ears to the ground, like those hunters' dogs that hear the slightest sound signalling wildlife outside.

"You mean he plans to make me a senior king?"

"Indeed my lord, this is his plan, on condition that you prove that you are worthy of being trusted with such a huge responsibility, by finding the right potion.

"Selone, you know I am not a doctor. Where will I get the potion?"

"You will hear, my lord, that this potion is very hard to come by. That is why he said you should find it yourself, as *you* are the one who desperately wants to be a senior king."

When he finished saying this, he took a break. He behaved like someone about to break heavy news, thinking of ways and measures to break it so that it is acceptable to, and will be understood by, those listening.

"The potion needed here is human liver."

Selone's eyes became soft like that of a girl looking at the man she is romantically involved with, but then changed immediately – his eyes pierced like a pin stabbing those facing him; nobody could compete with those eyes. He looked at Mosito without blinking, waiting for his reply.

Selone's words hit Mosito's heart like a million needles entering a body with paralysing force. Fear engulfed the very core of his being, and he went ice-cold, even though it was hot. His brain stopped functioning. His body visibly froze.

Selone was staring fiercely at Mosito. "My lord, I can see you are afraid, but if indeed you need your kingship, you should prove your bravery, and show that you are human and that you can rule."

Mosito tried to talk but was tongue-tied. No word came out of his mouth. He could not utter a single sound.

"Selone, please give him time to think it over," Sebotsa came to his rescue when he realised that the King was in trouble, but his suggestion had no effect. Selone's eyes bore into Mosito, as a snake stares at a bird or a frog.

Finally Mosito managed only, "A human liver?"

"You heard me well, my lord. They need human liver. Fresh human liver taken out of a very healthy *living* being, and that person should come from the Bahlakwana tribe. He should be huge and strong."

He stopped and waited for Mosito to answer, but not a word came from the King's mouth.

Selone continued: "As I was being instructed to tell you all of this, I was shown a tall, well-built, handsome man, light in complexion. He had a slight, old injury on his forehead. When I told him that I did not know the fellow, your father said *you* would know him, as he is one of your servants."

On hearing this, Sebotsa's eyes distended widely. He looked at Khati and Maime and all of them communicated with their eyes and clearly knew who had been chosen by the ancestors.

"Yes, indeed, there is a fellow who fits that description," nodded Sebotsa. "His name is Tlelima and he belongs to the Bahlakwana tribe. He was actually here today, but because you do not know everyone living here, you perhaps did not spot him."

"Selone," said Mosito, "I am completely overwhelmed by this revelation. A king is someone who is supposed to protect his people. I simply don't see how I could do this. My conscience will not allow me to do that and honestly, I don't agree with it."

Selone responded this way: "You are the one who requested my services, my lord, and I am only relating to you what I have been instructed. There's no way other than this one I am telling you about."

"My king, you are yet to learn that everything we tell you is the truth," said Khati. "Do you remember that immediately after the death of King Lekaota, we came to you and suggested a similar procedure?"

"I remember."

"Today you should be convinced. The person revisiting this story is a total stranger, who does not know that a similar thing was suggested some time ago."

"All I can say is that with my ears I hear what's being said, but my brain is unable to comprehend it. A human liver!"

We all remember how angry Mosito had become when Khati and company had suggested this matter and how he had ordered them never, ever to come to him with such ridiculous suggestions again. What is peculiarly different is that the matter has been raised once again, but this time by a total stranger with piercing, bewitching eyes, demanding answers, without mincing his words.

Mosito was paralysed. His heart had sunk. His voice was gone and he felt like a person who had been ill for a very long time and was now on his death bed. With shock, he realised how weak and vulnerable he had become.

"My beloved king," said Maime, "I think you must consider this carefully. Take your time, calm the storm in you, consider carefully what the ancestors are telling you to do and get the potion. We, as your loyal servants, are here for you. We are your dogs and you are the hunter. All you have to do is to blow the whistle, we will rush out there sniffing high and low, looking for the creature and bring it kicking and screaming. Your village needs to be fortified so that the roots of your kingship penetrate deep into the belly of the earth. All you need to do is give orders, my lord."

"My father, on his death bed, ordered me to always listen to and rely on my conscience and he *specifically* said that if my conscience did not agree with something, I should not do it. I therefore cannot and refuse to get involved in this horrible deed of killing a human being in order to be a senior king. I absolutely refuse."

"It seems you are not really listening to me. I told you that I had been instructed by that very same man, your own father. He told *me* to tell *you* exactly the things I am telling you right now. The instructions he gave me show clearly that, while he was alive he was as uninformed as you are right now, not knowing how some of these things needed to be done. Today he is doing things differently because his mistakes have been revealed to him. We, who are alive, are on the side where we only deal with matters as they are happening to us. Your father is now a living dead, he is in a better and more informed place; he knows and sees everything before it gets to us. He has the authority to empower those he chooses; he is a god and has chosen his son to rule over a bigger and better territory. Can't you see that? The latest instruction supersedes the ones he gave while still alive. This information seeks to strengthen you.

"You should be recognised for your bravery; you should execute this order without any hesitation if indeed you value your kingship. Let me once again show you the dangers that are threatening you if you refuse to heed these directives. You have just escaped the most deadly trap emanating from these ancestors whom you are refusing to obey. But, if you don't want to take instructions, it is fine with me. After all, I'm not the one in danger. I'm not the one seeking kingship. I'm not the one finding snakes in my room. You and only you can try and avoid disaster by delivering to me the potion required, so that I can make the horn needed to give you kingship that is sustainable until the day you die."

Selone took his fierce eyes away from the King, looked down and then looked at all the other men present.

Mosito felt increasingly weak, as he was sinking deeper into a pool of confusion. He could not even begin to consider the plan that had been suggested. In his weakness, the only thing he knew for sure was that he was not going to use human liver for any reason, whatsoever. The only thing he knew was that using another person's liver was an intolerable thought. It would require him to kill Tlelima and so commit murder – a crime that was not only prosecutable, but, above all, was unacceptable in the eyes of God. He had difficulty telling these men in firm words that would not be hurtful that he did not agree with what Selone had just told him.

Finally, he said, "I have heard you all, but right now I am really disturbed. My conscience does not agree with this and right now I feel I have to rest. Maybe tomorrow I will wake up rejuvenated, and with a conscience calmed enough to agree to give you what you need. Right now, I cannot imagine doing anything of that magnitude. I am fatigued and desperately need some rest."

Mosito was anxious and felt he was just holding his head above water. How on earth was he going to come out of this unscathed? He was terrified and knew it. He was aware that he was fooling himself by thinking that when he was alone he would find the power and the courage to fight those evil suggestions and come out victorious.

When everybody had left, Mosito remained behind alone. It was already late in the evening and he knew he had to leave the court house, but he was feeling ill and weak and also deeply depressed, desiring absolutely nothing. When he finally got home, the Queen was still awake in bed. She had acquired the habit recently of not going to sleep when her husband was with his advisors. She would wait for him to tell her everything afterwards. This night, she had known beforehand that sleep was not going to come their way, because Mosito had indicated to her during the day that whatever they expected had finally come together and she anticipated that the discussion would take place that very evening. So she lay on top of her blankets, alert for her husband's footsteps.

Mosito entered their room and threw himself on the bed with his hands and feet splayed like those of a dead person. The Queen was shocked.

"What's the matter, my father?"

Mosito's heart sunk deeper than ever. He lost all remaining energy and could not answer his wife.

"I am just asking, what's wrong? You have thrown yourself on the bed like somebody who is really ill."

"I am ill, very ill, and the illness that's destroying me is eating away my soul."

He briefly told his wife what had been discussed. His tone did not change, it was dead – the voice of a person who might be buried the next day.

"'Mathabo, I am so very ill. My ailment is wedged deep into my soul. Please be kind and stop nagging me. I need time to think, to become spiritually healthy again, and will start the discussion with you again as soon as I feel better."

Like all other people, a woman is someone whose patience has its borders; it can be stretched for a certain period, but not further. From then on, she will stop pretending. At this moment Mathabo's patience ran out. The potion drama had been playing for quite some time now. It had become like an uncomfortable shoe, or an egg that is urging a hen to be laid but there is no place to lay it, so, under such pressure, the hen lays the egg anywhere, even on stones, because she no longer cares whether the egg gets broken or not.

"Mosito, my patience is at its end! Night after night I've spent without sleep, grappling with this matter you initially made your own private secret, and now you are refusing to discuss it with me! Listen here, Mosito, do you understand that my life, the life of Thabo, our son, and your life are in danger and hanging by a spider's thread? Don't you see that this matter needs urgent attention, so that you can be firmly positioned in your kingship, permanently and with enough power? Please, stop burdening me with a burden too heavy to carry."

She talked in a voice that was meant to hurt and her words penetrated King Mosito in such a way his heart nearly stopped beating. His wife was saying words that he never thought she had in her to say. Like needles they pierced his body, splintering the bone and entering his marrow. They were like those Selone had uttered with his eyes firmly rooted in his. Selone's words were cruel, hurtful and offensive; the meanness behind them paralysed Mosito and left him exposed and vulnerable.

'Mathabo spoke like the female twin to Selone. But instead of making Mosito weaker, *her* words recuperated him. His heart started beating faster and he could feel healing and rejuvenation pulsing through his body; her words gave him energy and power, reversing the pain and suffering Selone's words had caused. Her words made him recoup his power. When Mosito stood up from their bed he was a new person, confidence and authority coursing through him. He was animated and his voice had regained the volume and timbre almost lost when Selone needed answers and instructions about when and how to find the potion.

"'Mathabo, this matter had an unexpected and unforeseen development, and I found the content onerous to the extreme."

"But what was the outcome?"

His voice was now full of authority and he spoke with self-assurance like a person who knew the difference between right and wrong.

"Selone said the crucial element of the potion was revealed to him by my father in a dream, and it is to be human liver and the person who has the qualities described by my father, is Tlelima."

Even 'Mathabo was rattled by these words. She did not expect the matter to turn out in the drastic way just described by her husband. But it was the news that her husband's life was in great danger that shocked her most and sobered her up. The veil of fog that was in her brain quickly lifted and she started to talk.

"I imagine that everything is at a very sensitive stage right now and I completely understand how hearing this must have shocked you, but what was your response?"

"Can't you guess without being told?"

"Amongst the gifts I was born with, prophecy is the only one that I did not receive."

"I told Selone that I was unable to give him what was required."

"Oh! In other words you are not accepting the lenaka that he was about to prepare for your kingship?"

"Certainly not!" And it looked like this was the end of the matter.

'Mathabo was silent for a moment, looking at her husband as if seeing him for the first time. "And your reason?"

Now it was Mosito's turn to look at his wife as if seeing a new creature foreign to him. "I can't believe you ask me this. Don't you understand that if I agree to get the potion, I will have to spill blood and therefore agree to commit murder?"

"I'm fully aware of that."

"So if you already know it, why do you ask for a reason?"

"I ask because you have to get the lenaka."

"Even if it means killing an innocent person?"

'Mathabo again looked at her husband with astonishment.

"You know, I thought you understood me by now, my husband, but clearly you don't. If you truly know me you would have known that I have the kind of personality that does not change. If I have goals and targets, I don't allow obstacles in my way. That's my personality. If mountains threaten to interfere with my progress, I break them down into soil. Now, if I, a woman, have that attitude and courage, what stops a person like you, a man, from having the same attitude and bravery multiplied a thousand times?"

Mosito, woken recently from his temporary paralysis, spun again into powerlessness when he heard the words his wife poured on him; his insides collapsed like someone who had received electric shocks. He had somehow believed that his wife was going to be more understanding and sympathetic, agreeing with his arguments, but she was clearly siding with his father's old advisors and he knew there was a difficult road ahead of him, negotiating with a group of primitive people. Redirecting their thinking and their ways of reasoning was going to be a mammoth task. Deeply disillusioned and disheartened, he wondered what kind of language he should talk to be heard by his wife.

"A king is a servant of God who is mandated to take his people to greener pastures. The responsibilities and duties that come with it are large and extend beyond human understanding. A king is the only shepherd put in place to guide and protect God's flock. He should jealously protect the law, while at the same time he *is* the law and if he doesn't protect those laws, he cannot expect others to observe and respect them. Remember that a little monkey mimics its elders."

He paused, looking at his wife, with eyes begging for kindness and understanding, with something close to the kind of prayer one often has when faced with severe difficulties and simply want a chance to do what is right. Mosito's pleading eyes were stopped dead by 'Mathabo's hardened approach – cold and hard, like a stone used to make mill stones.

"My view of kingship is this," said 'Mathabo. "It's like owning a flock of sheep. When you own a flock of sheep, you have the authority to do as your heart dictates. You may sell the whole flock, you may slaughter some, or give some away; you could lease them out to other farmers... The choices are endless and you could do whatever your heart commands, because you have the flock at your disposal and nobody will oppose the king for doing what he wants. You have the right to catch, discipline, beat and preside over their matters, dismiss or expel them and no one can accuse you of being in the wrong. The communities are put under the guardianship of kings to serve, and the kings must achieve their goals using their people. Amongst your flock of sheep, there is a special one and that sheep is named Tlelima. You are the owner of this special sheep and have an obligation to use it. So, what's the problem? Because of the authority and power you as the owner have over this sheep, you have the right to do what is necessary. What's stopping you from using it as you have to? If Tlelima dies knowing that the direct result of his death is an effort to rescue your kingship, he would certainly consider himself the luckiest person to be born. He is providing a service that no one else is capable of and will die knowing that he had done a great deed. Surely he will be at peace with that."

"You are an utterly corrupt person, 'Mathabo, and your reasoning is quite sick. Tlelima is a man like me, he has a wife and children, who all love him the same way you and Thabo love me. Try and put yourself in Tlelima's wife's position. Would you appreciate it if someone with authority over me would one day have me as a sacrificial lamb? And you become a widow as a consequence of that? And Thabo an orphan? Do you have a clue how painful it must be to be orphaned for such a deed? Listen and understand what I'm saying: this murder then happens to me not because of war or anything like that; not because it is something that could have been avoided, it happens because an unbelievably selfish person feeling entitled to preside over others, has sat down, worked out a plan and executed it. How devastated do you think a family should feel?"

"The fact, my dear husband, is that no one will ever want to try and make a sacrifice of you, so your argument has no basis."

"I actually don't care what you feel or think; I am definitely not going to follow that line of reasoning."

"So you find it difficult to sacrifice the life of one of your many subjects, but prefer to put your own life at risk?"

"That's exactly how I feel."

Now 'Mathabo was sobbing, "What you are actually saying is that the only person you care about is yourself! Why don't you start by killing Thabo and me now? Since you refuse to comply with the requirement from the gods, your days are numbered. I think that instead of remaining here with all sorts of problems and poverty when you are dead, it would be better to take me and my child out of these miseries that would be our new way of living."

"Good! I like the way you've just reasoned. You've articulated your miseries so eloquently – even beyond my death, so why do you want me to do that to Tlelima's wife and children? May I ask: do you honestly believe that being deliberately widowed and orphaned is pleasant?"

"You are sympathetic to people who do not care about you. You also seem to have forgotten that monster of a cobra sent to destroy your life."

Mosito froze at the mentioning of the snake, and felt his body shrinking, filling with fear. The picture of the snake flooded his mind fully and he found it impossible to erase it; it was as though it had been written with tar. Nonetheless, he got hold of himself, concealed his fears, recollected his thoughts and continued with the argument, though no longer as charged and fired up as before. "Listen, it is not Tlelima who is bewitching me!"

"Oh! So you already *know* who is behind this bewitching?"

"I never said that. I was simply trying to show you that you are reasoning in a wrong way."

We have already mentioned that every person's patience has its limit – a point it won't go beyond. 'Mathabo had exhausted all avenues. Her patience completely ran out, so she turned to the only weapon left, the one most painful but the most effective.

"Do you mean it, Mosito, when you say your mind is already made up and that you refuse to comply?"

"What must I say or do for you to understand that I am totally against the killing of an innocent man?"

"Oh I see now, you are scared. What kind of man is so easily frightened? Fear is a word used only by women and seldom found in a true man's vocabulary."

"Oh no, 'Mathabo, don't come with that! A lot of people practising these types of rituals have been found out, prosecuted and hanged. I am totally, utterly and completely against such practices. The minute I agree with it I would be an accomplice, t'sohana-ea-neta. Where would you hide your head if I died the shameful death of being hanged, a death reserved only for the lowest? I repeat; I am not participating in such activities."

"All those people you refer to made stupid mistakes, so don't equate their stupidity to yours."

"I am disturbed spiritually, my soul is in tatters and I am asking you to have mercy on me. Please stop this matter and leave it, because it causes me a lot of pain and frustration and I might end up losing my mind."

Mosito was exhausted. He could no longer keep up countering her line of reasoning and needed a break. He prayed for divine intervention, but his prayers landed on the ears of leshoma, a deaf person.

Suddenly, 'Mathabo jumped out of bed. Flustered, her husband remembered the snake and thought maybe there was another one, or some other kind of disaster. But 'Mathabo wanted to demonstrate her anguish and was grabbing at her last weapon. All other methods had failed; she was clearly dealing with a very tough skin, the skin of an elephant on which very few weapons work. She went straight to where Mosito's gun was stored, picked it up and tried to give it to him. "Here, take it and take away my life so that this pain and suffering can stop at last!"

Mosito was tongue-tied.

"If you don't know how it works, I know: here's the trigger, here's the mouth and here's my heart!" And then 'Mathabo began to cry hysterically.

Mosito loved his wife and he also knew her well. In debates, she always wanted to be the winner. She wanted to lead everything and simply demolished any obstacle in her way. Knowing her for what she was, he realised that nothing would stop her from achieving her goal.

In a last attempt to stop his wife, Mosito also jumped out of the bed.

Mathabo spoke, "There is only one choice: my life or the life of Tlelima. Please stay where you are and do not come closer,

169

because right now I know where the trigger is and will pull it. Remember that in the past women used to kill themselves by hanging themselves or jumping off cliffs, so that they could make a swift end to their suffering. Choose between myself and Tlelima."

She turned the gun on herself and pointed its mouth at her heart and watched every move her husband made.

"Please, 'Mathabo, put the gun down. I'm begging you."

"So that you can take it? You will have access to this gun only when I have accomplished my mission."

"I beg you, please put the gun down and let's discuss the matter and not opt for violence."

"Will you then listen to me? And remember: I'm not forcing you to do something you don't want to do. Your opinion is your opinion. My opinion is mine. You have a choice between listening to me or not, but bear in mind that the choice you make will determine what I do with my life. If you still disagree with everything I say, do not feel yourself restricted. By God Almighty, each and every one of us has choices and preferences. After you have decided, I will know exactly what to do. And who knows, when I am dead your life might improve and you will live happily. You will marry a new wife – there are many you could choose from – and she will agree with you about everything because she will be educated like you and will support your dismissal of the useless council of uneducated people like Khati and company. It is obvious that they are the ones delaying the progress you would like to achieve with your friends Pokane and Khosi, both behaving like puppets because your so-called education has hardened your hearts. This new wife will be best friends with them as they eat you alive; you will not realise it as they will be smiling while doing that."

"'Mathabo, please listen!"

Slowly, he approached, but then pounced on her, wrestling to retrieve the gun, but 'Mathabo was swift and read his intensions.

She pulled the trigger and a deafening bang reverberated through the house. She fell on the floor with the gun next to her. Mosito knelt down and examined her quickly, but, to his relief, found no wound. He inspected the gun and found it loaded, but not with a bullet, with topisi ea mosili, compressed ash. During the pulling of the trigger she was shaking so much that her hand had moved away from its target and missed her heart. There was a little bit of soot on the wall from the gun. 'Mathabo had fainted momentarily, but when she came round, she was in a state of shock and sweating copiously.

The door burst open. Khati stormed in, discernibly shaken, but before he could open his mouth, Pokane and Khosi also ran in looking alarmed.

"What has happened, Master?" asked Khosi, unable to hide his shock. The breath from his lungs sounded inflamed, like that of a rat trapped in a calabash, knowing that its life is about to end.

Khati also freed his tongue: "King, what's going on?"

The presence of Khosi and Pokane then changed the mood in the house. Mosito became rigid and uncooperative. He had the typical mood shift he usually suffered when they were around.

"Nothing. I tried to wrap the gun in some cloth, it fell and a shot went off. Go, get out and have some sleep. It is late."

At this point his heart was blood red. He felt like loading the gun with live ammunition and randomly shooting at them. Threateningly, like a lioness protecting her cubs, he glared at them. "I am serious. Get out."

They all left.

By now 'Mathabo had calmed down and she could speak normally again.

"Next time I will put in real ammunition, and because I will be alone, my hand won't shake. You have demonstrated that my life is nothing to you. When compared to that of Tlelima, mine is like that of a locust."

On that note she stood up, went back to bed, got under the blankets, covered her head and started to cry once more.

The anger that consumed Mosito when he saw Pokane and Khosi made him aware that he no longer sympathised with anybody. He understood that it was by the grace of God that his wife was not cold by now and that, if she had died, it would be because of Khosi and company. He also appreciated that he would never be allowed to make peace with kindness. Some people were out there, standing on the mountain tops, throwing heavy stones at him, and in return he was talking about orphans this and orphans that. Who knew if Tlelima was not the source of all these strange and evil things happening to him and his family? And that was why the ancestors wanted Tlelima dead. Who would know? Today he had survived being called a widower, but tomorrow he might not endure an onslaught. Even if he were to hide the bullets, 'Mathabo could jump off a cliff, hang herself or throw herself into the deepest part of the river. Knowing her approach towards disputes, he understood very well that, even though she had not succeeded in ending her life today, this would not be her last attempt. If his wife was to succeed, how would he cope without her, who was going to look after his household and how would he deal with the shame? He became very disturbed thinking of all the things that would go wrong if he lost her. The depression he had earlier when he came home from the khotla incapacitated his soul and he descended into a depression that was even deeper.

"'Mathabo," he tried, lovingly.

"What? Stop irritating me, please. I am trying to calm my troubled soul and map out what it is that I should do tomorrow, in order to succeed with what I failed to execute today."

She covered her head in blankets again and he heard her lost crying. Mosito was moved and felt pity for her. After some time she quietened down and even fell asleep. But the King couldn't sleep. He got out of bed and went outside in an effort to calm himself down. But he came back from outside with the same problems he'd had before he'd got up. Removing himself physically from 'Mathabo did not remove the problems he had with her.

"Are the things Selone tells me the honest truth, and nothing but the truth?" he asked as a way of reassessing his thoughts and regaining composure. He also tried to remember what he had learned at school and found that nothing had prepared him for this and it was never suggested that a time might come when he would be required to do all these strange and dreadful things that Selone and company expected of him.

"And again, are the white people correct in saying that our traditional healing is baseless and useless? By the look of things they also seem to practise wizardry, the only difference is that their wizardry is practised openly, unlike ours, and anyone who wants to learn is welcomed with open arms – so everything they do is considered normal and harmless. A few days ago, Khati drew my attention to the fact that the Europeans do use human parts where they deem it necessary. He said they mostly deal with dead bodies, because when a person dies, they operate on the body to investigate the possible cause of death. The question he posed was, how certain are we that, when they return the body for burial, it still has all the parts? I don't know, but he was convinced that the body returns from the mortuary with some of its parts missing. And those missing parts are used by the European doctors to make a lenaka, which is why Europeans have this scary presence about them. He said that was the reason why every time a European appears, an African suddenly feels helpless. It is because they have used the body parts from one of us."

What Khati had suggested weighed heavily on his psyche. He could not but agree with Khati's explanation. It made perfect sense. What other reason could exist for the fact that a few hundred Europeans could rule thousands of Basotho people, unopposed? It was the body parts that made the Basotho fear and respect them. The other thing Khati mentioned was that European houses were seldom struck by lightning, while African houses got hit on a yearly basis. All of this showed one that Europeans were exceptionally good when it came to fortifying their properties. If they had the knowledge for blocking lightning, one could just imagine how unstoppable their knowledge would be when it came to dealing with small evils.

"Now, suddenly, something makes perfect sense: the other day at the offices of Qacha's Deputy District Administrator, I found a European who had no time for me. He really dealt with my case in a disrespectful and derogatory manner. I felt so intimidated when I reached his offices, which was strange, because he was not the first European I have met. It must mean that he had a very strong and tough lenaka, and I think it won't hurt if I could also get myself a tough and mean lenaka, just like that of the Deputy District Administrator." Pondering on this, Mosito suddenly felt foolish that he had for so long refused the help of traditional doctors, who could have assisted him with herbs and rituals that could stop forces of nature, such as lightning. He returned to his bedroom, got into bed, struggled a little bit, but eventually slept. He now knew what to do.

14

Mosito gains the potion

Mosito woke towards dawn, feeling much better. His head was clear. He re-examined everything that had happened between him and his wife the previous night. He also thought about what Selone had told him the day he had interpreted the bones. He saw and understood that his life was hanging by a spider's thread, as his wife put it. Bringing into his thinking the things Khati had said about European witchcraft, he spent a long time contemplating all the arguments and ended up by convincing himself that his wife had been correct when she had said "it is foolish to spare someone's life at your own expense".

"A Sesotho proverb against misplaced retaliation says, 'Ha e iphetetse ka e e hlabileng' – do not avenge yourself on something that is already wounded – and it is appropriate to my life. I am now focused on one thing – Tlelima will be the ingredient for the potion," he decided.

Mosito woke his wife, and as always she woke up angry and said harshly, "What are you up to now? You disturb my sleep! And I had to struggle for it because of you. What do you want to offer me this time?"

In a soft voice Mosito replied, "Dearest, I woke you up to tell you my true feelings, the feelings I have reached after thinking for a long time. I love you, your life to me is the light and I shall preserve it and be your servant at all times. I am happy about your advice and I have convinced myself that what you said is true: 'what does it help to pity someone while by so doing you put your own life at risk?'"

Mosito's wife was surprised. "Did you really arrive at this through your own feelings? Don't point a finger at me tomorrow and say, 'It was 'Mmathabo who pressurised me into something I did not believe in.'"

She deliberately phrased it like that to make her husband think that she had reached a final conclusion about her own life, but, in reality, she wanted to drive Mosito to a point where he had to be firm in his mission; he should run into the fire without thinking about returning.

Mosito fell into this trap. His anxiety about his wife attempting suicide stopped instantly when he heard that she was not even attempting to support him. At that moment his heart turned into a beast's heart, not caring about anybody's life. As we know, he was an educated person, and he thought of Shaka's story, how Shaka had decided to turn himself into a beast, because of the hardships he suffered.

"I am like Shaka," he thought. "I was born a king, but because of people's evil deeds, I have to lose the kingship blanket. I have never robbed anybody, or treated anyone badly in any way, but where did it bring me? Reptiles are sent to agitate me. When the enemy threatens, one has to defend oneself in many ways, and when matters are really bad, one may shield behind somebody to escape danger."

After thinking about such matters, he turned back to his wife.

"I have considered this matter carefully and have decided on it thoughtfully. I therefore repeat that Tlelima will be the sheep I sacrifice to the ancestors, to buy my kingship, and buy my stature."

"It is good that your feelings are now settled. You have spoken like a real man, who loves himself and is guarding his life as well as that of his children. Thabo now will never become a slave, and even when you are no more, he will bless your bones. Now I believe that you really love me."

There was no further conversation between husband and wife. Although Mosito tried to relax and get a bit of sleep, he remained awake until sunrise. While the sun's rays were warming everybody, the King did his best to spend the day being pleasant, friendly even towards those two he so deeply detested and despised. Although many accepted that their king was in a happy mood, Khosi and Pokane were not deceived. They smelled something rotten and warned themselves that this happiness would be shortlived.

"You know, Homeboy," Khosi said to Pokane, "how it is when a storm is gathering, you find the sun very hot, and people go about half naked? The thunder roars, but far off, so dim that a person with weak hearing would not hear it at all."

"You have said a mouthful. The pleasure the King displays today is not real. One foot is limping, although not everybody will notice. My conscience leads me to believe that something very big is in the offing. King Mosito is plotting, and I do not know when that plan will become visible, but it is definitely there. We have to move carefully so that sparks don't scorch us."

He laughed as though it was a joke, but he was very serious.

That evening Mosito met the trusted elderly men as had recently become a daily routine.

"Gentleman, yesterday we parted with little agreement between us, but today I am glad to inform you that your point of view and mine are the same."

Maime was the first to interrupt. "Oh Ntate, I am speechless and cannot explain how delighted I am! You can take up your privileges in full now, and get the salary you deserve, and we, your underdogs will also benefit." Maime winked at Khati discreetly to acknowledge that the weapon they had used in this heavy war had been very successful.

Khati understood and joined the response: "You will see me, my lord, we are not small boys, but experienced men, knowing the road like a very tame pack animal. We shall never mislead you, my lord, because we love you.

"Today even the late King Lekaota, wherever he is sleeping, will rejoice to see that you have heeded the advice of the people he trusted the most. Today you will be a man, you will be a king and where you move among people, they will shiver; they will attend to you, and reserve your seat."

But the King had not finished. "I also have to tell you that I haven't agreed to get that particular ingredient of the potion. It disturbs my conscience, but I would be very happy if you could assist me so that I can get over it and have peace in my soul."

All kept quiet and looked at the King.

"The thing that worries me is that there is a known government law that when someone is found dead, he cannot be buried before the district surgeon has examined him so that his next of kin and the government should know the cause of death. When we have executed our plan, what shall we do with the corpse so that it should not be seen and examined?"

They all looked down. It was clear that nobody had any idea. At last their eyes turned to Selone, indicating that he was the one who should find a solution. He saw that and understood.

"Oh, but that is a very minor thing," said Selone. "Remember that in this job I am not a young horse or ox to be broken in, which could jump around and throw down what he carries on his back. I could give you the names of the victims who have been sacrificed to pacify the ancestors. But, as a doctor, I am bound to keep secrets – and up until this day nobody knows where they ended up. The incidences are as many as my fingers and you can believe me: only one of them nearly got us in trouble, because the negligence of those who were handling that victim led them *not* to act according to my instructions.

"The victim was found and taken to a doctor, and it was discovered that some organs were missing, but that case ended there. When I deal with such matters, my lord, I use very strong herbs. Even if the police get a lead, I dismiss that easily by using boreba, our magic, to make them forget the case and attend to something else."

Yes, Selone addressed them with the serious face of a man who knew what he was talking about and who did not need to hesitate during an execution. All listeners sensed that they had a veteran in front of them and felt safe and encouraged.

It was three days before Christmas. Following Selone's advice, the only one of them who knew how much work such a deed needed, the whole thing was postponed.

Some tried to object, saying that procrastination was the thief of time. "No, no, not at all," Selone warned. "You should rather know that haste doesn't pay. Now that the King has softened his heart, we have to work at our pace. I have stopped the crisis for a while and it won't return soon."

Selone smiled reassuringly.

"Remember, our forefathers lost many battles because they lacked planning. They never sat down and planned the wars properly. When a king woke up one morning, and felt like attacking some tribe, his word was final. Men would come out armed, without prior planning on how to attack, and from which direction. So when the war suddenly turned they didn't know what to do. They simply assumed that the enemy was too strong, then chose to flee, each one trying to save his own life, and, in the process, got killed.

"But those who have studied how Europeans fight tell us that before soldiers go to a war, they start by verifying the number and strength of the enemy. Then the commander sits down, takes a map and indicates the different approaches his soldiers will use, as well as determining the route the soldiers will take when the fight becomes too heavy. When they retreat, they retreat in an orderly fashion so that they can regroup to fight again but this time from a new position. This prevents the killing of many soldiers, despite a fierce defence. In the same way we must plan carefully how to catch our victim.

"Knowing for many years what is involved in a scheme like this, I suggest that we need to plan it during a festival because then people drink a lot, walk home at night, walk carelessly, and due to drunkenness, many fall off cliffs. All these things assist the work towards a successful conclusion. We have to make use of the pitfalls of carelessness. Let us wait until Christmas Day, so that we can trap our victim when people have had too much to eat and drink and are less observant about what is going on around them."

He convinced them and they agreed to wait for Christmas.

As the day approached, all the people in all the villages were preparing themselves: smearing their houses and courtyards with fresh mud, brewing beer, preparing different dishes of food, because nobody wanted visitors to leave their home without having had something to eat or drink. So, each homestead was fully prepared for a stream of visitors and all eagerly waited for the day.

Mosito was the only one who was not affected by all the cheerfulness and various activities. He wished the day could be shifted back and never dawn, and the feeling was unbearable when he was alone with no distraction. At such moments, a flame of feeling would flicker steadily as if it was going to grow and help him think in a humane way. But as soon as his conscience began reprimanding him, he would walk out to be among people, and once there, his conscience stopped haunting him. Also at night he slept badly. Most of the time he had nightmares, woke up and tried to make light of them, consoling himself that one day, things would all be well.

"Imagine when a warrior in war kills someone with an assegai for the first time. He also has sleepless nights when he thinks about the poor man dead because of him, but after a while that feeling stops. That's how it will be when the work is done: sleeplessness will stop and I will sleep like I always did." Mosito was speaking to his inner self in loneliness, trying to console himself, managing somehow to live until the special day.

On the last night before Christmas Day, the hunters met for the last time to arrange how the victim should be caught and to get instructions from the main hunter. Khati had been instructed to select young men he trusted to catch the King's victim. This night he had brought them along. They arrived and all sat down, quietly.

Khati said, "My lord, as you instructed me, I have selected the men who will carry out your instruction. I have also told them to attend our last meeting to get the details from your mouth. Here they are: Senyane, Bohata, Papiso, Letebele and Molafu. I selected them because I know them, my lord. They are very brave young men, reliable, talk little, and love their king with all their hearts. Senyane and Bohata are Tlelima's great friends, and they will be his watchdogs the whole day until we need him."

Suddenly Mosito's heart began to beat faster. The plan was gaining momentum. This was it and he was fully committed – there was no retreating. He listened to his racing heartbeat, as if he had just run up a flight of stairs, missing some to reach the destination sooner. He halted as if to think.

"We are waiting on your word, my lord," said Khati.

Mosito sweated and felt bewildered. He dug deep into himself to gather some courage, speak and give instructions. It is true that the devil, always waiting, often helps in many ways after he is sure that someone cannot withdraw from his promise. Mosito's weakness was evident to all, but the devil aided him. His weakness stopped abruptly and he began thinking about his kingship, his name and his fame. His voice became strong, and, when he spoke, it penetrated the hearts of all listening.

"You, young men, who have been introduced to me, you are here to assist me. My position as the king is in jeopardy because of the changes that will take place when the community fund is introduced. I need a victim as an ingredient to get the right potion to help me restore my rights as a king, the rights I am about to lose. I need a victim and that victim is Tlelima. I want you to get him."

He paused to gain some courage, and give the young men a chance to digest his words. "I say this victim should be caught by you. But, note: you should not kill him. I need him alive and whole. If Tlelima tries to fight, you should hold on to him, and may not spill his blood, as that will weaken our potion. His blood should be spilled by my hand; that is the herbalist's instruction."

There was silence. Each person talked to his own heart, asking whether it was in accord with what the King said. All felt their conscience accepting that, when the King had spoken, his word was final: the victim should be brought to him alive and not a single blood vein should be cut.

"Have you understood me? Should I repeat the instruction?"

Without shaking or nodding their heads, their eyes and faces said everything: the command had sunk into their ears and would be carried out.

"So let me conclude. The last and most crucial point that you should understand is that your mouths must be shut – shut for good! You all have wives and there should not be a single one of you who, overpowered by love for his wife, lose his senses and talks to her about this. The one who does that, will die together with Tlelima, and his death will be more painful than Tlelima's. But it's not necessary to belabour this point, because if you did not know what I'm talking about, you would not be in this house at this moment."

"My lord," said Molafu, "I joined this mission with my whole heart, pushed by the love I have for you, and I am very aware of how you are oppressed by your seniors. My mouth will be sewn with sinew thread, and only my death will untie it."

"Because of how you have declared yourselves," said King Mosito after the other young men had affirmed what Molafu had said, "I am very proud of you, and promise that after the mission has been accomplished successfully, each of you will receive a reward of twenty pounds.

"But remember, I want to make it clear: I am not bribing you. You are my subjects, you work for me, carrying out my instructions without expecting payment, but I find it appropriate that, when you perform a duty such as this one, I reward you accordingly, so that in future you perform such duties wholeheartedly."

Everyone indicated his gratitude.

"Now, when we have grabbed the victim, where must he be taken to?" asked Molafu, who had been chosen to be the spokesman of the other young men.

"That is the very last point. I am happy that you asked the question, Molafu, because it signals to me that you have embraced this mission fully and do not wish that there should be any mistake."

"My lord!" said Molafu.

"Do you know the area where the Sejabatho meets the small rivulet next to Baterefala? That is where you will find us, and where the main work will be done. You will find me there with Khati, Selotsa and Selone. You, Maime, will be with these young men, support them carefully, there should be no mistakes. When you grab him, make sure that nobody sees you. There should be no crying or yelling so that people hear noises, inviting passersby to investigate... Senyane! Bohata!"

"Our lord," the two said with fierce eyes, indicating their zest. After they responded so positively, King Mosito took out a bottle from a box. "You are the ones who know Tlelima and you have already accepted that you will be his watchdogs. So take this bottle with seawater." He gave it to Senyane next to him. "I am not the one to teach you tricks. You are the ones who will see how this water can help you in your work."

"Our lord," said Senyane, accepting the bottle with two hands.

"I hope that is all. If there is anything I have forgotten, Khati will remind me."

"You have said everything, my lord; there is nothing I can remind you of."

The young men left beating their chests, indicating a vow to carry out the instructions from their king against all odds.

The Christmas Day sun rose in a clear sky. Everywhere one heard the birds singing, happy in the warmth of this special day. Roads and tracks were not lonely. Multitudes, files and files of people, were going to different places. Some were going to see friends, to ask for Christmas beer; some were returning to their homes from church, where they had spent the whole night, waiting for the Son of God to be born, some were on their way to church services that would start during the day. Some men appeared on horseback with ornamental plumes, on their way to a men's big dance, at some villages happy women ululated, over the hill a praise singer was heard singing praises, reminding himself of the past. Everywhere people met, they demanded a Christmas box. This was a peculiar thing and surfaced in various forms: sometimes a coin, or a calabash of beer, bread, a cup of tea, a handkerchief, an earring, a piece of steak or any other thing. Senyane and Bohata went to Tlelima's place and asked for a box. It arrived as a calabash of beer. They drank it at once, and the three of them prepared to leave together.

"Oh, please, Tlelima," said his wife, Lipuo, "do not go far away, please. On Christmas Day many accidents occur due to drunkenness. It is better to remain around here. There is a lot of beer here at home. You could drink until sunset. You could even drink tomorrow!"

"That is true, wife-of-my-father's-cattle, but if I am with these two young men, nothing can harm us. If there is any threat, my stick will strike and leave people scattered on the ground. But I am with them, so you need not worry."

"What you are saying is so true, my friend," said Bohata. "If there is any trouble, the bones will rise from the graves, I swear, by my sister Mookho. Look here, Lipuo, this boy who married you is a man, he *knows* how to use a stick. He was born with a kierie in his hand, I swear to God!"

"Maleshoane gave me the same warning. As far as I am concerned, if they talk like that, they bring bad luck. We can leave it there and it will disappear. Remember, if we say that a knobkierie carries blood clots, we may just as well go and start a fight!" said Senyane.

"Oh, no, now you are up to something wrong!" Lipuo sounded furious.

Senyane laughed with gusto, "You easily fall into a trap, Lipuo. I was merely teasing you to make you angry, because when you are cross, I love you even more, my sister – then your beauty piles up a thousand times."

All four of them now laughed, and all was well.

"Well, that's it, Lipuo. We thank you for your box, and we are now going home to see what is in Maleshoane's box. The day is still long, we will come back."

As they went out the door, Lipuo said, "So on this day when you enjoy the box, I no longer get a kiss when you leave? You will see Maleshoeane's won't be as nice." She said it happily, and her voice was that of a wife who loves her husband.

"Oh, I nearly made a terrible mistake, my dear," Tlelima said with pretended excessive regret. "I will get heartburn from other boxes if I do not kiss you. I am holding you by the ears, kissing you, my loving bride!"

They kissed each other happily and Tlelima left with his friends. When they got to Senyane's home, Maleshoane brought a drink known as 'Tears-of-the-Queen', but who is this queen who has so many tears that they fill up vats and can be drunk by the whole world every day, and never run dry? Senyane filled three glasses, they drank. He and Bohata sipped a little, whereas Tlelima simply swallowed his in no time.

"Just have this one, brother," said Senyane to Tlelima. "I spent the whole night with this thing and I feel that now I must stop."

"Bear in mind that I also went all out last night," said Bohata.

"Fellows, you are capable of killing a person. I have always imagined that as you love me, you would grab the lion by its jaws if it was attacking me and you hadn't warned me in time." Tlelima took Senyane's glass and gulped it down. "I think you have reached the limit. What is now remaining is mine alone, and I will let you sip a bit from time to time."

"Do as you please, brother, everything is yours." Senyane was saying this, happy that Tlelima would obviously continue as they had started.

"Maleshoane, don't you have a smaller bottle that we can use for provision? This one is too big and will attract attention. What remains we shall see tonight."

Maleshoane brought a nip bottle and Tlelima filled it up and put it in the pocket of his trousers. He stroked the bottle's mouth several times as they went around in the village, moving from one house to another. Towards midday, they reached Rooijane, and had to taste its beer.

Towards late afternoon they were close to the mountains and Tlelima indicated that it was time to move towards home as he had drunk enough, and wished to reach home before dusk, so that his children could see him. "Gentlemen, I love my wife. The way she spoke this morning, I do not ever wish to disappoint her. As it is, I was wrong to move so far away from home. That dark beauty of mine, she drives me crazy, brothers!" It was clear that Tlelima loved his wife dearly; he spoke about her as if she was a real jewel to him.

"No, Tlelima," said Senyane hastily, "do you take instructions from a woman? She has also gone out for Christmas box, you will see her later. Anyway, let us leave after sunset; it will be better because it's cooler. You know, brother, on Christmas Day the wizards do not move in the night."

Their friendship was real, so Tlelima was game to prolong their stay until it was cooler. He admitted that the day's heat had been rather severe, and coupled with the drinks, it was unbearable.

"Gentlemen, do you know that I was invited to visit Baterefala?" As Bohata said that, he winked slyly at Senyane, making sure Tlelima did not see it. "There is a young man I worked with, who arrived last week and he invited me. He will be very unhappy to learn that I was here and did not go to his home."

It is always difficult to understand how the mind works of a person who is drinking too much. There and then they decided to visit Baterefala and arrived at Thebe's place. Tlelima had been sipping from his bottle the whole day and was much drunker than his two friends. They had been drinking moderately because of the task ahead. While they were drinking, chatting and laughing, Tsietsi arrived. Because of the joy of that day, he invited them to come to his place to see what he had to offer. Senyane encouraged the team to oblige.

"Brothers, I am not accompanying you," Tlelima told Senyane. "When I leave this place, I want to go straight home. I have had enough."

Senyane did not oppose him. "If you feel that you've had enough, brother, it is fine, stay here. We won't be long, because it's already dusk. When we get back we will go straight home. Besides, we have been offered a lift, taking us not too far from home."

In his mind, Senyane was saying, the devil deserved thanks for separating them from their victim. This was the time that they should be far from him; besides, there were now enough witnesses who could give evidence that they had left him there.

Senyane and Bohata stayed at Tsietsi's home and there was a lot of beer, but they were just sipping a bit; the main thing was chatting and singing to while away the time. When they realised it was close to midnight, Senyane sent for Tsietsi's daughter, Likeledi. "Please go to Mr Thebe's home and tell Tlelima, the visitor who is there, that he must go home, it is late. Tell him that we feel too drunk and are reluctant to tackle the uphill road back. He is there, waiting for us, but we are already on the way to our homes, so run; be quick!"

After instructing the girl, he said to Bohata, "Brother, let us move, our home is far."

Likeledi left and they followed her. When she arrived at Thebe's, she delivered the message to Tlelima. When he heard his friends were on their way, he left and joined the road down the hill.

"My God, those two do not know me! They went away, leaving me here, while they are the ones who brought me here! I will injure someone!" He said that only because he was tipsy and did not really mean it. When he joined the road, he started by calling Senyane and Bohata. They were somewhat ahead of him, and heard him calling, but deliberately kept quiet.

"We have managed successfully to shake him off," Senyane whispered to Bohata, "so we must not let people who might pass here think that we were with him. The people at Tsietsi saw that the two of us were alone when we left. He was not with us, and there is no one who can say that we met somewhere. And remember, he is drunk and we are as well."

Bohata laughed softly and said, "Everybody is drunk and that's a fact, brother!"

They walked faster, and when they got into the fields, they slowed down until Tlelima reached them.

"My God, I want to beat you up right now! What are you trying to do when you leave me behind! I tried to call you but you didn't respond!"

"Man, we are soused, brother," said Bohata, but speaking softly, "We are so drunk that we think we shall end up sleeping in these fields. I am completely soused!"

They went on and on stressing their drunkenness, each one trying to stress that he was drunker than the others.

They moved on until they reached where the road passes next to the field of a man called Tuka. When they got there, they had to walk where the road goes through the Sejabatho mountain ridge. Senyane and Bohata had been given strong instructions not to let Tlelima escape and they were determined to carry them out with great care. They knew that four other watchdogs were behind them, cautious that Tlelima did not notice them. The four men – Maime, Papiso, Letebele and Molafu had walked behind until they reached Baterefala. From time to time they had been supplied with information about developments. They knew that Tlelima had remained at Thebe's place when the others went to Tsietsi's home and that Senyane had sent Likeledi to tell Tlelima it was time to leave.

They quickly moved higher up from the road, taking a shortcut through the fields, so that they were in front of Senyane and company. They hid themselves. When the three men passed Tuka's field and were about to reach the mountain ridge, Maime and his dogs emerged from the field. They were silent and walking fast. The moment they emerged, Senyane staggered and fell heavily to the ground, as if drunk.

"There you are!" said Tlelima to Bohata. "I do not want to go along with people who are controlled by beer in this way! Now he is going to create a big job for us." He bent down to try and help Senyane, but realised that he was a heavy, useless bag.

"Senyane! Senyane!" said Tlelima. "Wake up brother, let's move on. It's late!" He tried to hold Senyane with both arms, attempting to pick him up, but discovered that he was heavier than a bag of salt. "Hold his legs, Bohata, let's get him up, even though he created this problem. If he hadn't insisted so much, we would not have left home. Now, here he is, and has created such a big problem, I don't know how to resolve it!"

Bohata held Senyane's legs, while Tlelima was at the shoulder side, and they carried him. Senyane slipped his arms around Tlelima's neck, but weakly, as if they were the laces of a cradle skin. They took a few steps forward but the load was too heavy.

"Just put him down, brother, my trousers are falling down. They are too loose," said Bohata.

As they put him down, Tlelima felt a blow behind his ear, hard enough to hear bells ringing, and his legs collapsed like thin thongs. Senyane's arms around Tlelima's neck suddenly turned into an iron knot that gripped his throat. His eyes rolled back in his head and Tlelima went down easily.

Instantly strong ropes made of tough mountain grass ringed his hands and legs. They were not simple decorations, but very tough ropes with knots that needed some fat to untie. One rope was in his mouth and tied behind the ears, tied so hard it could never be untied again. Then they took a big piece of sekhakha – we do not know whose wife it belonged to – and blindfolded him so that he could not see where he was being taken to.

Everything was done as quickly as possible, and everybody was doing exactly what they had set out to do. No one spoke or asked what should be done, nobody gave instructions, supporting the old doctor, Selone's belief that nothing beats sitting down and planning strategies. The victim was handled in such a way that he could not defend himself or shout for help. When everything was done, they carried him on their shoulders, and in absolute silence went into the field, walked across until they reached the place where the Sejabatho meets the smaller rivulet next to Baterefala. At the ridge they went down swiftly until they reached where the King and his three assistants were waiting.

"I can see without being told that my instructions have been carried out successfully," said Mosito after the young men had put their load on the ground, sweating.

Selone said, "Remove the blindfold so that he can see where he is!" Selone was as wild as a beast.

First the fist on the ear and then being strangled by Senyane had caused Tlelima to faint for a while, so when he was being manhandled he had not felt much pain. The blow had made him dizzy so he had not realised that he was being throttled by

Senyane, whom he had thought was drunk. He had regained consciousness when the young men had gone down the ridge, but because he was blindfolded, he had not been able to see where he had been taken to or by whom, and he could not make out where his friends were. He had tried to listen to the voices, but those carrying him had been silent. When his blindfold was untied, he recognised the people carrying him and those now surrounding him. But because his mouth was tied, he could not speak. He also discovered his legs and arms were fastened tightly. He felt exhausted and stretched himself, already begging his torturers with his eyes.

Because of how things were in Lesotho at that time, Tlelima understood, without being told, what was in store for him. He thought of his wife and her advice in the morning when he had left home with Senyane and Bohata. His thoughts jumped further. He thought of his son, Thabiso, who was three years old, and his daughter who was eleven months. Now that he saw that there were only a few minutes left of his life he wondered what would happen to them, having to face the difficulties of this world alone? His eyes were full of tears, and in his throat sat a huge lump he could not swallow.

"We have brought the victim, my lord," said Maime to the King. "We caught him unaware, and because of the fist of Molafu, he could not even make a noise like a kid goat. I think if we untied his mouth, he would be able to tell us whether his head is aching."

Molafu stretched his fingers one by one and they gave a clicking sound. "I was certain that my fingers were broken because his skull is as hard as a black stone," said Molafu, feeling important.

"Time does not belong to us," said Mosito. "Untie his mouth and hands so that we can start the job! Molafu's fist story will follow later, gentlemen, when we have our potion."

Tlelima's hands and mouth were untied, but his legs remained tied. Tlelima tried to stand up, but they quickly held him down. "This crook we must watch. If he can rise here he might cause pandemonium," said Papiso, stepping on his hand and foot.

"My lord, what wrong have I done that my children should be left in this manner?"

"The problem is your liver, if you really want to know. It is a pity that I cannot get it while preserving your life; I'm therefore bound to take your life, in order to get your liver." Mosito's conscience was giving him no rest, but he ignored it.

Tlelima's muscles were torn and in pain, though his body was numb – nothing he had ever experienced had prepared him for this. "Oh please, Sir! Pity my children, please! If I were a bachelor I would say, no problem! What will happen to my children in this cruel world?"

"My lord, this person talks too much. He will spoil the potion," said Selone. "The best thing is to continue the work, and here is the knife to start the job!"

The knife in his palm was already opened. Mosito took it with a hand shaking as if he suffered from a trembling disease, but he persevered, wanting to finish as quickly as possible to get past this horror. But time and time again, Tlelima's prayers landed on the hardened heart of Mosito and his conscience shook him and gave him no rest.

"My lord, if you spare my life," cried Tlelima, "I promise not to breathe a word. You are also a parent, my dear king, and because of your son, Thabo, I beg you, please, be merciful. If you were in my shoes at this moment, how would you imagine your son Thabo would survive and make a living?"

As he was lying on his back, tears rolled down into his ears. Not tears of fright, because he had never in his life known fear, but tears of a broken heart when he thought of those he loved, those he was living for, those whom he would die for, if necessary – his children and his wife – whom he was about to leave before the time stipulated by his Creator.

He turned his head, and looked into Senyane's eyes. "Senyane, my friend, are you among them? You who fetched me from my homestead, my wife resisting? Bohata, do I also see you? The others I don't care about, but you!" His voice choked in the tears of a ruined heart.

"My lord, start by taking his tongue, so he stops talking while we are at work. It will affect my medicine." Selone's voice, as he ordered Mosito to perform this nauseating act, was exceptionally harsh, leaving the King no alternative but to act. The young men held Tlelima tight.

"God, Father, look after my orphans!"

Molafu wrenched Tlelima's mouth open, pulled out the tongue, shifting slightly to make space for Mosito who gripped and pulled even harder and then cut it off.

"Instruct your God again, please, that he should remain looking after your orphans," said Khati, looking pleased with himself. Mosito threw the tongue into a tin for all the body parts.

Tlelima was being held so viciously tight that he could not even jerk. A human face can be so warped with pain that we lack words to describe it. Tlelima continued to breathe and ruckle, although it was evident that he no longer longed for it, wishing for an end to this torture.

"Cut him open, my lord, and take out the liver!"

Selone's words made all of them hold the victim even tighter. The knife penetrated, Tlelima went into a spasm. As he closed his eyes with shock, Mosito twisted the knife and soon took out the liver and threw it in a tin.

"I need the eyes," said Khati, taking the knife and without any qualm digging out Tlelima's eyes.

"My piece is the spleen." Selone took the knife and cut it out.

"I want the genitals," said Molafu. He took a knife and cut them off. They cut at his body; each taking what he needed and all were satisfied.

"Now I want the heart which is the foundation of life and the spirit of the bravery that this gentleman displayed. It was unfortunate that the ancestors chose such a hero, but still, they selected him because of that heroism and his liver, so that the potion can be strong," said Selone. He took the knife, went into the chest and dislodged the heart. It was still beating so vigorously that it slipped from his hand and fell on the ground.

"You are a tough Mosotho! This will produce a strong horn." Selone picked up the heart and put it among the other parts.

Once the heart was removed, the life of a human being, the light of Tlelima's life went out. His body collapsed and that was the end of this hero of the Bahlakoana clan – a hero because if he had had the opportunity to yank loose, he would have avenged himself on three or four who accompanied him on his journey, disingenuously moving together, sharing tobacco and Christmas box.

Even so, when the truth hit Senyane that Tlelima, his friend, was dead, he became afraid. He, Senyane, was what he was because of his friend, was that not true? When he arrived home, how would he face Tlelima's wife? And what would he say when she asked him where he had left her husband, because she had specifically asked them not to go far from home? Tears filled his eyes.

"The work is done." Mosito's voice was a trembling, hoarse whisper and everybody could see that this act had shaken him terribly and stretched the muscles of his heart. "There is still one thing to do." The King whispered so quietly, he could hardly hear himself. "The corpse must be buried where it will not be seen.

Tomorrow evening we shall take it to the Senqu River and throw it into the deep pool above the Mohlapiso drift. I don't need to remind you that your mouths must remain sewn tightly closed."

Khati arranged everything. The young men took spades, it dug into the sand. The corpse of Tlelima, which was in pieces, was thrown in and covered up.

"You have all heard, young men," said Khati. "Tomorrow we will be here again to take the corpse to its last resting place."

They all left quietly, everyone fighting with his own thoughts. When they were near home, each one took his way, walking warily like a dog with its tail between its legs.

15

The alarm sounds

After Senyane and Bohata had left with her husband, Tlelima, Lipuo bathed her children and dressed them for Christmas Day. Then she visited her friend in the same village to ask for the box which was in such demand that day.

In the afternoon she returned and gave her friends some food. Everybody was happily discussing women's affairs while the sun was setting; the night arrived spreading its mokgahla, covering up all the children. However, Tlelima did not return home. But because it was a special day, people everywhere feasting, and those who drank moving all over the area to participate in the various pleasures, she did not worry.

When supper was ready, she fed her children and let them sleep. She stayed sitting up for a while, waiting for her dear husband to arrive so that she could give him what he needed before they went to bed. When she realised that it was getting too late, she went to bed and assumed that they had probably gone further from home than they intended and would soon return. She fell fast asleep.

When the first cock crowed, she woke up suddenly. She took a box of matches and lit the lamp. She looked at her husband's side of the bed, but there was nobody. Now she was worried. The first cock had crowed and he was not home.

"We've been married for five years and he has never slept out when he's gone out drinking. Even when he was very drunk, he has always come home, struggling until he got here," she said to herself. "If he is to sleep out elsewhere he always tells me beforehand, so that I am not unnessarily concerned and worried about him."

She was disturbed, although there was still some hope. Because it was Christmas time, perhaps he had drunk far too much at the place where he had been and simply fallen asleep. She took a lamp, checked her children and found them peacefully asleep. She looked at them; they both resembled their father in one or other aspect. She removed the lamp so that they did not wake up, and put it aside. Once outside, she went straight to Senyane's place. She knocked and Senyane's wife told her that he had not returned yet. She walked to Bohata's home. He was also not back.

"Why do you bother yourself about people who have gone for Christmas food to so-and-so's mother? They will eventually return. They're probably so drunk that they have to sleep it off."

"Well, then, I feel better. If they are all not back, I know they are still together, the three of them, and they will come, hand-in-hand, in their own time."

She went home and found her children still sleeping peacefully. She then took a glassful of the medication that heals all the ailments of the human soul, so when she woke up, the sun had already risen.

When the young men who had accompanied the King returned from their hunting expedition via different routes, they did not go straight to their homes, but gathered at the royal place to divide the loot they had taken from their victim. Most of the work had been done while the hunters were under the influence of liquor, and they had not cared much about the pleas of their prey. Their friend, Mr Liquor had given them bravery, or should one say, lent it to them. But then again, when one borrows something from someone, there comes a time when it has to be returned. Mr Liquor had also decided the time had come to leave with everything that belonged to him.

The young men were suddenly alone with their thoughts. Having nobody to discuss anything with, they began to realise that during their actions they had been accompanied by a friend – their conscience – who had all along been hiding, because he and liquor were great enemies. All their dealings began to emerge in different ways in their consciousnesses. They realised for the first time the evil and cruelty of their deeds. Conscience, their daily friend, the one they grew up with, was forcefully descending on them. It reprimanded them, but in vain. Havoc had been wreaked! Nothing could be reversed.

They arrived at the royal place with distressed hearts. Accompanied by their consciences, they were shivering and filled with regret when they entered the house and saw in the lamp-light their clothes heavily stained with the blood of their victim. Their feet desired to be dumped into another darkness, where they would live forever and not see the dirty work they had done.

Yes, all were shivering, except Selone. His conscience had died long ago, when he was still a young boy. Mosito produced six bottles of Tears-of-the-Queen. It was a symbol of happiness, but to all of them happiness was far away. In its place was seated fear.

Mosito did not waste time, just filled up a glass and slugged it down, filled up a second one, and also gulped it down. The others did not hesitate. Each one filled a glass or mug and swallowed down as much as possible in an effort to restore their friendship with liquor. They finished the bottles promptly.

After a bit of the deceptive bravery returned, it was time to divide the loot, but the participants sensed that their excited frenzy during all the stages of their mission had evaporated. They made some small-talk about it, but it was not of the kind people make when they do something that pleases their hearts.

When each had received his share, they left, one-by-one, and went home. At home, they were welcomed by soft hands and their heads rested on bosoms, like babies.

When Lipuo realised that the sun had risen she jumped out of bed. She looked at her husband's side of the bed: it was exactly as it had been the previous night. She did not even wait to sweep, but went straight to Senyane's home, and when she got there, his wife informed her he was back, but still asleep, as he had arrived when the second cock crowed, and was so drunk that he could hardly lift a foot.

"Maleshoane, wake him up, my dear." When Lipuo said that, her lungs shuddered involuntarily.

"What is the matter, my friend, you seem frightened?"

"I am surprised to learn that Senyane has returned, but Tlelima is still away, and yet they left together from here."

Without any further talk, Maleshoane went into the house and shook Senyane, removing the blankets from him to wake him up.

"What is wrong, Maleshoane?"

"Wake up quickly. We have a visitor!"

Senyane woke up reluctantly, struggling to get up from his bed. His legs were weak, his head was about to burst, his eyes bloodshot and dark brown, and because they were large, they became wild, like those of a beast of prey, when he opened them wide. He struggled to the door, and when he got out of the house, his eyes locked with Lipuo's, where she was sitting at the reed enclosure in front of the house. He was overcome by remorse and felt ice-cold.

"Where did you leave Tlelima?" Lipuo asked him, her eyes sharp and probing Senyane's red eyes, so that he quickly had to avert them.

"Has he not returned?"

He tried to speak as if he was still drunk, but the truth was that when his eyes met Lipuo's, the remaining drunkenness disappeared at once. He instantly recalled Tlelima's words when he said, "God, Father, look after my orphans!" The words pierced his heart like a sharp hunting spear.

"He is not home!"

Lipuo's answer sent a chill down Senyane's spinal cord, and when he spoke again it was in a very soft spirit, so soft that everybody could see that he was lying.

"What could have happened to him? Yesterday we left him at Thebe's house and went to Baterefala. I went to Tsietsi's place with Bohata and when we were about to leave, we sent a child to inform him that we were leaving and he must follow us. When we didn't meet him on our way, we assumed he had left just after we had left him at Thebe's. But if he is not here, he must have spent the night there."

Lipuo left and went to Bohata, but there, too, the answer was the same. Then she went to the royal place, where she met Khati and told him that Tlelima was missing, and those who were with him were home. Khati took her message to the King, who seemed unruffled and told Khati to inform Lipuo to stay calm. Her husband might have just slept somewhere, and would return home soon.

A woman has her own way of viewing a situation. Lipuo's fear was telling her something had happened to her husband. Whenever he had gone away with Senyane and Bohata, under all circumstances, they were always together. The village people used to call them iguanas.

"Dear Khati, inform the King that my conscience does not allow me to accept that Tlelima slept out. I therefore humbly request the King to send a message to Thebe at Baterefala, to enquire where Tlelima is."

Khati went and came back saying that the King currently had no messenger to send and that she should stop pestering him, her husband would return home. Lipuo saw red. She only controlled herself because the King was in court, and she could not confront him there.

"Khati, tell the King I am not accepting that Tlelima slept out, but let him know that, from here, I am going to the police station at Qacha, to inform them that the King refuses to help me look for my husband."

She left and when she got home she sent a child to Pokane, to inform him to come immediately. When Pokane got the message, he came rushing. "What is the problem, Lipuo, that you sent me a message so early in the morning?"

"Ntate, Tlelima left yesterday with Senyane and Bohata and he has not returned, but those two have. I have been to the royal place to ask that they send somebody to Baterefala where they say they left him, to ask where he is, but the King says I should wait. Now, what should I do?"

Pokane kept quiet for a moment, thinking. "It is a bit strange that Tlelima should remain behind when the others came home, but still, I think you should wait for a while, because he could have become too drunk and decided not to venture out in the night. Just be patient and see whether he does not come today. But if by tonight he is still not home, then there was certainly some trouble, and we will have to sound an alarm."

"Because it is you saying that, I will wait and see, but I am so worried and was thinking of going to the police station."

Pokane left and Lipuo felt her worry subsiding a bit.

That day passed the same as the previous one, feasting, with food in abundance. People ate, as it was part of the custom of the Basotho: if they had had enough the previous day, they would return to ask whether they had not perhaps broken any utensils when they had been eating and drinking. They would then be given what remained.

People continued indulging the way they had done the previous day until sunset. But amid that happiness, there was no peace in Lipuo's heart. She watched all the roads from Baterefala, but saw no trace of her husband, and by the time the sun went down, no one could report having seen him anywhere.

Dusk. Early evening. Midnight. But no sign of Tlelima. Eventually, poor Lipuo lay down and prayed in a sad mood, waiting for some sleep.

As we know, a huge task was still waiting. Towards midnight, the young men came one-by-one from the village and went down the hillock. They were to meet among the poplar trees, where the road crossed the Sejabatho. When everybody had come, they moved down along the river to where they had been the previous night. King Mosito was also with them. He was uneasy, thinking of the people who had done similar deeds in the past and been hanged. To calm his terror, he wanted to make sure that he was present to see the corpse removed and positioned where nobody would ever see it again.

When they got to the place, they dug up the corpse and carried it along the Sejabatho until it joined the deep 'Meiri pool in the Senqu River. On the banks of the river they wrapped the corpse in a mokgahla, tied it with thongs, tied a huge rock to the body and carried it up a precipice that was dangerous even in broad daylight.

There was a flat rock next to that precipice, where fisherman usually sat while fishing. Below it, there was a cave, in which many people believed a big water snake lived. The whole pool was very, very deep, unlike other pools in the river, where there was sand where one could walk before reaching the deep area.

The men decided that was the place where Tlelima would be laid to rest. The water was calm, as though the pool was stagnant. Its flowing was only noticed at the drift below the deep area where you could hear the sound of its movement over the boulders.

They got to the flat stone at the precipice with their heavy load. They swung it to and fro, and when one of them said, "Let go!" they flung it into the air and it landed in the river and sank at once.

But what had just happened? Where did the cry come from? They were alarmed because when they threw the corpse into the water, they saw someone following it and disappearing into the water.

"Help, oh please, help me!" It was Papiso, struggling in the water.

"Help, please, I am drowning!"

The men on the banks were silent. They saw Papiso dive and come up, battling with the tanned hide. He let go of it, as it was pulling him down, but because he could not swim, he surfaced once, yelled and then went down for good. Where he had sunk, they only saw bubbles for a while – when those disappeared, it was the end of his life. They suspected that while they were swinging the corpse, Papiso had not been aware that he was next to the edge of the deep pool. When the corpse was thrown into the air, he slipped and followed it.

"Gentlemen, Papiso has drowned," Khati shouted, when he regained his tongue. "Go Molafu, Bohata, Senyane, you who can swim. Go get him out!" They all looked at each other and stepped backwards from the deep pool. Mosito was stunned and did not know what to do. The others all accepted that Papiso had been drawn down by the fito in the deep pool.

When they realised that he was gone, and gone forever, they walked back home. Tlelima was dead, and his wife was already making noises. And now Papiso, who had been with Tlelima at some stage during the night Tlelima was killed; Papiso's wife would also start making a noise. How should they handle the affair?

While they were still brooding about what they should do, another foolish mistake dawned on them! The corpse had been thrown into the deep pool covered in a tanned hide. What would happen if the corpse was mysteriously recovered and someone recognised the hide? Would the owner be held responsible for Tlelima's death? He would have to explain how the corpse had ended up wrapped in a hide whose marks belonged to him. But they tried to console themselves that they had tied it firmly enough, and it would not easily escape the weight of the big stone.

The sun rose and the sky was clear. Lipuo knocked on Pokane's door. The door opened and Pokane, still in pyjamas, peeped out. Lipuo cried, and cried, and cried. Pokane knew without being told that conditions were serious. His eyes asked the evident question: had Tlelima not returned?

"Tlelima still hasn't returned." Tears flowed over her cheeks. Pokane didn't say anything. He went into the house and came out dressed. He told Lipuo to wait a while, rushed to Khosi and found him just getting out of bed.

"Brother. Conditions are serious. The woman woke me up and she's crying."

"Whose wife?"

"Tlelima's wife. She says her husband has not returned since Christmas Day. Those he left with returned the same day."

"And now?"

"Let us go to the King and inform him about this case." They left, went back to Pokane's house to fetch Lipuo, and continued to the King's house, where they found him sitting outside with Khati, Selone and Maime.

When Mosito saw the two men and the woman he saw red; his unusual response rose and he spoke in a very harsh tone.

"Haven't I told you that I don't want to see you here at my house? When will my instructions ever be respected?"

"My lord, here is a woman, and she is crying," said Pokane. "We have come because of her."

"Am I to wipe the tears of a woman I do not know? Why is she crying? Am I the...?" He swallowed the words that were already in his mouth.

"My lord, Tlelima has not returned," Lipuo said, with tears streaming down her face.

Mosito's anger did not subside. "Am I supposed to look after your husband? Have you ever seen me with him, that you should come and bawl to me as you do?"

"I do not say that, my lord. I was merely requesting that you help me to find him."

"Where do you think your husband has gone to?"

This time Mosito tried to control his anger, aware that it might cause people to suspect that something was irregular.

"How would I know, my lord, because he left home with Senyane and Bohata? They have returned, but I have not seen Tlelima since he left."

Suddenly Papiso's wife stormed in, her eyes sharp and flashing like that of a fierce bovine. "My lord, my husband Papiso left yesterday at dusk with Molafu, and has not returned home. I spent a sleepless night. I have just met Molafu, and he says he does not know where he has gone to. Now, my lord, I am appealing to you for help."

"He left with Molafu?"

"Yes, my lord."

"Did they say where they were going to?"

"They did not say, but when they were at the door, I heard Molafu speak about their victim but I could not hear where the victim was, and what it was doing."

"These cases are important, my lord, and we have to be alert," said Khosi. "They might smear you with mud unnecessarily."

Mosito's eyes flashed. "Why are you here? Are their husbands swallowed by me? Do you want to besmirch my name? Do I know where they have gone to?"

"I do not say you know, my lord, but as you are the people's father, you are the only one who can instruct men to go out and look for lost people."

"Where will the King start to look for lost men, when nobody knows where they went?" Khati also thought the idea ridiculous. "Let me say: it is unnecessary and a waste of the King's time that he must instruct men to look for drunkards. Where will they look for them? Tell us, maybe you know better! The disappearance of people during the festive season shouldn't bring concern, as everybody knows that Christmas food lasts for the whole week; people are feasting and possibly they are still with friends?"

Maime also gestured that any follow-up on these cases had no purpose, but Pokane thought differently. "Even if they are in the village, it is imperative that they should be sought. The more serious case is that of Tlelima. Today is the third day he's been missing and he is not a person who usually sleeps elsewhere."

"If you refuse to instruct men to look for Tlelima," said Lipuo, "I am going to the police station, and you will tell them why you refuse to help me look for my husband." She was angry and no longer cared to whom she was talking – king or not.

"I can see that you are a mindless young woman!" said Mosito. "I am not your husband's shepherd. Am I the one who said: marry a drunkard, who sleeps out and forgets that he has children? Maybe a beating will teach you who I am!" He stood up instantly, went into the house and came out carrying a sjambok.

"Steady, my lord," said Sebotsa, who had just arrived, and found the case already under discussion. "Steady, my lord, you will create more trouble by doing that. These are women, my lord, who do not know what is happening."

The other men all asked for reason, supporting Sebotsa. The King stopped and calmed down, speaking in a normal voice but firmly, like a king should. The messengers were summoned and given horses to go and look for Tlelima at Baterefala.

The Thebes told the messengers that, when the child had told Tlelima that the other two, Senyane and Bohata, were going, Tlelima had also left immediately to meet them on their way. That was the last time they had seen him and they had not heard anyone say they had seen him elsewhere.

More men were summoned. People left their drinks to go and seek the missing men. Messengers were sent all over the main village and other smaller ones in the area. Soon everybody was disturbed. It was the first time people had simply disappeared without any trace in the district. But, because of the great disease – the disease of ritual murder that had spread all over Lesotho – people were rattled and panicky, asking themselves whether that dreadful disease had arrived in their area.

They searched everywhere they could reach: on plains, mountains, hillocks, and in dongas, thinking that perhaps the men had fallen somewhere, because they'd been drunk. But all in vain.

At sunset, men returned home to the beer pots they had left in the morning, to quench their thirst. The next morning very early, Mosito sent messengers to Ratšoleli's to inform the king there that two of his men had disappeared. Another was sent to Qacha to inform the police that two men were missing. When it became warmer, men went out again, but they became more and more reluctant, feeling that it was a futile exercise after the previous day's thorough but unsuccessful search.

Later in the day, the police arrived at Mosito's village. The guilty ones were immediately panic-stricken, expecting an arrest, but the police were looking for Molafu, who left with the search parties. The police asked that when Senyane and Bohata arrived, they, too, had to go to the police station at Qacha to explain their story about Tlelima. In the evening, the search parties returned. They had had no success and it was clear that nothing further could be done. But still, the messengers kept on searching around all the villages, all the way to Mohlapiso.

16

Drug of forgetfulness

In the evening following the disappearance of Papiso, the King invited all those who had assisted him on the mission of sacrificing the victim. When all were present, the King spoke to them.

"Fellow men, we did a great job, even though it ended badly because of what happened to Papiso. The matter puts us in a serious and dangerous position, namely that Papiso left home with you, Molafu, but when you came back, he was nowhere to be seen. However, this is perhaps not such a big problem, because you will come up with a plan and explain how you had parted ways with Papiso. We do not need to teach you what to say, as you are a grown man.

"What really concerns me much more are the words that Papiso's wife overheard, 'phofu ea rona,' when you, Molafu, referred to the victim. I am very unhappy about these words and foresee that it will be difficult for you to find an innocent explanation for what you meant by them. We all know that such words are used only by people who intend to harm somebody. I have called you here today so that we can destroy this matter. It must evaporate like mist, leaving no trace whatsoever. You will now hear the latest development from Selone."

Selone said, "My lord, fellow countrymen, you already heard the King explaining the danger we will be in if the matter reaches the wrong ears. I am appealing to you all to stay calm because keeping matters from getting out of hand is my speciality. Today, I am going to use boreba on you all: the miraculous stupefying drug, so that the police, the families of these two people and whoever wants to confront you, remain forgetful around you and find it difficult to interrogate you. This will make sure that they simply close the case and move on to other things."

He undressed his upper body and kept on only his trousers. With a razor blade in his hand, he started with the King, making incisions on his joints, the forehead and next to his heart. When he was done, Selone worked on all the others: Khati, Sebotsa, Maime, Molafu, Senyane, Bohata and Letebele. Then he gave each of them a small stump of medicine the size of your little finger and said, "The name of this medicine is boreba. You must keep it safely and never be without it, it should be with you all the time. And every time you talk to people or to the police about these two missing people, you must get into the habit of biting a little bit of this medicine, chewing as you talk. There is absolutely nothing that can happen to you or hurt you then. Talk freely. I guarantee that, if you keep and use this drug as instructed, you will be surprised at how strong and powerful it is. You, yourself, won't even know where the matter ended."

They dispersed and went in their different directions towards their homes.

When Molafu and Letebele were a bit further from the khotla, Letebele said, "Molafu, what happened to the promise made by King Mosito regarding our contribution and our assistance in killing Tlelima?"

"I also remember that he promised this and that, and now has simply forgotten to give us even half of what he promised. He could at least give us something; with even a little bit we could do something for our families. I am starting to suspect that he might not give us a single coin. I only entered into all these shenanigans because Khati said there would be a reward, otherwise I would not have involved myself in this disgusting and horrible mission. I have a number of problems and thought that if I participated perhaps I could make a quick buck."

Molafu cleared his throat and said, "You are right, man, because I don't think any one of us would have participated without some form of imbursement. I am the only one who might have participated with or without remuneration, because I love and respect my king. I love him so much that I am prepared to do anything for him to retain his kingship, so that he is treated like the rest of the kings in Lesotho."

Letebele was quiet for a while, but when he spoke again, he spoke like a person who did not understand what Molafu was talking about or what he meant when he talked about Mosito's kingship. "To be honest, my friend, my conscience is giving me no peace, especially when I look at Tlelima's wife and children. Just imagine, man, if it had been you who was killed; what chance and future would your children have?"

"Stop thinking like that! Why are you behaving like a coward? The death of that man could be likened to that of a soldier who died in a war, defending his king and country. In such cases, do you ever hear people mourning about what would become of their children?"

Letebele kept quiet, appreciating from the way Molafu answered him that he was unhappy.

"We have been ordered to keep quiet about this matter," Molafu repeated, "and right now we do not even know if some people are not listening to our conversation. People will start being curious."

"Indeed, my friend!"

That was the end of the conversation, and they parted ways.

A week passed without word or sign about Tlelima or Papiso. No one came forward claiming to have seen or bumped into either of them in the village or neighbourhood. By now, everybody was convinced that, wherever they were, they were not alive. Everyone wished for their bodies to be recovered for a proper burial so that the families could begin their rituals.

One very early morning, a man named Maleke from Nqhoaki went fishing. Catching fish was second nature to him. He always caught the biggest ones, ones the size of a horse's neck, that sometimes broke the line. He usually cast his net or line at the 'Meiri pool, where he knew there were a lot of fish.

The fish hook he used was impressive and as thick as a knitting needle. The line was also strong. People warned that one day Maleke would end up catching the monstrous fito that presided over the rivers, especially when he continued casting his line near the cave where people suspected the snake lived and was often seen relaxing. But Maleke laughed them off, saying there was no such thing as a fito.

This morning, he positioned himself very well on the rock, then prepared the hook and cast it into the water. He used the hook that was meant to catch barbel and sat relaxed, waiting and watching his fishing bob in the deep waters.

Small bait usually caught fish so small that Maleke threw them back into the water. Now he waited patiently for the bigger fish lured by the bigger bait, but not even one took a bite. He was beginning to feel a little bit discouraged. His bob was floating serenely, showing that nothing was even nibbling. Then he decided to retrieve his line. It was easy to pull in the beginning, but as he kept on pulling, the line became heavier and heavier. For a while it felt impossible to get it to move and he suspected that he had caught an enormous fish. He pulled and pulled, but nothing moved. He became scared and thought of cutting the thread and running, because perhaps he'd indeed caught the monstrous snake that he was so often warned about. Anxiously, he got up, but then, overcome with all kinds of fear, quickly abandoned everything and ran up the bank onto the plateau. He stood there paralysed with fear, not knowing what to do. "Should I cut the fishing line? If I cut it, the hook will be lost, and they are very hard to come by – only in Natal."

At that moment, two men came down the path from King Mosuoe's direction to cross the Sejabatho. Maleke decided to wait no longer and called them. Initially reluctant, they however walked over to him.

"Men, please help me retrieve my fishing line from the deep water. I think I have caught something really big because when I pull it is too heavy. One person can't pull it."

"Have you caught a fish or have you caught the snake? Nobody catches fish in this dangerous part of the river, except the Europeans, and they succeed because they are also snakes. I grew up near the Senqu, looking after cattle – this part of the river is very dangerous. No one plays here." The speaker took a few steps, and then retreated.

"Please, Motiki, let's help him," said his partner, Tefo. "Don't fall for the lies that there is a snake in this river. Have you ever seen it with your own eyes?"

In the end, Motiki agreed to help. They all descended from the plateau to the flat rock.

"Here is the line," said Maleke, and showed them where he had tied the fishing line so that the fish would not swim away with it. He untied it.

"You find it difficult to pull such a short line!" said Motiki, "Let me see how it goes." He pulled and pulled, but nothing moved. "Good heavens! You certainly caught a monster there!"

The three joined hands and pulled together but nothing budged. They pulled and pulled with all their might, to no avail.

They pulled one last time and something moved, and when they again pulled harder, it moved a lot easier. Eventually when the hook resurfaced, it was hooked to a blanket. Terrified, they looked at it drifting in the water, and nearly ran away, because they had never heard of blankets being caught from rivers before. Wearily, they stood there, drained with shock. It was not the whole blanket, but just a torn piece of it. They suspected that it had become ripped off because of their forceful pulling.

"Men, this is scary," said Maleke. "The blanket that came out the water is a clear sign that the owner is still in the water. It might have been someone who drowned in a small river and floated down. What are we going to do?"

"I can't swim, but if I could, I would be diving down right now," said Tefo.

"But if there is a body, it should have been caught or noticed long ago. The river is unable to keep a drowned corpse down. As soon as someone drowns, his lungs are filled with water and he floats, and is later found, spat out by the river. The river can only keep living beings," said Motiki.

"Maybe this one is trapped between the rocks," said Maleke.

"And being guarded by the snake-owner of this place," added Motiki.

They decided to call other fishermen who were helping people to cross the lower part of the river to come and search with them for whatever was in the water and had the other half of the blanket with it. Maleke rushed to the plateau next to the European house at the lower part of the river and screamed for help that they should come as quickly as possible, there was something very strange in the water.

Everybody, including the herd boys, dropped everything they were busy with and came running. On the bank of the river they also saw the piece of blanket and agreed that someone who could swim should investigate what was going on down there. By now, there were about ten people gathered at the scene.

Motanyane volunteered to swim, immediately stripped off to only his underwear and dived into the water. Everybody present looked away because they were scared that it might be the last time they saw him alive. He swam deeper and headed to where they had seen the piece of blanket. He dived and was gone for a while. He resurfaced with empty hands.

"People! There is human body under the water. It's too heavy for me to bring up as it's trapped between the two rocks. That's why it's so heavy."

They sent a young man to fetch ropes. When he returned, they fastened the two ropes together and tied it around the swimmer's waist; the other end remained with them on the flat rock. They agreed that he would tug a few times on the rope as a signal that they could start pulling him. Then Motanyane swam to the place where the body was and dived. After a few seconds, the group on the rock started to pull, but the body did not come. It was obviously heavy. They all pulled together, and Motanyane surfaced with a naked body in his arms.

"Oh, man, this is Papiso!" exclaimed Maleke. "Now, how did he get here?"

"Evil deeds are at their end," said Motanyane, looking even more shocked than those he was with. "There is something else left in the water. I could not see clearly but it looks like another huge and heavy body. But hey, now I am tired. I can't go back. Someone else must volunteer. I did my bit."

At this stage, the fear of the big fito had already disappeared, because Motanyane had demonstrated that it was possible to return unharmed.

"Let me try," said Tsela, a giant of a man, who easily defied the Senqu in full flood, crossing as if it were nothing. He stripped down to his underwear. They tied a rope around his waist and instructed him to give a signal, like Motanyane had, when he was succeeding. Tsela dived into the river and was gone for quite a while. They felt him using the rope sign and immediately started pulling him. He resurfaced, pulling a large object, wrapped in a hide. Now everybody gathered there were in a state of shock, when they saw what Tsela had brought to the surface. They untied the rope around the hide and came face-to-face with a body in a terrible condition. The body had been severely mutilated.

There was only one thing to do: to notify all people in the surrounding villages of King Nqhoaki and King Mosito. Within minutes, people were gathering to see what had been discovered in the river. Both corpses were identified as those of the two missing men, Tlelima and Papiso.

The police were notified about the latest development. Immediately, they were on the scene, ever-ready, like scavengers: inspecting the bodies, asking Maleke, Motiki and the others questions about the place and position of the corpses and the sequence of events. Thereafter, the bodies were loaded into a police van and taken for further investigations by doctors and then to the mortuary in Qacha.

The families and the general public waited to hear the outcome of the post-mortem. It was released quickly and stated that Papiso's death was due to drowning and that foul play was suspected. The second corpse revealed that when Tlelima had been thrown into the river he was already dead. The doctors found he had sustained injuries all over his body and some body parts were missing, removed with a very sharp object. The bodies were released to the families for burial.

Now, the real work of finding the perpetrators began. Government police were seen all over the two villages, sniffing like dogs, trying to unravel the mysteries regarding the two dead men. They acted typically, like hunter's dogs. At King Mosito's village the mood was sombre when the corpses were laid to rest; the weeping from widows and children could be heard in the neighbouring villages. Their grief had an extra twist to it: the deaths were not God's way of recalling his people back to his Kingdom, they were man-made.

In the meantime, Selone jumped into action, burnt drugs, and impressed all those involved. Incisions were the order of the day, in an effort to strengthen the boreba. By now, King Mosito was totally dependent on Selone's expertise in traditional healing and rituals. He was relaxed and even bored by the investigations and enquiries.

In the same week that the corpses were found, an unusually tall young man arrived at King Mosito's place, looking for a job. He presented himself before the King, wearing a tattered and torn piece of grey blanket, usually used for horses or dogs, which was much too short for his build. He had no trousers on and it looked like he had never owned any in his life. Instead of trousers, he wrapped a very dirty piece of cloth around himself, which looked as if it had never experienced water, since it had landed in his hands.

"Where did you say you come from?" asked King Mosito, after fully inspecting this giant of a young man.

"I am from King Molapo's village, my lord," answered the giant.

"If you are from King Molapo, what brought you here?"

"I have already said I am looking for any form of work, my lord."

"Lesotho is such a huge country. You mean you have walked across almost half of this country and nowhere could you find any employment until you reached my place? How come you've been ignoring all these other kings nearer to where you come from, and conveniently choose *me* for employment?"

"I didn't just pass them, my lord, I did ask some of them for employment and also worked at King Ntaote's place for a little while. While working there, I heard people praising you for your kindness and decided to come and beg you to offer employment to this loitering soul: me."

Being famous is an attribute loved by all, and Mosito was also caught in a web, wishing to be famous and known all over the Kingdom of Lesotho, as part of the effectiveness of the potion. "Right now I do not have any specific job I could offer you. The only employment I can give is to look after my animals."

The face of the young man lit up, his soul was strengthened and he looked so happy. "Wherever I have been, minding animals was exactly what I did, my lord."

"Good. If you are happy with that, you are employed. The payment of all animal minders, as you know, is five shillings per month, or, if you don't want monetary remuneration, three sheep per year. What's your name?"

"My name is Seleso, my lord."

That concluded their terms, and the young man was employed.

The following day Seleso began his duty of herding the King's animals, as had been agreed. He did his job so well that he impressed everybody. The cattle came home well-fed, and the milking cows' massive udders could hardly contain their milk.

One day, while he was minding the animals in the valley near Sejabatho, there was a letsema, where communities gathered to hoe a field jointly. The field was where Seleso was with his herd of cattle. He joined the gathering for food, was well-received, and because there was enough food and traditional beer, really enjoyed himself. After the meal and beer, he felt a bit tipsy and returned to his animals, but they were nowhere to be found. He looked all over the valley, but found nothing. Then he climbed a plateau and saw the last of the herd disappearing into Molafu's corn field. He dashed to get them out, but it was too late. The owner of the corn field was already taking control of them, and so angry that he yelled all sorts of profanities: "You will get to know me; you bloody vagabond belonging to no one or nowhere!"

"Oh! Please forgive me, Father," said Seleso.

"You say, 'Oh, please forgive me, Father!' Can't you see the destruction these animals caused to my corn field? Today you will experience that I am Molafu, not Mrs Molafu!" Molafu uttered those despicable words as he was also tipsy. He advanced to strike the herder, Seleso, with a stick he had in his hand. The giant blocked a number of dangerous strikes aimed at his head, and sensing that Molafu was drunk, slightly side-stepped Molafu's charges and blocked him. Molafu stumbled, but somehow kept his balance. Seleso then charged, and hit Molafu on the forehead, spilling his blood.

When Molafu felt blood running over his face, together with the drunkenness it made him lose his head completely, and he yelled, "You took me by surprise! I'll teach you manners. Tlelima was a psychopath like you, and we put him straight!"

"I'm not Tlelima, so be warned," Seleso said, beating Molafu in the ribs. The fight turned ugly and became more vicious, until people at the letsema came running to separate the two.

In the evening, Seleso was called by the King who asked what had happened. After listening, the King said, "You see, if you go around looking for liquor and neglecting animals that then destroy people's properties I will not pay you, because the money must now pay the corn owner for the damage done. Molafu suffered a wound on his forehead, so I also have to pay for fat to heal his wound speedily.

Seleso was humbled and embarrassed. "I have heard you, my lord. From now on I will be vigilant in my duties, my lord."

"So what are you waiting for?" asked King Mosito, when Seleso stood fidgeting instead of leaving. "I've dismissed you."

"I want it to be noted that, even though I was at fault and negligent for not properly minding the animals that ended up destroying Molafu's corn field, it was not my intention to injure him. That happened because of his threats on my integrity. Molafu told me that I was exactly like Tlelima and that they were going to do to me exactly as they had done to him."

Mosito froze with shock and tried to look sideways to make sure that no one was within hearing distance to pick up Seleso's words. Nothing had prepared the King for what he heard Seleso, a total stranger and new to his village, saying.

"What did you say?" asked Mosito in a low voice.

"He said they were going to do to me what they did to Tlelima." When he said this he raised his voice somewhat.

Mosito dragged him into the house, "Listen to me very carefully, Seleso, this will be the first and last time I hear you mentioning Tlelima and Molafu's names. Do you hear me?"

"My lord, am I wrong to say that Tlelima was the fellow whose body was found badly mutilated before I came here? I thought I should tell you this in case I also disappear, so that you could hold Molafu accountable for my disappearance."

Mosito, visibly shaken, put his hand in his pocket and withdrew a one-pound note and gave it to Seleso. "With this money I shut your mouth. I do not want to hear you referring to or relating this to anyone, ever! You see, we really don't know what happened to Tlelima, but if you continue talking about this, you will find yourself in serious trouble."

There were times when Seleso could act like a real fool, as he had that day, drinking beer while tending to the King's herd. Now, he asked, "The person who knows what happened to Tlelima confessed, my lord. Why aren't you informing the police so that they can come and investigate? It is your responsibility to alert them about the latest developments, as they are busy with their investigations right now." Wasn't Seleso a total fool for not noticing how uncomfortable and jittery the King had become during the discussion?

Mosito shook his head. "Once I have spoken, I have spoken. You are stubborn and refuse to listen to my orders. Should I ever hear you discussing this matter with anyone, you will see what I will do to you. You will be rearranged with my own bare hands. Remember: if you disappeared, no one would care, because you don't have a family here and nobody even knows where you came from."

Seleso was embarrassed and noticebly shocked. "Oh my lord, please forgive me. I wasn't defying your orders. I will definitely do as I was ordered. My mouth is shut." He looked at the pound note he had received from the King, "This is a sign that you care about me because you are like a father to me. I repent, my lord." So Seleso agreed to maintain his silence, all was forgiven and forgotten and Mosito ordered Seleso to leave.

The large man left the King's place in a daze, shuddering at the thought that an assassin could be waiting for him outside as he walked back in the dark. When he got to the khotla, he found men warming themselves next to a fire. He squatted down with them.

"Oh fellow men, let me tell you, this boy who joined us now knows his story around tackling an opponent and defending himself!" said one of the men seated around a fire. "He's swift as a leopard. You see him here, the next minute he's there, tackling the opponent from behind." Everyone laughed.

Then Khati asked, "What did you say your clan name was?" and looked at Sebotsa.

"I am of the Bataung clan, Ntate," answered Seleso. He was immediately alarmed. What did his clan have to do with what was being discussed? And why was this interrogation about his clan coinciding with the day he had fought with Molafu?

"Oh, I see, that's the reason you're so brave," said Sebotsa. "The Bataung are a very brave people. They are as fierce as lions. So that's why you could injure a man the way you did."

When the time came, they all dispersed and retired to their different sleeping places. All was quiet. The next morning the sun rose and it became warm when people, to their surprise, saw that King Mosito's herd of cattle was still in the kraal. They checked on Seleso at the little hut where he slept, but he was nowhere to be found and nobody knew what had happened to him.

Khati rushed to King Mosito and reported Seleso's disappearance.

"Was he present at the khotla yesterday evening?" asked Mosito.

"Yes, my lord. He was with us. Some praised him for his strategic ways of tackling his opponent and his skill with the lebetlela. We stayed up late, but when everybody retired, he went to his usual sleeping place, together with other boys. And the boys are saying they went together to their different beds."

Mosito became apprehensive and tried to reach a convincing understanding of Seleso's disappearance. Could it be that Seleso had been scared by last night's orders and revelations? And if that was the case, where could he have run to? He remembered the money he had given Seleso and came to the conclusion that Seleso might have decided to abscond, now that he had been paid before the month was up.

Mosito said to Khati, "I don't think we should worry about vagabonds who roam all over the world not knowing exactly what they are looking for. In the first place, I did not know which entrance he used getting here, and, right now, I don't wish to know which exit he used running away from here."

The discussion ended there and Khati went to his house.

17

Handcuffs decorate

It was a Wednesday. It had rained the previous night, so the broad daylight was lovely and crisp. Most of the people were home because they had finished hoeing the fields, except for a few who had planted late in the season. Most families were spending their days now chasing birds away from the sorghum fields. Everywhere one could hear the twitter and chirrup of birds and the shwishing sound of clay balls, thrown to frighten away the birds.

It was almost three months since Tlelima had disappeared, and talk about his death was beginning to subside. Despite the fact that the doctor had indicated that the man had been murdered, it was evident that the police were failing to make headway in the case and determine the suspects. The disappearance of Seleso was also something of the past. After all he was just a vagabond and nobody really cared or bothered about him.

But his disappearance puzzled Pokane and Khosi. The King had not informed anybody about him. They had once asked the King to send out some men to look for him, but he had openly ignored their request, displaying his resentment towards them.

On this beautiful day, Pokane went to Khosi's residence. The two of them sat outside. Their work in the fields was finished and in earlier years they would have gone to the King's courtyard. But because the King had no time for them, they stayed at home.

"Homeboy, I am worried that we're going to be the next victims after Tlelima," said Pokane. "I am anxious. I don't go out after sunset, and, when someone knocks, I don't open until I'm sure about who it is and what they want. If I have to go out at night, I take my revolver with me."

"Man, you are behaving like a real coward, Homeboy." Pokane teased him with a laugh. "But actually, you have a point there. People can no longer trust each other, and fear everybody. You cannot even trust your friends any more, because they could be the people ensnaring you with a rope around the neck."

"But what I found most surprising was when the King refused to look for Seleso. He did not even bother to inform the police," said Khosi.

"And Seleso disappeared the very same night he fought with and injured Molafu!"

"And you know what; they say that Khati, on that same evening, asked him what his clan name was."

Pokane was shocked. "I don't believe it! Where did you hear that?"

"From the boys who were at the kgotla, while the people talked about the fight around the fire."

While Pokane and Khosi were having this discussion, the King was at court with Khati, Sebotsa, Maime and Selone.

"My lord, I have stayed long enough at your village." said Selone, "The time has come to move on and visit other friends. Perhaps there are also miseries, such as those I found here, which need my attention."

King Mosito looked down in thought.

"I hear your story, Selone, but is it not possible for you to settle here? Go and fetch your children. I have lots of fields and you can plough as much as you want. A person like you, who has proved

225

himself through his work, should stay here and be my doctor because I already know your work and how good it is."

All the men supported the King's words.

"You leaving this place is the same as a person who demolishes the shelter that has been protecting him against extreme sunshine," said Khati. "I also support the King's wish. You should stay here and be the nation's doctor."

"I understand, my lord, I shall think about it and weigh it up, when I get home. You will hear my decision from me."

"Alright, I will hear from you."

"My lord, but as for now, I have decided to leave tomorrow, and would appreciate it if I could be shown the calves that belong to me, so that I can mark them before I go. Seeing that I am not going straight home, I request the King to keep them until next month, when I will take them along with me on my way home."

"In the evening, when the cattle return home, I shall point them out. Although not everything you told me has materialised, what I have seen so far has convinced me that you are a reliable person. You have been honest in your work. Just look at what happened since we chewed the stupefying drug? The dogs sniffed everywhere, until they gave up and went back to their kennels."

Mosito laughed uproariously and stamped his feet on the ground.

"That was just to demonstrate my ability. Those are small matters. Much more is still to come," said Selone.

"Ever since you prepared the potion for me, I can feel that I have been a different person altogether. Whenever I meet the magistrate now, I feel dignified. I can see that he respects me far more than he used to do in the past. I've even noticed this when I am at Ratšoleli's..."

What he wanted to say died on the tip of his tongue. No one heard him. We too, shall never know what he was about to say.

A sergeant and ten policemen walked brusquely into the courtyard. The men saw them entering, and all boasting was cut off, as if by a knife. People began shivering in the hot sun, as if they were sitting on ice blocks. Sebotsa closed his eyes and then opened them, rubbing them to see more clearly or perhaps wondering whether he had turned blind. All the people's faces turned ashen. They did not know whether to stand up or go out. They were pinned down as if they were sculptures.

The chief officer went up to King Mosito, and said, "King Mosito, please note that you are under arrest. You are charged with the gruesome murder of Tlelima. Note that whatever you say could be used against you as evidence. Do you have anything to say?"

Mosito was dead silent. The chief officer handcuffed him, Selone, Khati, Sebotsa and Maime – they all received the same bangles as their king.

"Furthermore, we instruct you to hand over to us the following people: Molafu, Bohata, Senyane and Letebele."

"I do not know where they are, my lord," said Mosito.

Some policemen went into the village, and, in no time, returned with them.

By this time, the whole village was throbbing. Women cried bitterly, dogs howled as if they could sense that things were bad. Mosito was allowed to mount his grey horse, so the handcuffs were removed from his wrists so that he could ride, and he took his position in the middle of the police. The others were escorted by the police, and everybody could see who the culprits were.

When Pokane and Khosi saw the police, they ran to court to hear what the police were looking for. There they witnessed the arrest. They saw their king and friend of so many years leaving his homestead clothed in terrible disgrace. When he saw them, his eyes looked away, and on his face was written great remorse and embarrassment.

After the police left, Khosi and Pokane saddled their horses and followed them to find out exactly what would happen to the King. When they got to Qacha, they pleaded with the police not to lock up the King in the awaiting-trial rooms, but the police refused to listen, pointing out that he might try to interfere with the evidence.

Amidst all the scandal, only two people's hearts were consoled: Tlelima's and Papiso's wives.

Although the men were locked up, they could receive visitors in order to prepare their defence for the initial preparatory hearing. On their second day in the cells, a herbalist arrived. "My name is Thulare," said the man, when he introduced himself to Mosito.

"Yesterday, I slept at your place, my lord, and it was while I was there that I learned that you had been detained. I knew your father when he was still alive, and visited him frequently. He would tell me that you were at school down in the Cape. When I got the news, I decided to come and meet you, and to see if I can help. If you have any doubts, you can ask Khati and company, because they know me."

Khati concurred: he knew Thulare, but did not know that he was a herbalist, only that he used to visit King Lekaota from time to time.

"It is true you wouldn't know that I am a herbalist, because, unlike the other herbalists, I do not go about carrying bags and making a noise."

"I understand you, doctor. So, what now?"

"I've come to you to release the parts you have. It is only with them that I will be able to mix the medicine that I need to stop this case. What I need most is the liver of the person you alledgedly murdered. I tried to speak to your wife, 'Mathabo, but she dismissed me straightaway. Of course she does not know me and it was the first time she'd met me. You should understand me very well, Sir: I am not forcing you to give me what I need, if you do not trust me. I am fully aware that nowadays it is difficult to trust anybody. People have turned enemies on their friends. I do not blame the Queen, who pushed me aside, because how can she give that parcel to a stranger, someone she'd never heard of and whose name she didn't know? So, it depends on yourself whether you want help or not."

Mosito sighed and sat quietly for a while. He did wish to be dismissed from this case but it would not be wise to trust an unknown person and admit that the liver was somewhere and available.

"Well, the truth is: I don't know, because even the alleged charge is foreign to me. I know nothing about the person I was supposed to have killed. I was not there, and they talk about a liver, which I do not have, therefore, there is no way I can help you, even though I wish so badly to escape this ordeal."

"Then it doesn't matter, my lord, if these things didn't happen. I was hoping that there *was* such a thing, that it was true, so that I could use my knowledge and help you. But if you are innocent, then you do not need my help. You will win the case. I am therefore leaving now."

He stood up and prepared himself to leave.

"Just wait a moment. I want to discuss something with Khati. Perhaps there is a way you could help us."

Thulare said he would return after a while, when they had finished talking, and left.

"Do you say you knew this person while my father was still alive?"

"That is true, my lord, but as I have already stated, I didn't know him to be a doctor. I knew him only as a visitor who occasionally

229

visited King Lekaota. He hasn't been to the village for a very long time. I do not know where he comes from now or what brought him here today."

"What do you say? Can we give him the thing he wants? What must we do, Khati?"

"I do not know, my lord, one never knows. If I were certain that this man is a doctor, as he puts it, I would say, give it to him, maybe he can help us. But I am not sure, and it is difficult to say you should give it to him, not knowing his intentions. Who knows whether he's not a police spy? That's the thing that worries me."

"It's true, he may be a police spy, but on the other hand, wouldn't we have known him if he were a spy visiting villages? I have a feeling that he may help us, especially when you say that you knew him as someone who occasionally visited my father."

"Well, my lord, I don't say we cannot trust him, but was merely voicing my doubts. Perhaps it is through the grace of the ancestors that he arrived now, when you are in such a predicament."

"Would it be a mistake if I wrote a note to my wife requesting her to hand over the liver to Thulare?"

"No, my lord, not a letter, never a letter. Just instruct the Queen to give him the parcel where you have saved it."

"The Queen will never do such a thing without evidence from me. She will only accept a letter, because she knows my handwriting very well."

"Then that is fine, my lord, write a note."

Thulare re-entered, and found them ready.

"Thulare, I've decided to trust you. I heard how Khati talks about your friendship with my father and will give you a note to give to Queen 'Mathabo, so that you can help me."

"That is in order, Sir; explain to her that the only reason I want the liver is that I need it to mix my medicine. If I can get that, everything will turn out well."

Mosito asked for a piece of paper from the police, and wrote a short note to the Queen: instructing her to hand over the parcel to Thulare and describing where it was hidden. Thulare left happily. The following day he returned with the horn-potion he had prepared for Mosito with Tlelima's liver.

"This medicine, my lord, I have prepared for the big case, the one in Maseru, because this, here, is only a preliminary case. Tough arguments will be heard in Maseru at the Supreme Court."

Mosito thanked him sincerely and sensed that his ancestors still loved him. Thulare bade them farewell and left. As they sat there, they all suddenly felt much better.

18

Comrades in disarray

The first night Mosito had spent in the cells with his men had been marked by distress.

For a man of Mosito's status, brought up under great royal care, to sleep in a cell was a terrible experience. He had arrived at this crisis by listening to the elderly advisors and Selone. Selone had deceived him by saying this act would never be known, but here it was known, and here he was jailed. He had no idea how to get out of this mess. He was filled with foreboding, but there seemed no escape. The only hope he still had was that nobody had seen them when they performed their deed, and therefore there would be no evidence that could link them to the crime, and they still could walk out free. Thulare's visit gave him some hope. Mosito waited for the preliminary proceedings to commence, so that he could be freed.

But Mosito was not alone in worrying about the case. The men who'd been arrested with him were also grappling with it, each lamenting over his own case and hoping to be released. Everybody felt that, should they be freed, they would have learned a great lesson and would never make the same mistake again.

We already know about the major part Maime had played while the mission was being planned. He was the one who had taken it upon himself to talk to the Queen and had joined the mission wholeheartedly. On the other hand, his aim had been merely to please the King so as to get a favourable place in his heart. Until their deed had been exposed, he was sure that things were shaping up the way he had wished. Yes, just when his hope was nearing its fulfilment, this mishap occurred, and now all was in vain. When he thought about his wife and children, he began looking for ways to save himself, and wondered what those arrested with him were thinking about the case.

He decided to challenge their feelings and devised a way to test how deep they were. So Maime sat alone to the side, looking miserable, his head supported by his knees.

Letebele came and sat next to him. "My friend, why are you so gloomy? Why are you turning yourself into a loner?"

"No normal person can *not* be miserable when conditions are as they are. I'm thinking here we are, probably facing death, and what about my wife and children?"

Letebele looked at him. "You should have thought about that *before* you joined the mission. Thinking about it now will not help you in any way. The trap caught us."

Maime looked back at him despondently; tears even welled in his eyes. "If you did not have a wife who is pregnant, then I would say that you speak like that because you do not know the despondence of leaving children before the time determined by God."

"That's exactly what you should have thought of when you were told to kill Tlelima. He also had to leave his children. I, although I leave my children as orphans, find it fitting and should just persevere and take the punishment I deserve. My children will remain behind like those of Tlelima, because *I* wanted it that way."

Maime looked at Letebele for a long time, trying to work out whether Letebele was sincere in what he was saying, or whether he was just talking this way because he did not know how far he could trust him.

"Letebele, I hear what you are saying, but I know that what you have just said does not reflect your true feelings."

Letebele looked at him, and while looking at him became more and more astonished. "How do you know that these are not my feelings?"

"The animal we call man, I know him very well. Can you dispute what I said about your feelings?"

Letebele was amazed and dumbstruck.

"Your true feelings are far different from what you have just said," Maime insisted, "but because you do not know how far you may trust me, you do not speak the truth."

"You are right. Denying will not help us, Maime. Matters are as you say. My opinion is..." but Letebele became so overwhelmed that he could not continue.

"Your opinion is to find a way to escape from the snare holding you, but you fear to say that to the others arrested with you, because you do not know what they will say."

There was no answer from Letebele.

"Let me alleviate your fears, so that you can talk. I have the same idea that you have. Let me phrase it this way: Mosito promised each one of us a reward."

"That is true, but we did not get it, or let me rather say, I did not, because I do not know about the others."

"But you helped him to accomplish his mission."

"Yes, and the negligence that occurred cannot be placed on my shoulders."

"So are you satisfied about the fact that you should hang from your neck as an accomplice, without the promise you deserved?"

Letebele was a bit hesitant, but one could see he was discontented.

"I am asking: are you satisfied? You surely know the money he promised you was not much and cannot really sustain anybody. But if, at least, the money had been paid, if you should hang, at least your children would have some consolation."

"I do not know whether I am making a mistake," confessed Letebele, "but my feelings dictate to me that I should tell the truth, so that even if I hang, the truth is known. When I joined this mission, I did not act in accord with my feelings. I was influenced by the promise of money. Besides, Khati threatened me that if I did not join, they would deal with me as they were going to deal with Tlelima."

Maime continued, "I joined willingly, but now I feel that I was a big fool. But if the two of us could agree, I think there is a possible outcome. I was told that the government pardons people if they turn state witness and tell the truth as they know it. I am not completely sure about that yet, but if that is the case, it is the only way we could save our souls."

Letebele was unsure. "I do not think that such a thing exists, otherwise all these people would plead guilty and be freed."

"No, it's not as simple as that. You see, a man such as Mosito, he is the main accused, because the mission was for his benefit. If he pleads guilty, he will be tying the rope around his own neck, and will not be pardoned. But the two of us, although we have a hand in the crime, we are not like Mosito, because this was not really *our* mission. We joined when it was already in motion."

Letebele felt a little hope rising in him. "Now, where can we get the truth about this matter?" he asked.

"I do not know. We should ask the police to explain it to us, because this pardoning can turn out in one of two ways: we could be pardoned, or we could tell the truth as we see it, but the court might decide to turn it against us. Then we would be in big trouble; very difficult to get out of. But I still feel that we should give it a try."

They waited for the police to visit them so that they could get information about their plea. In the evening the security officer arrived to check all the cells. When he was about to leave their cell, Maime went to the courtyard, as if he was going to pass water. Before the officer left, he walked past Maime who gave him a small note: "Sir, I ask for your help. Please inform the sergeant that I would like to see him about an important secret! There is something I wish to discuss with him. Maime."

The officer left the cell and went to the sergeant with Maime's note. After reading it, the sergeant said, "I do not know what he wants to discuss with me privately."

"I do not know either, but I noticed that since his arrival, he seems like someone with a guilty conscience. He always sits alone, deep in thought."

The following day, the sergeant and corporal fetched Maime from the cell. "Maime, I hear you want to speak to me privately?" the sergeant asked.

"That is true, Sir, but I am not alone; there is a friend of mine who also wants to be present."

"Who is he?"

"Letebele, Sir."

"Let him come. Go and fetch him, Teboho," he ordered the prison warder. After two minutes, Teboho came with Letebele.

"We have brought you to the meeting, Letebele," said the sergeant. "I hear there is something you wish to discuss with us. Is that so?"

Letebele looked at Maime, who nodded.

"If you want to discuss something related to the case you are involved in, be warned that whatever you say could be used as evidence against you in court. It should be clear to you that you are not forced by anybody to speak; you are the ones who have volunteered to speak."

"That is true, Sir, we are volunteering. We feel it would be better for us to die after we have told you the truth," said Letebele.

"That is in order. Now, what do you want to tell us?"

"It would be better if you, Maime, set the ball rolling by giving the details from the beginning, because I only joined you in the middle, or to be precise, towards the end."

Letebele was being careful because of the sergeant's warning to them that carried no indication of the possibilities of a pardon if they told the truth.

"Sir, I shall start by saying the killing of Tlelima is true, and we know the facts from the beginning to the end because we were involved...following it. Now, here we are, arrested, so we think it necessary to tell the truth, so that God will be merciful when we die and accept us into His kingdom."

Maime paused and sighed to show his concern, and then continued carefully.

"I repeat: we know every detail of these events, because they were ours and we do not want to whitewash them."

"Steady," cautioned the sergeant. "I told you that nothing forces you to confess anything. Please understand that. When the case takes place you cannot say that we forced you to talk. I warn you, that, even if you don't say anything, we, the police have enough evidence for the case to proceed. Should you wish to reverse your decision and not say anything, all is still well. What you have said up until now shall be erased from our minds. You must know that, on several occasions, culprits made the police lose a case because they lied in court, saying the police beat them up to say what the police wanted them to say, or alleged that they were bribed to tell a lie that incriminated innocent people. This we detest, because it taints the good name of the police force, and, in the eyes of justice, we appear to be corrupt: failing in our investigations and incriminating people by assaulting them. Do you still want to continue speaking?"

Letebele answered. "Sir, Maime and I discussed this matter a number of times and asked ourselves what we should do, and each day we reached the same conclusion, namely, to tell only the truth and shame the devil. Although we might be tying ropes around our own necks, we still want to proceed."

"If that is how you feel, we will listen. Prepare pen and paper, Corporal."

Maime started at the very beginning, where everything originated: the minimising of the councils, Mosito's court case, Khati and Sebotsa's advice and how Selone joined them. His own part, where he spoke to the Queen, he did not mention because he realised that might implicate him. He continued until he reached the last meeting where the young men had joined them. He paused for a while, and then said, "From this point, Letebele can continue, because the next day, which was Christmas, all of us were together."

Letebele proceeded. "Yes, we were. After the evening meeting, we were instructed to watch our victim and catch him when it was dark, so that people wouldn't notice us, and take him to where the sacrifice would take place."

"Where was that?" asked the sergeant.

"Where the Sejabatho joins the smaller rivulet at Baterefala."

"But the corpse was found in the Senqu River?"

"That is correct, it was found there. That was the place where we had to dump it the following night, so that it disappeared for good."

Letebele narrated the events from the morning of Christmas Day and how they caught the victim. He narrated everything we already know, not adding anything extra or leaving out any detail, even the death of Papiso. He gave everyone the share he deserved. It is very rare for someone to narrate events as he did. When he had finished, he sighed and said, "These are events are as they unfolded, Sirs."

Maime seconded him and concluded, "The events are precisely as he has narrated them, Sir. There is nothing I can dispute. I confirm everything and we two hand ourselves into the care of your hands to do with as you please."

When he said that a teardrop shone in one eye. He thought of Tlelima's children, and Tlelima's last words before the knife started its deplorable task.

"Do with us as you please," echoed Letebele.

The corporal read back everything he had written down and then asked, "Have I written it all down correctly?"

"Very precisely," they both said.

"Take this paper and read it by yourselves so that next time you don't allege that I did not write what you told me, but wrote my own version."

"It is unnecessary to read. What you have written was narrated by us and you read the events as we dictated them. Everything is correct and we are satisfied."

"Sign here to confirm that what I have written here was said by you, and that you narrated everything out of your own free will, with no force or intimidation."

They signed willingly, satisfied that they had told the truth.

"This paper," said the sergeant, "we shall preserve to defend ourselves the day you want to dispute this in an attempt to try and exonerate yourselves and put the blame on us that you spoke under duress."

It is something that puzzles many people: why can an accomplice in a murder case be given freedom, simply by becoming a state witness? State witnesses help the police to obtain good evidence, solid enough to properly prosecute criminals; the kind of evidence they would not easily obtain. This was the reason that Maime and Letebele were finally released as state witnesses.

"But beware," said the sergeant when he released them, "If you have told us a lie, and it is discovered later that you made false statements about innocent people, you will be charged with lying under oath. On the commencement of the court proceedings, you have to swear that you will tell the truth. If there are witnesses that oppose you, you will be charged."

They were released and went home, instructed to call daily at the police station, to show that they had not absconded.

When Mosito heard that Maime and Letebele had been released, he was devastated. He knew that they had been released because they had turned state witness and would therefore strengthen the case of the state against him and his co-accused, adding more pressure to the knot around their necks.

"Now, conditions are at their lowest," said Khati when Mosito told him of Maime and Letebele's release. "On the other hand, my lord, it is a small matter, we shall win this case."

"How? Their witness will dispute our case! I don't see how we shall escape."

"According to my experience with such cases, the evidence of state witnesses should be supplemented by that of someone who was *not* present when such a thing happened; someone who heard something or saw something. In our case, such evidence cannot be found, because everything was conducted in a highly secretive fashion. So, nobody has heard or seen anything, except if the police bribe a person."

"Khati, to use the Sesotho expression: despite precautions, secrets become known, but let us leave it at that."

"Another point in our favour is the doctor," Khati added. "The one who came to see you. The way he spoke was encouraging to me, and it is clear that he was sent by the ancestors. For me that is an indication that they are on your side, and will not allow you to be killed so easily – especially after you have adhered to their wishes sent through Selone. Selone also apparently said that if he could get the herbs that he left behind when we were arrested, he would work out things in such a way that witnesses will be proved to be liars."

Finally, the preparatory court proceedings commenced. The state witnesses gave evidence, questions were asked and answered. When the preliminary proceedings were completed, everybody was informed that the case would be referred to the High Court in Maseru. They were disappointed, because all they'd had was hope – hope that the evidence would be insufficient, and they would be released.

19

Court case

"Silence in court," shouted the policeman standing to attention at the entrance of the Maseru High Court in a voice used to giving commands.

At once the people rose from the benches. The noise stopped instantly. All remained standing as if they were pillars. In the courtroom itself it was so quiet that one could hear a fly buzzing past, yet it was full to capacity. Some people were leaning against the windows because they could not find seats, others were standing outside.

Then the judge came in through one of the two closed doors, followed by four assessors, two Basotho and two Europeans. The judge was dressed in red to indicate that he was the one carrying life and death in his hands. Those who saw him for the first time imagined that the red signified the blood of the people who were sentenced to death. He was completely bald; only on the sides, above the ears, a sprinkling of grey hair indicated the years gone by. He sat on a chair reserved for him, the two European assessors sat on the right and the two Basotho assessors on the left.

Now the people in court also sat down. The tension subsided and they relaxed a bit. Here and there some whispering was heard. In front of the judge, but towards the right was seated another bald-headed man, like the judge, but he looked a little younger. Next to the judge's table sat the prosecutor at his own table, facing the door on the west. On his right were seated two advocates, also at their own table, for the accused. On their tables were stacked papers and big law books. At times, one might think these books paged themselves, because one never saw an advocate wasting time paging through – when he touched the book, his finger went straight to the point he wanted to make.

Opposite the table of the judge were seated the accused, squarely facing the man in whose hands their lives resided. They were in seats cordoned off, so that only their heads were visible, except for the taller ones, whose shoulders could also be seen. Behind them stood a policeman to remind them that they were accused of murder, and that no escape was possible, unless they convinced the ones in front – the bald-headed man dressed in red, together with his assessors – that they were innocent. They all looked at the judge, expecting mercy.

In the centre of the court room, but next to the witness box, there was another table, and on it were exhibits the police believed had been used in the killing of the victim. In the middle of it all was a tin. There was also the table of the secretary of the High Court, with another secretary recording proceedings in shorthand, so that not a single word should be missed.

The court secretary stood up. He was such a slender fellow you would think he had fasted all his life. He wore a black gown, held his head high and had spectacles. When he stood up, he was a picture of tranquillity. Everybody looked up expectantly, but he first cleaned his spectacles, put them neatly above his nostrils so as to read carefully and took a paper among the many in front of him. The men who had been accused stretched their necks to hear what he had to say.

"Mosito Lekaota!"

The owner of the name rose quickly and looked at the secretary.

"Are you Mosito Lekaota?"

"I am, Sir."

Mosito cleared his throat which felt ice-cold. All eyes were on him. The one answering there was a handsome, neat young man, light in complexion, but at that moment pale in the face, indicating that blood was not circulating properly. The women who were present remarked on his youth and attractive figure. Many people were seeing him for the first time. They only knew his name on account of his high educational level among the kings of Lesotho. The secretary looked at the paper in his hand and all eyes were once more on him and away from the accused.

"Mosito Lekaota, it is alleged that on 25 December, 1945, at Qacha's Nek, at the village of Mosito, you killed a person by the name of Tlelima in cold blood."

The secretary removed the paper he was reading from, put it on the table, took off his glasses, cleaned them with his handkerchief without looking at them, put them back into their case, put it on the table and looked at the accused without looking at them.

"You have heard the accusation. Are you guilty or not guilty?"

Mosito cleared his throat, but could say nothing. His throat felt like an old, parched leather milk container. With a hoarse voice, as if he suffered from TB, he said, "Not guilty."

The secretary carefully took his glasses out again – one could see that he was doing something he knew very well and did splendidly. When he had put them on, resting on the nostrils, he called upon the other accused: Selone, Khati, Sebotsa, Senyane, Bohata, Molafu. To each individually, the accusation was read and the question was: "Guilty or not guilty?" All pleaded not guilty.

The secretary collected his papers carefully, turned his back to the accused and faced the judge and his assessors.

"Your worship and assessors, these seven accused are here on the allegation of a gruesome murder. They have been brought to this court to plead their case and they have pleaded not guilty. I therefore put their case in your hands, to determine whether they are guilty or not guilty."

The secretary sat down and relaxed whispers were once more heard. The accused also looked somewhat relieved. The judge picked up his spectacles, put them on, and arranged his papers carefully on his table, which looked weathered, as if it had belonged to old cannibals in the days gone by. He was small in stature, but when he looked at the accused, his eyes seemed to read their feelings, as if from a piece of paper.

"Mr James!"

The owner of the name jumped up. "Your worship!"

This was the prosecutor. He was famous and his nickname among those who knew him was Mathapisa, The Tanner. He usually cross-examined the most difficult, most argumentative, accused until they were as soft as tanned hide, and ultimately admitting everything. The accused shivered when they faced him. His fame was enhanced by his legal qualifications, because his name was written: James Bell, MA, LLD, DCL, KC; and all these qualifications were earned through real studies – there was no honorary degree.

"You may commence with your evidence. Where are your witnesses?" asked the judge.

"I have seven, your worship."

The judge jotted down something on his papers and said, "Proceed and give the court an indication of how the case will ensue."

Mr James Bell bowed his head to indicate respect to the court and stood bolt upright, playing with the purple band of his black gown, which he had clearly done since he had appeared in court as a young lawyer for the first time. When he was certain the court was attentive, he proceeded.

"My case is short and the evidence in hand clear. The state will deliver evidence that on the night of Christmas Day, on the twenty-fifth of December 1945, the accused caught the late Tlelima, after a series of meetings and various preparations made before said date. When they caught him, they murdered him mercilessly by cutting him open while alive. The doctor who did the post-mortem will give evidence that the corpse had no eyes, liver, tongue, heart, male organs and other small parts to be named.

"Then we have a letter, which accused number one, Mosito, wrote to his wife, instructing her to hand over the flesh cut from the deceased. The case shall be based on further evidence from the two who turned state witness and that, in turn, will be supplemented by people who saw or heard something to support the evidence at hand."

He paused for a while, looked at the judge and his assessors, and said, "This is the outline I am indicating to the court, and if your worship allows me, I shall call upon the first witness, Maime, a state witness."

The judge nodded his head and the prosecutor instructed the policeman in charge to call Maime. Maime entered, his eyes looking wild, as if he was about to flee. The policeman pointed at the witness box. He walked into it as if it was a lion's den and something would devour him any minute. The secretary stood up, raised his right hand, twisted two fingers and asked Maime to repeat after him.

"I swear that the evidence I shall give will be the truth and nothing but the truth, so help me God!"

The secretary sat down, paged through his legal books, inserting a piece of paper here and there, marking what he might need during the court proceedings. Maime's throat was dry. He alternated between feeling freezing cold and feverishly hot.

From the tables of advocates, their eyes were sharply on him, as if about to demolish him. The prosecutor stood up, cleared his throat, took a glass of water in front of him and sipped. He looked at Maime, then at the paper in his left hand; the right hand was twisting his gown's arm in a kind of habit, indicating importance. Maime was absolutely terrified.

"Your name is Maime, is that true?"

"Yes, Sir."

The voice was whispering, not really audible.

"When you speak raise your voice, so that what you are saying can be heard."

Maime looked at the person in red speaking. As that was his first experience in court, he did not know that it was the judge. Nevertheless he said, "Yes, Sir" and tried to raise his voice.

"You stay at King Mosito's village?" asked the prosecutor.

"Yes, Sir." Now the voice was better.

"Just have a look at those accused and tell me whether there is anyone you know among them. Look carefully."

Maime looked at them once and said, "I know them all, Sir."

"Can you name them?"

"Yes, Sir, I can," and he said their names.

"Among them, who is Mosito?"

"He is the one in the middle of the box."

"Alright, I can see you know him. Do you still remember this past Christmas day?"

"I remember it well, Sir."

"Tell the court what happened on that day."

Now Maime's tongue was loosened. He related all that occurred, which we already know. The prosecutor helped him here and there, to put the record straight. He led him properly and took him to the day the letter from the Paramount King was received, stating the establishment of the new national fund, as well as the changes envisaged, and came to where the idea of a ritual murder was planned and executed on Christmas day.

When the prosecutor had finished, he sat down and looked at the judge and his assessors. Maime had stood for a long time and was tired. When the prosecutor sat down, he thought that his turn was over.

"The court shall adjourn for five minutes," said the judge.

All stood up, the judge and assessors left and people went out to stretch their legs. Many, however, remained in their seats, worried that those who had been standing outside would come in and take them. In court, unlike at a shebeen, one cannot come back and say, this is my seat, I was sitting here before.

The doors were opened and the policeman shouted for silence. People stood up, the judge entered, sat and everybody also sat down. Mr John Murphy, MA, LLD, KC, was next up. He was the advocate for the accused, assisted by Mr Joubert du Plessis, BA, LLB. They were also bald, and appeared to have been long in the legal wars.

Mr Murphy, slender and tall, had bushy eyebrows and eyes as sharp as a hawk's. The Basotho, because he was familiar with such cases, nicknamed him the Rope Cutter. When a person was on the verge of being hanged, Mr Murphy managed to win his case.

Before recess, while James Bell had been speaking, John Murphy had looked very annoyed, apparently surprised by what his learned friend was saying. This he indicated by leaning backwards, yawning and looking irritatedly at his watch. He would survey the courtroom, yawn again, shake his head. This was a trick advocates used to draw the court's attention to the fact that the speaker was being vague and wasting time.

But the moment he stood, all this fatigue was gone, also his annoyance. He was energetic and his eyes bright with lively energy. Maime was taken back to the witness box. He was surprised, as he thought he had finished, not knowing he was about to be cross-examined.

Mr Murphy looked at him with piercing eyes, showing that he did not have Mr Bell's friendly attitude. We do not know whether it was for fancy reasons or legal ones that all the advocates wore spectacles. Mr Murphy also took out his, and wore them on the crooked nostrils of his long, sharp nose, which resembled an eagle's beak. He put them on carefully to indicate that he had an even better way of putting on his glasses, took a paper and looked at it. To those in front of him, it was as if he was looking over the spectacles. When he had finished reading what was on the paper, he took them off and held them in his right hand, which kept bobbing in the air like someone's sewing machine. This attracted the attention of the court because the gown's arm flew around in the air like the tail of a willow bird in the reeds among finches. All eyes in the courtroom were on him.

"You say you are Maime?"

His eyes were severe; the aim was to scare the witness so that he would not be able to answer questions reliably.

"Yes, I am Maime."

We should note that he did not add 'Mr' or 'Sir', as the others before him, because he was in a fighting mood, and like the witness who had preceded him, felt stubborn.

"You are King Mosito's confidant?"

"That is true."

"You love him very much?"

"I love him."

Maime answered this question in a way that showed he thought the question irrelevant to his evidence.

"I understand you are a person who speaks the truth at all times."

"Who said I am lying?"

"Don't answer a question with another question. I say, do you always speak the truth?"

"Yes." Maime looked annoyed.

"Do you always tell your king the truth?"

"I tell it; is there anyone saying I once told him a lie?"

"Look here, Maime, understand that I am asking the questions, not you. I ask, are you sure you have never told King Mosito a lie?"

"I told you. How many times should I tell you?"

When Maime said that, his huge voice returned and shook the court room, penetrating through the ears of the people standing outside. The advocate put on his glasses, looked at the paper in his hand, and said, "I understand that you are a person who always speaks the truth."

"Yes indeed, that is true!"

"Do you still remember the day the King was invited to Ratšoleli's place?"

"He was invited on several occasions. I do not know which occasion you are referring to."

"How many times?"

"I do not know, but they were many."

"Could it be three times?"

"I do not remember."

"This year, was he invited?"

Maime thought for a while and said, "No, he was not invited."

"Last year? Was he ever invited? How many times?"

"I do not know, I have already said it."

The advocate spoke facing the judge so that he should hear what he was saying.

"But the things you have just said you know very well?"

"Yes, I know very well."

"Why?"

"Because I saw them with my eyes."

"When the King went to Ratšoleli's place, you did not see him with your eyes?"

"I saw him with them, how else would I have seen him?"

"But you do not know how many times he went there?"

Maime was quiet, looking up at the ceiling.

"Answer me!"

"I do not see what I should answer. You let me repeat the same thing I have already told you several times!"

"How many times have you told me?"

"As many times as I told you."

"State the number of those times."

"I do not remember, but I know that you asked me more than twice."

"You say you do not remember the times I asked you?"

"I told you that I do not know."

"But you say the court should accept, and believe the things you have just stated here, which took place about four months ago?"

"Yes!"

"How do you remember those, when you can hardly remember what you have just said here?"

"I remember them."

"I put it to you that the things you have just said are false. You have put them together."

Maime was quiet.

"What do you say?"

"What do I say where? You are telling me, not asking me."

"Is it true or false? Let me return to this point. You say you have never told King Mosito a lie?"

"I said so on several occasions."

He looked at the paper and back to Maime again.

"You said you do not know which day I was referring to when I spoke about Ratšoleli?"

"Yes, I said so."

"Do you remember the last time?"

"Yes, I remember."

"Why do you remember that day?"

"I remember it because I stayed at home, whereas usually I accompany him."

"We understand when you remember it. Just tell the court why on that day you remained home?"

"I was sick."

"What was wrong?"

"I had an upset stomach."

"Are you sure?"

"Yes." Maime agreed hesitantly.

"Did the King know that you were unable to go with him because of an upset stomach?"

"If you are now telling me this, it seems we have exchanged stomachs so that you know something about my tummy that I don't know."

"I say you were lying!"

When he said that he looked fiercely at Maime, and Maime felt uneasy. He asked himself how the advocate got to know this fact. It was possible that Khati had told him. Could they really betray him in that manner? Yes, because he had also turned against them. He was in trouble about whether he should now tell the truth or not.

"I put it to you that you had no upset stomach."

He hesitated then said, "Well, that is true, my lord."

Maime's answer indicated to the advocate that he had now broken his molar tooth, and he decided to confuse him even more while he was being tamed.

"It is clear that you are a person who thrives on telling lies?"

"The things I have stated are true." He was annoyed that a person who had not been present should say he is lying.

"Now that you have just acknowledged that you told your king a lie, the person you respect, how do you expect this court to believe that you are not lying against King Mosito?"

"I say the court should believe me because I told the truth."

The advocate cross-examined him on his evidence, but Maime answered easily. The advocate was busy with him for a long time, but after two hours it was accepted that his evidence was solid. Here and there had been some gaps, but the gist of his evidence stood the test of time. The advocate sat down.

Mr Bell was on his feet. "Your worship!"

The judge looked at him, nodded as he was ready to listen.

"I wish to ask the witness a few questions, and also clear the dust that my learned friend tried to create."

"Go ahead."

"Maime, you answered my learned friend that it was true, that you lied to King Mosito and said you had an upset stomach, which was untrue?"

"Yes, that is true, Sir."

"Why did you say so to the King?"

"I was instructed by Khati to meet Queen 'Mathabo and ask her to help us to speak to the King about the ritual murder affair."

"Help you in which manner?"

"To talk to the King to stop the ritual murder mission."

Here out of the blue, Maime told a lie because he felt his conscience troubling him. He was aware that if he told the truth that he had wanted the Queen to encourage her husband to indulge in a ritual murder, he would complicate matters that would implicate *him* and it would be obvious that *they* were the ones who forced the King to go ahead. That he could not afford.

"So, you are saying that you were against this mission?"

Maime looked towards Mosito and his group and found them frowning, because of the stink of his lie. Still, he had to answer.

"We were very much against that, Sir."

"And that was why you did not wish the King to know that you had remained home to talk to the Queen, because you were opposed to it?"

"That is correct, Sir."

"You did that because you did not wish to see your king get into trouble?"

"Correct, that was my reason, Sir."

But as he said that it was as if all the people could see that was a lie.

The prosecutor nodded to the judge and sat down. At once Mr Murphy stood up.

"Your worship, I concluded my task with this witness, but I feel I have to ask a few questions about what he just said."

The judge nodded his head.

"Maime, I am with you again, my friend. You said you remained behind to talk to the Queen to convince her husband to stop the idea of a ritual murder?"

Maime realised that now he had created a terrible problem for himself that he had not foreseen. He had told a lie, but it was evident that Mr Murphy knew all the facts regarding this case. What should he say?

"I put it to you, Maime, is that true?

"It is true."

"Will the Queen also say that it is what you discussed with her?"

It was one thing to affirm when one knew one was at war fighting for one's life, but quite another to say that the Queen was lying.

"I say: do you swear that the Queen will agree with you?"

"That, I cannot tell."

"How can you not tell, when you speak the truth?"

"Well, I do not know what the Queen may wish to say. I only know what I said."

"If she says that you did not say that, but that you were trying to get her to convince her husband to take the route of ritual murder, what will you say?"

Maime was quiet.

"Will you say she is telling a lie?"

"I can't say she is telling a lie. I respect her. She is my king's wife."

"You do not answer me. Will you say that she is telling a lie or not?"

"I shall say..."

"Yes, what will you say?"

"I shall say she is telling a lie."

Maime's conscience now rattled him badly.

"Well, we will hear what the Queen says."

He nodded his head and sat down.

Maime left the witness box after the gruelling session with sweat streaming down his body. The proceedings were adjourned until the next day at nine o'clock.

The case proceeded for another five days, with the court listening to the evidence of the state witnesses and the accused. At times the evidence of the accused weakened and the bald ones quickly closed the gaps with arguments that improved the evidence accordingly.

On the fifth day, all the witnesses on both sides had given evidence. The judge concluded that the following day the court would listen to the prosecutor. If the time allowed, the court would also hear the advocate of the accused. The advocates on both sides spent the night consulting various legal sources and preparing their concluding arguments; adding a touch of elegance and quoting some relevant sources.

At nine o'clock the next day, the proceedings commenced. The arguments were stronger and more authoritative than the previous ones, each person trying his best to argue his point.

The prosecutor stood up, looked from side to side, requiring with his eyes the attention of the court. "Your worship and the honourable court, I shall be brief. The evidence delivered in this court is such that even our learned friends should accept its truth."

He said that, looking at his so-called learned friends with utter disdain. It was perfectly silent in the court, so silent that one could hear the pen of the judge while he wrote.

"I put it to this court that the main evidence is solid, your worship. It is the evidence of two people who were involved in the mission. My learned friends tried their best to indicate that the first state witness, Maime, was a liar, and that his evidence should be dismissed. But the answers he gave me when I interviewed him the second time showed convincingly that he was not a person for lies. He only did that because he wanted to lead his king in the right direction."

He drank some water from the glass in front of him.

"So, your worship, I request that the court accepts this evidence as true. The discrepancy that might be found in the evidence of the two witnesses is something common. The court knows that, when two or more people witness something happening and they narrate it later, each one will do it in his own way, because people never view things in a similar manner. If it does happen that they describe an occurrence in a similar way, such people have been coached. Even if the evidence of the state ended with the state witnesses, it would suffice for the court to find the accused guilty. However, the case has been strengthened by evidence from other sources. The doctor's evidence supported the state witnesses in that the deceased had no eyes, heart, liver and other organs, which the witnesses said had been removed. The first person to cut was the owner of the mission, Mosito. Apart from that, the evidence of the state witnesses is supported by the one named Khera, who said that he was relaxing next to the rocks where the deceased was caught. While resting there, he recognised the voice of the late Tlelima who was talking to Senyane, saying he should wake up. He also recognised the voice of Bohata, who wanted to attend to his loose trousers. Khera saw a group approaching and manhandling the victim, because there was bright moonlight. His evidence tallied well with that of the state witnesses. I therefore see no need to look for other evidence. Now I get to the evidence of Lipuo, the deceased's wife."

He once more wetted his throat with some water from a glass.

"Lipuo told us that, when she went to the King to report that her husband had disappeared, the King became angry, and, if the men who were around had not intervened, he would have assaulted her. Why was he behaving like that? The woman had good reasons to go to him. He was the king, after all. There is only one reason: he was trying to hide something, that is, where the missing man was. He was inflamed by a guilty conscience. More decisive evidence was given by the cattle herder, Seleso. He got to the King's place looking like a vagabond, and was offered a job. The day he fought with Molafu, Molafu said he would do to him what he had done to Tlelima. Mosito, when he heard that, was shocked, pleaded and paid Seleso never to repeat what Molafu had said. If the King had been concerned about the death of Tlelima, he would have regarded Molafu's words as a clue to help him find Tlelima's killers. But he did the opposite, and did all in his power to stop the gaps. If Seleso had not fled that night, I have no doubt he would be among the dead. Or, if they had known that he was an investigative spy, he would certainly be among the dead now."

He had some water again and continued stripping naked the witnesses for the accused and told the accused how he saw them. After two hours he said, "Now I near the end of my speech." He spread his right hand like a woman smearing the floor, drawing patterns.

Everybody realised that he was now attacking with his last weapons, more dangerous than the ones he used till now. "Your worship, the last state evidence is from accused number one: the letter that the court already knows about." He waved it in the air happily for all to see, looking askance at the advocate of the accused, as if saying there was nothing you could say that would refute this letter as evidence. The accused's advocate seemed flustered on his seat and spoke softly to his colleague.

"I repeat: this evidence is enough to render all doubts irrelevant. The handwriting corresponds with the writing the accused did here in court and experts testified that the handwriting was from the same person. Accused number one instructed his wife in this letter to give the doctor, Thulare, the liver got from the deceased, so that Thulare could prepare some medicine that would render this case null and void. The accused jumped around, but has failed to explain how the liver got into his hands. His advocate suggested that it could be a sheep's liver, but that was dispelled by the wellknown expert, Mr DD Brown, MA, DSc, PhD, FRS. Mr Brown ascertained that it was the liver of a human being. I further wish to remind this court that Thulare is a senior man in the police force: sergeant of the special investigating force in the police services. He is well-respected in the government and community for being a loyal officer. I say all these things to discredit what my learned friend tried to intimate, namely that Thulare was an unreliable witness, based on how he got the evidence."

He paused for a while, giving the court a chance to reflect.

"When you consider the evidence and piece it together, it's the pieces of a broken mirror reassembled to the original shape. The evidence tallies so well and leaves no doubt that I therefore appeal to this court to examine it thoroughly. It will find the accused guilty of ritual murder."

He took a sip of water again, bowed his head and sat down, seemingly satisfied for having won the battle. He was obviously feeling proud for putting his arguments across in such a splendid manner.

The court adjourned and it would meet again at two o'clock in the afternoon.

The people came out into the sun convinced that the rope was looming low over the accused, despite Rope Cutter's reputation as rescuer of those on the brink of death. Today, the prosecutor was of a different calibre.

At two o'clock, the Rope Cutter was ready.

"Your worship!" He bowed his head to indicate respect, stood up straight and kept on picking at his gown. The court was silent. "It's a miracle that a learned friend such as this one can stand on his feet and assert that such weak evidence should lead to a guilty verdict! This evidence is so weak that one could not even hang a fly on it!"

All ears were raised, all eyes brightened. It was evident that this was an unusual bull kicking up the dust.

He proceeded to pull down the argument built by the prosecutor, wall by wall.

"Which evidence entitles the prosecutor to say the accused are guilty of ritual murder: the evidence of the state witnesses? The first witness, Maime, has admitted he is a liar, a man who does not hesitate to lie in the face of his king, the king he claims to respect. The court should note how I pressured him to admit that he had told a lie, but even that he couldn't do, and so lied again. I invite this court to accept that everything he said here was a lie.

"When I cross-examined him, he delayed, but in the end he admitted that he had told a lie and that he had not been ill. His aim was to remain behind so that he could discuss something with the Queen. Then he told yet another lie, namely that Khati had asked him to stay behind so that he could influence the Queen to speak to Mosito to *stop* the mission. According to Maime they were *opposed* to the mission."

He sighed heavily and drank some water as if to quench his thirst in order to speak in a normal tone. "Maime said he believed that the Queen would agree with him to stop the King."

Rope Cutter smiled a bit, and it was the smile of someone feeling good because he was demolishing walls built carefully by the advocate of the state.

"The evidence of the Queen is that Maime talked about how the King rejected the idea of murder – even after they had pleaded with him. Maime wanted the Queen to persuade her husband to yield and commit murder, because his kingship would remain shaky unless he was strengthened by means of a horn of herbs mixed with human flesh.

"The court heard the evidence of the Queen, and is satisfied that she is, by nature, a person who sticks to the truth. I, therefore, believe that the court will accept her evidence. The evidence of Maime, to my mind, is something he created out of his puerile head when he realised that he was going to be hanged. The truth is that Maime and his group are actually the ones who murdered the deceased and they merely involved the King, so as not to die alone.

"King Mosito is one of the most intelligent kings in Lesotho, educationally above them all. Because of his education, the idea of horns and herbs does not make any sense to him. It is, therefore, surprising that the court is expected to believe the story of Maime, who implicates King Mosito. Even his upbringing never taught King Mosito anything about the use of horns in government. His late father gave him the correct education, but the use of horns was never taught, as some of his subjects testified: he didn't even use popular potions to block hail or chase away birds. Does the court really want to believe that a man such as Mosito, brought up in that manner, would suddenly begin to believe in potions?"

In their section that was cordoned off, the accused were whispering, indicating that they were taken up by how Mr Murphy put his case across. The people in court were also enthusiastic because of the advocate's talk.

"Your worship and the honourable court, I humbly appeal that you reject Maime's evidence. The second witness, Letebele, is equally unreliable. Letebele said it was Selone who started to cut, while Maime says it was Mosito. If these witnesses speak the truth, can they differ so widely about such a deed? I would say one should reject their evidence totally.

"Cross-questioning Letebele, the court heard that King Mosito had taken his field from Letebele the year before last, and given it to Khati. This shows motivation for Letebele's false statement in court – his aim is to avenge himself. That is why his evidence smears Mosito and Khati, the ones who are linked to his field. Your worship, I wish you to understand that, even though a field might seem like a minor issue in the eyes of Europeans, to a Mosotho it means a lot. His whole life depends on ploughing the soil. Taking it is like stealing a thousand pounds from a person. So, that means Letebele has a major reason to vent his anger himself."

He looked all over the courtroom, his eyes brightly focused on the accused in the witness box, finding them gazing at him as if he was the one who would pronounce them not guilty. He continued.

"Letebele admitted that King Mosito is not someone who ever sends for him. Since Mosito has been king, Letebele has been a nobody. Now, why would Mosito send for Letebele when he planned such a dangerous job, knowing very well the man's anger about his field?

"If the court accepts this, it suggests Mosito is a fool. But, according to the evidence, this court knows that Mosito is not a fool."

The court adjourned then for ten minutes so that people could stretch their legs. Ten minutes passed like a minute, and in no time, court proceedings recommenced.

Mr Murphy was on his feet again.

"I am back, my worship, and if you allow me, I shall continue."

He looked at the judge, who nodded his head.

"Apart from these two witnesses, the other evidence is that of the doctor. The doctor's evidence need not concern the court too much, because a post-mortem works with people already dead."

But somehow, in his heart, Mr Murphy felt that he could not spoil the evidence of the doctor, because he, himself, had never seen a person murdered in this way, so he simply stated that a person had been killed by having organs cut from him. The evidence that the murder was for the use of potions in witchcraft could not be disputed, but he tried to formulate an argument.

"I do not see how my learned friend could find the evidence of the doctor supporting. A person was found without organs. The evidence is about how a person died, but *how* that death occured remains with Maime and Letebele, and they cannot be relied on. As we have seen, the advocate only noticed the points that supported his argument, so he quickly rushed over the doctor's evidence.

"The other evidence is that of Khera. How can this be relevant? Nobody believes Khera's story. On Christmas Day, everybody was drunk. Khera was drunk. In fact, he fell on the road, although he alleges he was just resting. When he woke up – his eyes still covered by the web of drunkenness, his ears still misunderstanding – he heard people speaking. He didn't even see their faces. He pretends to know that one of them was Tlelima, another was Senyane, another one Bohata. How did he recognise all those people? Through their voices. Through their voices! How can the court accept evidence of this kind? The court should also note that, when he was giving evidence, he was not talking fluently, and he admitted that, yes, he had taken a bit from the calabash before testifying. Now, if a sip from the calabash is enough to affect him – think of Christmas Day, when beer flows like water, and he had been drinking for the whole day, from morning till night! I should actually state that Khera's evidence should be rejected in total!"

He took a sip of water and looked around. His right hand went up and then came down, like a hawk attacking a chick, and forcefully landed on the huge book on the table. He stood, picking at his gown from time to time.

"Another witness brought in was Seleso. And, truly, just the way he speaks, I find him to be a fool. His evidence was pitiful; listen: he was drunk, he fought a drunken man, then he heard the name of the deceased and suddenly assumed he had evidence. Why did he run away? Because Khati asked him what his clan name was. When he told his clan name, the men commended them for bravery in war. Instead of feeling flattered, he decided to flee. If the state wastes money by employing people like Seleso in the criminal investigating division, the nation's taxes are thrown into the water. I do not in the least see how Seleso's evidence can affect this court.

"The testimony of King Mosito is supported. When Lipuo reported her husband missing, the King's anger that day was justified because of how the woman spoke to him. Even an angel would have taken offence. This woman said to the King: if you refuse to instruct men to look for my husband, I will report you to the police station, and you will tell them why you refuse and what you are defending. Those words were challengingly offensive, as they insinuated that the King knew where the deceased was. So, I am not surprised that the King lost his temper. She addressed the King without any respect, in despicable words!"

Thereafter, he had to deal with the letter given to Thulare. Mr Murphy knew that the King was in loose sand here and there was little one could argue in support of innocence. The only hope was to try and prove that the letter was written by someone else.

"King Mosito is a person who writes a number of letters every month to the state, and there was nothing stopping anybody who had decided to betray him from practising the King's handwriting, and then writing such a letter. Does the court really believe that a normal person, who knows all too well the *type* of allegation he is facing, would write such a letter, and give it to an unknown person, someone he is meeting for the first time?

"I request your worship to weigh this idea carefully, because, to my mind only a mad person would do that. If this court accepts that King Mosito is a normal, sane person, it ought to reject the idea of this letter; if the court accepts that this letter was written by him, it should admit that King Mosito is insane. Then he should be acquitted, because he wrote that letter not knowing what he was doing."

In a last ditch effort, he once more tried to defend Mosito: washed him, dressed him in sparkling white clothes and put a shining crown on his head. "Does the court believe that a person who is as educated as King Mosito, who has performed his work so diligently, can believe that the flesh of a dead person, or herbs, are things that will bring him great stature, honour and the kingship he does not possess? I conclude: all the evidence produced here stands on one leg, and does not prove anything beyond reasonable doubt. If the court shares my doubt (as I am convinced it will) the accused should receive the benefit of that doubt and be found innocent to the charge of ritual murder, in order to avoid a miscarriage of justice."

He sank into his chair and sighed heavily. He was evidently relieved that he had done his part in this difficult case. The court adjourned. Judgment would be delivered on Monday.

The people left, not knowing what to expect. When the prosecutor had put his case before the court, everybody had found the accusations obvious and the arguments clear; they could not see how the advocate for the accused could have any counter-argument. Then, when Mr Murphy had stood up and gathered points from this side and that side, dipping into some sand and sprinkling it on all that had been said, they began to view matters differently. They began to distrust their feelings and ended up entirely confused.

On Monday morning, it was as if a big feast was about to take place. At eight o'clock, a crowd of people had already gathered, so that, when the doors opened, they could get a seat inside. The number of police on that day frightened many people, but they came all the same, because the case had been endlessly discussed during the past weeks. Many were of the opinion that the accused would be found guilty, while others agreed, but said: watch out for the Rope Cutter.

The doors were opened and people scrambled in, determined to hear the verdict directly and not via hearsay.

"Silence in court!"

All eyes were on the door, where the judge would appear from. He entered in his gown as red as blood, and in the light of the possible verdict, the red again startled the onlookers. They tried to study what was written on his face or on the faces of assessors, but found them blank. They listened.

The judge arranged his papers, in order to read the verdict properly. He started with the prosecutor and the state witnesses. He pinpointed ideas so neatly that many felt that he acquired the position of judge through his expressive eloquence. He pierced holes in the evidence, and sometimes closed gaps. Then he went for the arguments of the advocate of the accused and the defence witnesses. He continued as he did with the first group.

He dismantled and put together facts and situations where necessary, and some began to feel that he was going to let the accused free. Yes, but the aim of the judge is not to hang or release, but to see that justice prevails, and therefore he has to look into all the loopholes, break things up into their different units and correct where applicable, so that, when he says this person is guilty or not guilty, he knows that his conscience is clear, knows that no one can point a finger at him and say he has been biased.

Each word was well chosen and there were no misgivings about what he said. Everybody in the courtroom was glued to his speech and listened attentively. Two hours passed, then three; eventually he said, "I have tried to clarify the speeches of the advocates, delivered eloquently, and indicating thorough legal knowledge. I arranged the evidence, putting forward what is acceptable to the court and pointing out where the court disagrees. When I examine the acceptable evidence and reject the unacceptable evidence, I find the case of the prosecutor as firm and unshakable as black ironstone. The advocate hit this stone with heavy rocks, which chipped here and there, but those are minor dents. Thus, I find all the accused guilty of ritual murder and my assessors are all in agreement."

He paused for a moment. All eyes were on the accused, and then turned to their wives, who had been attending the hearings daily, since the case had started.

"Is there anything the accused would like to say before I give the sentence?"

All eyes were on the accused now.

King Mosito stood up and went to the front, but everybody could see his legs felt weak.

"Your worship, the court has found me guilty of ritual murder. I would like to stress that I know nothing about this murder. It is something planned by people who hate me; I do not know what it is that they want from me. I shall go to the grave denying my guilt. Please have mercy on me! Apart from that, your worship and the court, there is nothing more I can say."

When he spoke his voice was hoarse, like the voice of someone suffering from syphillis or someone who had spent the whole night singing. It was not as strong as when he had been under cross examination. He had spoken with a forceful voice then; with the tone of one astonished by the impudence of a false and vague accusation.

The other accused also stood up, denied that they were guilty of the charge and pleaded for mercy – the mercy they did not have when Tlelima was pleading on behalf of his children.

"The request for mercy is understandable. When you get to the cells, request papers, write and request an appeal. Your letters will be sent to the relevant person with the right jurisdiction."

At that moment, the accused were all standing in single file, in front of the judge's table, in the middle of the courtroom. All eyes were on them, with their shaking legs. The whole house was as if electrified; people felt miserable, feeling the cold winter atmosphere in the middle of summer. In desperation, the accused, sweating, looked all over the room as if expecting help from somewhere.

The judge proceeded. "At this moment, however, the court finds you guilty, and the sentence is the only one appropriate to people like you. From here, you will be taken to the cells and when the hour has come to carry out your sentences, you will be led to the gallows and hanged by your necks; you will hang there until you die."

He collected his papers and disappeared through the door. The police went to the accused and pushed them out, pushing them mercilessly, to take them to the cells where they would be kept until their last day.

20

The light dwindles

The police took the accused in a police car, and locked them up in their cells. The accused knew that things were bad because they were not locked up in the usual cells but had been taken to death row. From inside, they could not see anything. The beauty of the country of Lesotho; the sight of people happily walking in the streets, attending to their routine work; children noisily playing everywhere; the Lesotho mountains that attract one's eyes with their exquisite colours – all this they parted with, it was wiped off from their world, because, where they were, they would never see it again.

The death cell enclosure they were in was built with sandstone, with thick, high walls. A person could see nothing of the outside world, save a blue space above in the day, if there were no clouds, or black clouds forming in the sky, when the heavens were sulky.

This was where they were kept, and they felt lost, condemned. They felt that even their God had forsaken them, had cursed them. They remained there until evening. No one spoke to them, nor did they speak to one another, each talking alone to his conscience, which showed each one their individual stupidity. They realised for the first time that not heeding one's conscience leads to disaster, but the lesson had come too late, the judgement had been passed. They were waiting for the chosen day, among so many days, which would come and adorn their necks with rope tie – free of charge.

That evening, each one lay down in his corner, alone, bemoaning his own folly and trying to invite sleep, that comforter of the depressed, but it was evident that they had also parted ways, because sleep respects itself and does not wish to mix with people who shed blood. As the night moved on, they had just a small taste of the sweet honey sleep had for them, but when one opened his mouth like the young of a quail finch, to have the honey dropped in, the hand would disappear and one remained behind with a quivering beak.

That happened several times to Mosito. When he eventually dozed off, he saw a shadow in front of him. He jumped and hit the wall. When his eyes got clearer, he realised that it was a person, not a shadow, a person different from ordinary people. He began to cry.

"Mosito, are you the one crying?"

It was a voice he knew very well, and he knew the shadow talking to him. He now wept uncontrollably.

"Mosito, my king, I have helped you so much with my liver to gain the kingship you were yearning to have, how can you be frightened by me when I am visiting you to congratulate you on achieving your reward?"

Mosito stood up, fumbled around, called on Khati and Selone and the others, but they were fast asleep.

"God, my father, please, be merciful on me, and remove this devil haunting me!"

"The name of God is the one you can call upon because you don't know it. If you knew it, you would have had mercy on me when *I* called that name, pleading with you to spare me."

Tlelima's crying when Mosito cut off his tongue entered his ears, piercing like a sharp needle. He pulled Khati's foot and shouted, "Wake up and help me. You who put me in this nightmare!"

Khati simply turned and slept on the other side. The heavy thunder from his nostrils continued.

"You should not blame Khati, because you did not listen to your conscience. Your father advised you before he died, and repeated it on his death bed, that you should listen to your conscience only, that it should be your only advisor, that if you adhered to it, and listened to Khosi and Pokane, you would not be where you are now. But by disobeying your conscience and forsaking your true friends, today reap what you sowed. Here is your parcel!"

Mosito saw the shadow stretch out an arm and give him the liver, oozing fresh blood.

"Take your parcel, my lord, because it is through this that you turned my children into orphans before their time."

Mosito shouted and kicked Selone and Sebotsa, but that did not wake them up, it made them sleep deeper.

"Where shall I receive forgiveness? Oh, God...!"

"I said you should not repeat that honourable name, because you do not deserve to use it. If you refuse to accept this parcel, I shall go back with it, and I shall not visit you again. The day I return, please note that I shall present this crown to you."

Mosito saw a rope with a knot put over his head and settling against his throat. He rushed again, and shouted loudly, kicked and scratched his sleeping friends. Instantly the shadow and the rope vanished. Khati and the others woke up.

"Why do you make such a noise?" asked Khati.

"How can you ask? While you were fast asleep, Tlelima was here, he was taunting me. For how long have I been trying to wake you up to help me?"

With a broken heart, he narrated what he had seen, but they had not noticed anything.

The rest of the night, Mosito did not sleep, he cried, his heart aching. When they woke up, they were given papers to write their request for mercy and began to hope that they might be pardoned. But even though they denied their guilt, the evidence showed they were guilty and they also knew that it was true.

On the following nights, Mosito slept normally. Tlelima no longer visited him. But the others also got their visits, equivalent to their part in the murder. Khati, Selone, Sebotsa, Molafu, Senyane and Bohata, saw the victim they had cast into a deep pool of the Senqu River wrapped in a tanned hide. They saw this victim alive, with no wounds, with a tongue and eyes, eyes that looked at them more accusingly than any accusation they had endured from human beings, the world and the court.

The one among them who suffered the most torture was Senyane, Tlelima's best friend. They had had a lot in common. Senyane was the last to be visited by the ghost, and spent the whole night sleepless, crying and hitting his head on the ground, but of course, all in vain. Tlelima was looking at him with the eyes they thought they had extracted, speaking with the same tongue that they had cut from him. His friend left him with the same promise as he had left for Mosito: that he would visit when the hour was nearing.

The day after the verdict, once it was clear that there was no way the accused could ever escape, their wives went to see them. That day was a day of weeping and not much could be discussed. At sunset, they were told that when the hour was near, they would be informed and they took the train home.

Pokane and Khosi also went to visit the criminals. They found them in distress; their eyes had become the eyes typical of criminals, avoiding people. Mosito felt even worse when he saw the friends he had grown up with, the ones he had departed from. They would go back to life, and he, to the valley of death.

When they said to him, "Homeboy, we see you. Trust in the Almighty. Maybe he will pardon you," he thought they were mocking him, yet they were sincere, talking from the depths of their hearts.

Then they had to go back to Qacha, to the pleasures of the country, where it looks as though God Himself resides. Mosito remained behind with his helpers; he, who was condemned, remained with them in a cell of death, where only the sky was visible.

Two weeks passed without any word about the pardon they had applied for. By the end of the third week, news from the High Commissioner in Pretoria came, saying that there was not the slightest reason why they should receive mercy; the judgement stood as pronounced and they had to be executed.

This sorry group was in great distress, with no one to console them, although, by this time, any consolation seemed like derision to them. No one visited, except the ministers on Sunday who brought some prayers. They realised that the world had forsaken them, had cursed them, and they convinced themselves that even God had abandoned them, because what happened on earth was linked to what was obtained in heaven. Therefore if the inhabitants of the earth rejected them, God would also not accept them in His heaven, but cast them into deep darknesses.

After the letter rejecting their appeal arrived, conversation among them stopped completely. When they did talk, it was to accuse one other.

One day Mosito said, "Selone, you wicked, evil vagrant; where is your stupefying drug now? Did you not say that this case would evaporate in the air?"

"Well, my lord, a person does occasionally fail, because..."

"You say, my lord, my lord! I am here because of you! I leave my son because of you!"

"Are my children not remaining behind? And please remember, we did not catch you, bind your hands and make you do it. You are the one who considered and accepted without any pressure!" Selone spoke without considering Mosito as a king. Was there any reason to honour him as a king, since Mosito had no power over him? They were both criminals, they were both killers, both were condemned, both would feel pain the same way, both would have a rope and the same person would execute similar punishment on each of them. Kingship could go to hell, as far as Selone was concerned. Mosito was not his king in any case, because his home was far away and he did not pay tax to Mosito.

Human nature is a very strange phenomenon. Even if a person has been told what will eventually happen, you will find him daily having some hope. Its origin might be uncertain, but he will cling on to it until the end. Who knows, possibly even when the execution has been carried out, having hanged by the neck until he died, when he gets beyond the grave – and we have no idea what happens there – he will still cling to that hope, he might even become stubborn, saying he has not died, he is as alive as before.

Criminals do not believe they will hang until the last day. Even more surprising is that, to those who visited them and tried to convince them that they should let go and forget about this world, make peace with God by giving themselves over to Him so that He could pardon them, they presented their stubbornness. Tlelima's killers never accepted their guilt, but continued to allege that their enemies plotted against them.

"You have to understand," said Reverend Tshepo, when he visited them one Sunday, "that God is kind and merciful; He takes pity on those He said would perish. But God has mercy only on those who confess their sins and are ashamed of them. Therefore, if you wish to receive mercy from God, you have to speak the truth, confess your sins and admit that you are ashamed of them, and you will be pardoned. You have forfeited the mercy of this world. To place hope in it is to trust an antheap without ants. I once more appeal to you: confess your wrong deeds.

"Bear in mind that the human soul is very important. It does not die, but the flesh, which we human beings in our stupidity regard as important, is nothing, because it dies and rots and returns to the dust it comes from. The human soul is from God, and because it comes from Him, it does not die. When the soul departs from the flesh, which is the picture of the soul, and returns to its Creator, the Creator wants the soul to return as clean as it was the day He blew it into a human being. When it returns clean, He will accept it and keep it among the other clean souls that are with Him and that live forever in happiness. But when it comes to Him dirty, full of the mud of sin, He will not accept it, and will throw it where all dirt belongs – the ash heap!"

He paused and looked at them full of kindness, his heart broken, because he realised that the devil had hardened their hearts, and that they would go and roll in the ash heap created by the devil for himself. The reverend's heart was distraught and tears welled in his eyes.

"My lord," he said, looking at Mosito. "You are an educated person, who should understand these matters better than the people you are with. Do not harden your heart and possibly kill your soul."

"Reverend, all you have said I understood and you spoke the truth, but there is no person who will admit that he did a certain act, knowing very well that it is false. I have said time and again, in court and here, that the accusations on which we have been found guilty, we do not recognise and we fully reject. If another truth is expected from us, I do not know where to find it. Would you believe us if we stood on our heads?"

It was not only towards Reverend Tshepo that they hardened their hearts. They were like that to all the ministers of different denominations of the Basotho and Europeans. The ministers would visit them time and again, trying to save their souls, but in spite of all their efforts, the men denied knowing anything.

A week after they'd received the letter reaffirming the judgment, their wives arrived. That disturbed them very much, because they realised their days were numbered.

"Have they informed you where the execution will take place?" Mosito asked his wife in a voice that seemed to belong to someone who had been ill for months.

"Nothing has been said. The letter only stated that we should come to visit you." Tears streamed down 'Mathabo's face. Her mind went back and gathered matters from the beginning. She saw her husband the day he had rejected Khati and his group, but he had been convinced by her, his wife. She remembered the day he had arrived home very disturbed, his feelings in turmoil by the suggestion to murder Tlelima to get his liver. Where he had again rejected Khati, she was the one who had persuaded him. So, she was the one who had betrayed the man she loved. She was the one who had taken a rope, tied a knot and thrown it over his head. She would be the one who pulled the rope so that the knot tightened, until the spinal cord snapped and life stopped. These feelings harrassed 'Mathabo deeply. Her heart chased her ceaselessly.

When Thabo grew up and heard about his father's death, as the news would then be known, how would he view her as a mother, who had made him an orphan? How would he love her, when she could not love his father? How would he respect her, when she had failed to respect herself? All these thoughts weighed her down, and she wished that death would visit her soon. She even wished she could die in her husband's place, because, when she viewed things properly, it was she who was guilty, although the guilt had been thrust on her husband.

"My sister, my love..."

'Mathabo blocked Mosito's mouth with a cry, "I do not deserve to be called my love, because the fruits you are about to pluck are not from love. Call me a traitor, a tempter, any other thing you can think of, but never call me by the name of love, because the love you had for me, I spoiled and betrayed. I separated you from your true friends, and matched you with the sons of vipers, asking you to welcome them in your bosom. Today, they are here; they are warm and have turned against you. They have bitten you and you are facing your grave." Tears flowed from her like water from a big clay pot.

"My love, your crying weakens me."

These last words from Mosito touched the centre of her heart. She stood up and went out shaking, crying uncontrollably in the streets of Maseru.

Pokane and Khosi also visited with Reverend Motete, who had welcomed Mosito on that glorious day of the feast, when he had returned after completing his studies. Although the old man's years were at an advanced stage, when he heard that the Queen had been called, he realised that the end of Mosito's journey was approaching. He picked himself up and went to see the face of his king for the last time.

When Mosito saw the minister, and the faces of the two friends whose advice he had dismissed, his heart broke, oozing blood that could not be stopped.

When they entered, he looked down and remained in that position. He responded to their greeting with his head drooping and hands covering his eyes. All the questions they asked him, he answered without once looking at them. The dirt of his actions had clothed him in unspeakable shame.

They spoke to him for a long time, trying to let him forget about his imminent death, but he could not. Eventually, Pokane and Khosi finished speaking. Reverend Motete, who had only greeted Mosito and had been quiet since they had come into his cell, knelt down for a prayer, but it burst out of him: "Mosito, my son, why did you not listen to your father's advice? Why did you not reserve my words on your return from college? Why are you now in such captivity?"

These were not asked to be answered. It was just a way the minister wished to relieve his own broken heart.

Mosito raised his head for the first time since they had entered the cell and looked at them once, quickly, then dropped his head again and covered his eyes. "Father Motete, my wife created this predicament for me!"

That was the end; they understood the conditions for the first time.

"Have you made peace with your God?" the old man asked, shaking his head, his beard covered with tears.

Mosito's answer was just to bow his head slowly.

"My son, there is little time left and you have to sweep all the dirt out of your heart to remain clean and receive the mercy of God. Because, to Him, no sin is indelible. Just one drop of His blood, dropped on the one who repents, fully wipes out all the dirt within a minute, as long as the sinner confesses and repentance is genuine."

They all kept quiet and spoke to their hearts. It was so quiet each could hear his own heartbeat sounding like something hitting hard stone.

"Father Motete, and you, the friends I grew up with, I feel ashamed to say what I am about to say, but I have reached a stage where I feel that there is no alternative, except the one given to me by the court."

Mosito was quiet and produced a tortured piece of cloth, which in earlier days had been a clean handkerchief, and wiped his eyes. He raised his head, his hands left his eyes and he looked at them, looked them straight in the eye, his own eyes weary but full of kindness and embarrassment. He spoke facing them, without turning away from them and in a soft voice, without the arrogance he displayed answering the prosecutor in court or asking state witnesses a few questions. The voice was as soft as that of a child when he admits a mistake to the parent he loves and respects, but whom he has wronged.

"I am guilty of the death of Tlelima. Khati and Sebotsa started the plan and my wife supported it. I listened to her and joined in, despite my conscience warning me and my father's last words ringing in my ears. My friends, I am very ashamed to see you here. Ever since I was arrested, you have been on my side, because deep in your hearts you could not believe that I could do what I have done, and felt strongly that I was innocent. My greatest shame is caused by the attitude I had towards you for regarding you as my enemies, throwing you away like pieces of rag. But you remained what you had been, advising me, although I did not listen."

He paused again and wiped away his tears – his shame chose those tears, they were not the tears of a frightened person.

"My wife created this ordeal for me!"

Reverend Motete said a short prayer that moved everybody, and they left him alone in his misery.

That evening, Mosito slept apart from the others, feeling as though he was being massaged by a salt that was healing bruises. He soon fell into the soft hands of sleep and forgot about his despair. But while asleep, the spirit of his ominous visitor visited him once more. When Mosito jumped out of the corner where he was sleeping, he found the visitor holding a rope. He knew what that meant.

There is a kind of fright, which is so severe, that the person experiencing it is unable to make any sound. Mosito suffered such a terror – it dried up his body parts, his tongue was parched.

"You see, I am a person who loves his king, who, when he makes a promise, does not forget. Today I have come because the time has come to reap the fruit of the seed you have sown."

Mosito tried to shout, but his tongue stuck to his palate.

"Are you aware that I have no eyes? Are you aware that I have no liver? Do you see that I have none of the parts that you removed? Are you aware that I don't even have a tongue?"

After the tongue had said that, the voice began to prattle incomprehensibly, to show how it sounded without a tongue. When Mosito looked at the shadow, it looked like the corpse of Tlelima, dripping blood. Where the eyes had been were just gaping holes, with clots and veins where the eyes had been plucked out.

He closed his eyes to avoid seeing it again, but it did not help. His mind was like a camera, and imprinted the picture where it would never disappear.

"I can see that today you fear me, my lord. You fear the work of your hands, but, not being unkind, I shall not harrass you any longer. I am leaving because you are about to come here where I am, where you will have to account for why you killed me so mercilessly."

Instantly the shadow vanished, and in its place appeared the shadow of King Lekaota. Mosito's fear grew because his father's face was angry in a way it had never been when he was still alive.

"Oh, Father, what shall I do?"

"If you had built with my words a kraal in your ears, and kept it in your heart, this would never have happened. I advised you when I was still alive; there is nothing else I can do for you. There is no pity for self-inflicted injury."

Then Lekaota was gone and Mosito remained in deepest darkness, shivering, not knowing what to do, tears flowing like water from his eyes and mouth. He fell on his knees and tried to pray, but Tlelima's shadow appeared in his consciousness, and he became confused and simply repeated the same word over and over again.

All the prisoners were individually visited by their victim. When it was Khati's turn to be visited, he tried to call the lovable name of God. The voice of a shadow without eyes said, "Khati, are you daring to call that name? When I called it, in my time of need, you mocked me. Just give back my eyes, so that I may look at you, talk to you, face-to-face!"

Khati screamed, but nobody heard him. The shadow disappeared and Khati remained, frantically colliding with the walls.

The night passed in its own time, time determined by the Creator. It cannot be pushed to come to an end before its time by someone who is in a hurry. Then night was over, and some light seeped through the key hole. The prisoners realised that it was dawn and they knew that the day's dawning announced something, as Tlelima had visited them for the second time.

On the day they had murdered, they had been brave, as if they did not fear death; on this day they were shivering, and at times some of them found their trousers somewhat damp, although it was dry where they were sitting.

So is death. It does not care whether one claims to be a hero.

The day became warm, although warm and cold meant very little to them. The door was opened, and they emerged from the death cell, stretched their legs in their open space, where they could only see the blue sky. The sky was clear, so clear that God's creatures outside, even the least significant insects, were happy, moving freely where they were, doing as they pleased. But for the guilty men the world ended inside the four walls. Their humanity was locked in there and would never find freedom again.

After breakfast, they were visited by an evangelist, because, although they had not been informed, it was their last day. The evangelist prayed and sang a hymn. "If you ask me about my hope, I shall say it is Jesus."

They sang with sad hearts, and, as there was no one else looking at them, they surrendered to the One who had the power to save their souls. They sang the verses out of their heads, with no hymn book, because the hymn was the main hymn sung in prison. All those who had been there, even if luck came their way, left the place knowing the same hymn. When they had finished singing, Mosito prayed a sad prayer, that of a broken heart, which will disturb the readers if it is written here. When he had finished, the evangelist said a few words, and left.

They remained behind with their misfortune. They remained on the thorny bed they had prepared for themselves, a bed they could not invite other people to sit on, to feel how thorny it was. Towards the late afternoon, they saw a jail police constable and senior prison warder, together with a European man they had not seen before. They were startled by his frightening appearance.

After the warders entered, greeted them and spoke briefly, the visitor who was with them asked, "Do you see me?"

They all confirmed that they saw him.

"It is a good thing that you see me. I was absent from the court hearing, and what you have been found guilty of, I do not know. My only duty is to carry out the judgment. If you are not guilty, that is irrelevant to me. I am just here to carry out the law, and that's all."

He looked at them, pitying them. Especially when he saw the four younger men, who were just at the beginning of their autumn life, to be cut short by frost before reaping time.

"Tomorrow morning at six o'clock, your judgment will be carried out according to the judge's instructions. You should prepare in your ways and build peace with your God, because there is nothing left that can save you."

Then he measured the height of each individual, and wrote in his little book. He put them on the scale and recorded the mass of each one individually, so that he could organise his ropes, so that each one received the length of rope that would fit him. When he had done all that, he went out through the door they all knew. The constables also left, the door closed, the lock clicked. They remained behind, miserable, their lips pale. They looked at one another accusingly, as if each was saying "I am what I am because of you!"

What their thoughts were as the time passed and pushed them nearer to the grave, no one could tell. Perhaps they were not thinking about anything. Perhaps they were thinking about their children, about Tlelima's orphans, the disgrace on their names, what they would meet beyond the grave. Before sunset, their wives visited them for the last time, but there was no talk, because the time was reserved for tears on both sides and people like Khati and Sebotsa learned to kiss their wives for the first time. One clung to his wife and the constables had to step in to separate them. Each one wished he could become a fly, sit on his wife's blanket and escape with her, to go and hide in some unknown place, far away.

Pokane and Khosi asked for permission to be allowed to fetch Reverend Motete and other ministers together for the night in the cell to be with their friend for the last time. The state gave permission, and they spent the night together with someone who had missed the way of humanity, made terrible decisions, thinking they would lead to the things he was wishing for. The whole night they sang hymns, not allowing themselves an idle moment to remember their imminent deaths.

Cocks crowed, crowed for the second and third time, and when they crowed for the last time, King Mosito spoke amid a hymn.

"Time is becoming short! You who are hardened, listen, and pray for yourselves, so that your hearts are softened."

He shouted, spoke alone and said, "Oh, Tlelima, forgive me, my friend! Where shall I find help? Oh, you the stars of heaven, shine and be bright, so that there may be light forever and ever! You the eye of the lovely heavens, shift backwards and do not dawn, the night should reign forever, time should not move. Pull the last minutes backwards, stay away for another hour, so that I can make true repentance, that my soul be redeemed and go to its Creator. Who shall I call on to have mercy on me?"

They held one another, and the hymn was sung vigorously and continuously to try and cover the distress in their voices.

Time is running out,
But what do you fear?
To believe in the Saviour –
Indeed you had been paid for.

They knelt down, prayed and sang:

When you ask me about my hope,
I shall say it is Jesus.
I am longing to kiss Him,
At His place in my home.

They accepted the song forcefully, pushed by something they did not understand. The door opened, their friend the executioner entered briskly and full of strength, and the constables tied their hands with handcuffs behind their backs. They put on the hoods that covered their faces and the murderers were the sheep ready to be slaughtered.

They were taken out in threes, not knowing how long the journey was to the end of their lives, led like the blind, but their eyes not gouged out like Tlelima's. Unlike him, they received some mercy, because their deaths were delayed so that death could stalk them, and not come straight to them while they looked on.

The rope did its job and by six o'clock in the morning it had completed its task. The men hanged by their necks until they died, just as the judge had pronounced; they had crossed the boundary between life and death. Being on the other side of it, where we do not know what happens, could they have met Tlelima awaiting them, seeking his eyes to see where to go, seeking his tongue so as to be able to speak to his Creator, seeking his liver and other organs, so as to appear in front of his Creator, complete as when He'd sent him into the world?

When you sow sorghum, you harvest sorghum. When you sow maize, you harvest maize, but when you sow devil's thorns you cannot expect to harvest wheat! Each person harvests what he has sown!

21
Epilogue

"People died painful deaths!" said Khosi at a packed gathering in the courtyard. Everybody was present, including Pokane, some young men and boys and others who had completed their senior certificate.

"Yes, people indeed died terrible and embarrassingly inconsolable deaths," Pokane repeated, with a familiar, sunken feeling, because it was difficult for him to remain consoled – they had witnessed the misguided and malevolent actions from beginning right up to the end. Khosi and Pokane saw how men from their own village had been led to the gallows. They stood on planks, and when the ropes were in place around their necks, the planks suddenly pulled open like a trapdoor, the nooses swiftly tightened, the bodies hung into the vacuum and their necks snapped – that was the end. Khosi and Pokane had seen the corpses after hanging, their necks broken, eyes bulging out and tongues protruding. It was the most horrific scene they had ever seen.

Pokane was quiet for some time and everybody tried to picture the frightening scene in their imaginations. Finally, Pokane continued. "When a person has died a natural death, the family is consoled by people saying one can do nothing if God wants back what he has lent that particular family. And the family is given solace. With what happened in our village, it was difficult for anybody to say anything to the families, because what can people say? What happened to them and what was done to others cannot be associated with God, whatsoever. The murder was entirely in the hands of these men and in their hands only. How do you invite God to comfort the families of people who killed others? They deserved everything that happened to them, they deserved to be hanged. The minute you mention God's will to the condemned men it would sound like a mockery."

Pokane was still very disturbed when he spoke those words. He had no way of contextualising what he'd seen in a way that anyone would understand. He said, "We the Basotho, we are a nation cursed more than any of the other nations of the world. In ancient times, during King Moshoeshoe's days, the Basotho nation was made popular because of their king's wisdom, his kindness, his inclusive love for his people. He was the one who saved the amaNdebele who were running away from their ruthless leaders. He welcomed and accommodated all those small tribes. He built a strong and wise people, living in peace and stability. He abolished cannibalism and begged the cannibals to come down from the caves to live among other people. His love and kindness were proven when he refused to kill the cannibals who had killed his grandfather Peete, because, he said, doing so would be like destroying the grave that his grandfather was housed in.

"Today, things have changed. Those who call themselves kings and who rule Lesotho use his name to justify their misdemeanours while they are the ones destroying the very nation that its architect respected, ruled and protected jealously. He had learned during the Lifaqane that a king is king because of his people. Today, people are harsh and cruel. The question we have is when will this dreadfull malice and cruelty end, so that we may all live in peace and with stability?"

He could no longer talk because he was heartbroken.

A young man by the name of Seisa, who was a teacher at a local school in the village took over and talked in this manner.

"It is very disturbing that for almost one hundred and thirteen years, the gospel of God Almighty has been preached in this county and yet we still practice these terrible things and shameful acts. One can say that it means the Church has failed in its mission to make people lead clean, admirable Christian lives. The priests have still not succeeded to truly convert people."

"What do you mean?" asked a young man named Phakiso, a district farming supervisor in Qacha. "Every Sunday the churches are filled to capacity with people claiming to be Christians."

"I mean spiritual repentance – a repentance that is truthful and reflective. Our repentance only scratches the surface; it doesn't penetrate the hearts of those who claim to be Christians. People practise it, so that when they die, a priest can come and bury them; because, when a body is carried to the grave and buried in total silence, it is simply excruciating. Some also believe that the only way to avoid Hell and get to Heaven is when a priest walks in the front of the funeral procession. I call it a misleading repentance because it serves to fool those who are not observant.

"Have you noticed that, if a king of a certain area surrenders himself to a certain church, suddenly a lot of his people follow him; even those from different churches. So what does that say? They didn't choose the previous or the new church because they have heard and accepted the teaching as the one they truly believed in; no, I am convinced that they 'repent' to impress their kings, so that they can meet him every Sunday in church. Or, they find it boring to stay home while their kings go to church."

"When you explain it like that, I understand," said Phakiso.

"I want to add and go a little bit further," said Pokane. "Since its first inception, the Church has failed in its mission. They didn't come here to win people's hearts by teaching them the ways of Christ, but to impress their senior supervisors abroad. They started off by terrifying everyone with hellfire and sulphur and burning eternally. They never made an effort to make people understand exactly what God requires of His own children, to understand that God is kind, loving and patient. People put one foot in the Church, while the other foot remains in deep, heathen mud. As it sinks deeper into the mud it pulls out the foot that was in church and it ultimately joins the one that was in the mud."

"You have hit the nail on the head, Pokane," said Seisa. "Some children obey school rules because they fear being beaten up by teachers. As soon as the teacher is out of sight, they break those rules. Other children obey school laws because they feel it's the right thing to do, even when they are not being watched by teachers."

They were quiet for a little while. Then Phakiso said, "So, what do you suggest the Church should do?"

Old man Mokali stood up slowly from an aloe stump he had been sitting on, shifting so that he could position his stance firmly to talk. "You might think that I am stupid because I am not educated in the European way, but there is only one thing that would heal this nation from senseless ritual killings: the murderers should be hanged publicly. The public should see the whole process with their own eyes. People should even be allowed to take photographs to be enlarged and spread all over schools in Lesotho. Or films of an hour long of their painful deaths. Films are better because you can hear the sounds. When people have seen what happens to transgressors, it will stay in their minds."

"Yes, that's exactly what is needed," said Mokali. "The murderer's pain, the rope cutting deeper into his neck and him tossing and turning."

"Indeed, old lion," answered Phakiso. "What do you say, Khosi, regarding the suggestions from old Mokali? I think they're brilliant!"

Seisa cleared his throat and said, "They are brilliant in the sense that they instil fear, but, as I explained, fear does not yield desirable results. We all know that the Second World War just ended and was started by Adolf Hitler; we know the manner in which he oppressed German Jews and terrorised their lives. This created assassination attempts, bombs exploded at his feet... Things like this tend to breed fear and fear only works for a little while."

Khosi, who had started this debate, had been quiet for a while, listening to others, but now added his voice again. "What you suggest has already been tried in other places. People were hanged publicly and that did not yield any results. In Britain, where this law was adopted from, they hanged transgressors in public. It yielded no results, people continued their criminal activities. The government of His Majesty the King in 1866 appointed a commission to assess whether the public display of hanging transgressors had any impact on the general public. The commission reported that out of 167 people hanged, 160 one of them had witnessed a public hanging. So it did not serve as a deterrent and the law on public hangings was reversed in 1868."

"If I may add, Homeboy," said Pokane, "public hanging is horrible. It hit those watching a hundred times. Those who witnessed public hanging spent weeks and months traumatised, unable to get those pictures out of their minds, and some people ended up losing their minds."

"So what, then, should be done?" asked Mokali.

"I think all these useless traditional healers claiming to do things by means of herbs and human parts should be stopped from practising their trade," offered Phakiso. "Anyone caught burning herbs and making sacrifices should be imprisoned without trial."

"That would not be right," said Seisa. "It would deny those practising genuine, legitimate and resourceful medical processes, which succeed where most of the European medical doctors have failed, the right to practise. Have you noticed that some ailments such as a bulging fontanelle cannot be cured with European medicines? The Sesotho medicine deals with such ailments effectively. If we follow your suggestions, a lot of useful and valuable traditional knowledge would be lost and people would suffer. My brain tells me that education is the only answer to this sickness of ritual killings, which has become so cancerous. Education should be made compulsory and accessible, whether a child is born rich or poor. And no child should leave school before completing their junior certificate. This should be implemented throughout the whole country, and within ten years, nobody would be fooled by those carrying little sacks of bones."

Khosi said, "You have packaged everything so well, but you must complete it: girls should be given preference over boys because they are the ones who can derail the situation. The hand that rocks the cradle is the hand that rules: if it had not been for women – I mean a woman! – Mosito would have not died like a dog. He had enough education, but because of the one who had no education, he ended up following in her footsteps. If women could be cleansed of believing in manaka and sacrifices, the job would be done. It is women who teach children that there is such a thing as witchcraft. The generation born out of a group of women who have been cleansed of that bad influence will grow into a good nation.

"Furthermore, the king's advisors should have a certain level of education. Our king was derailed by uneducated advisors." Pokane felt too emotional to continue.

"Let's go back to traditional healing," said Seisa. "It is imperative that the Basotho should be taught European healing in a proper manner, and that the European way of healing should be readily available all over the country. A Mosotho listens better if he learns from another Mosotho. If we could have more Basotho doctors qualified in the European way working in the country, there would be no room for evil practices such as manaka."

"I hear all you are saying boys, honestly, but something is lacking. You can see how poor I am. If a traditional healer comes to me and says, 'if you sacrifice Khosi, I will give you medicine that will make you rich', would I refuse? Never! I swear by my sister!" Old man Mokali said this looking very serious; clearly showing that he was talking from the heart.

"That is absolutely correct," said Khosi. "The government must intervene so that ordinary people have their livestock and food increased, to make sure that everyone is clothed and no one goes to bed hungry. Those at work should be remunerated accordingly, so that they live with their families comfortably and harmoniously. If poverty is eradicated, no one would be fooled by false traditional healers. Everybody involved in this trial was, in some or other way, interested in compensation. But if everybody had enough, not even a thousand pounds would tempt a person to participate in such horrible deeds."

His passionate words were followed by an immense quietness. Then an old man, Monokoa – who had been quiet since the beginning of the discussion – spoke in a low voice: "Oh Lord, our Father, the words spoken by your servants from this village are spoken because they are hurting and their hearts are shattered. Oh Lord, hear us and stretch your hands over us and cover our hearts with the gospel of love. We repent; make us new people. Have mercy on our country, Lesotho. Let our pleas reach your Heavens so that the Holy Spirit reigns in the heart of every

Mosotho. Let us connect and know that the life of every person is very important to each one of us, to our families and our country. Teach us, oh Lord, that a human life is very important and should not be crushed as easily as breaking a clay pot. Human life is more valuable than that of a louse. Teach us to kneel on our knees before You, Lord of Mercy. Hear our prayers, and turn this unfortunate deed into a blessing. Give us rain and blessings that cannot be countered."

When old man Monokoa stopped, he had tears in his eyes, like a child. When all the men in the kgotla realised that, they murmered, as though they had been prepared for this: "Let it be!"

Glossary and notes

bohadi traditionally cattle and other livestock paid by a bridegroom to the family of his future wife, to unify the two families

boreba herb used to cause a person to forget; 'drug of forgetfulness'

bulging fontanelle a soft spot on the top of a baby's head towards the front. If this feels firm and curves outwards (bulges) it may be a sign of fluid build-up and could result in brain damage; immediate medical attention is required.

fito a long mythical serpent. According to belief, when it moves from one place to another, it causes and is carried by a tornado.

Gun War (1880-81) conflict between Basotho and British forces from the Cape Colony over the right of Basotho to bear arms

iguana large, mostly herbivorous lizard that spends most of its life in tree canopies; originating from Central and South America and considered invasive to southern Africa. When used as a description of people, the connotation is that they are always seen together, such as husband and wife.

kampong location or village

kgotla courtyard

lebetlela stick (knobkierie) with a knob at one end, often used as a weapon

lefitori Sesotho blanket (the blankets have different colours and patterns that carry symbolic meaning)

lenaka (plural **manaka**) hollow cattle horn filled with a mixture of dried herbs and fat

letsema work party; gathering of people from the community to work in a neighbour's field. In return, the owner of the field gives food and beer.

Lifaqane a period of large-scale migrations of people in southern Africa, many of whom were fleeing from wars, especially at the time of Shaka

Maime heavy one (also the name of a herb)

manaka (singular **lenaka**) hollow cattle horns filled with a mixture of dried herbs and fat

mokgahla a roughly tanned hide

Molomomonate sweet tongue (also the name of a herb)

morena king (having royal blood)

ngaka herbalist, traditional healer

ntate father (a term of respect that can be used to address any adult man)

phofu ea rona idiomatic expression meaning 'our victim' (the literal meaning of 'phofu' is eland, a type of antelope)

Phonyoha escape (also the name of a herb)

pitso meeting

sekhakha a blanket that is spread over a grass mat before sleeping

t'sohana-ea-neta anything next to you, affects you

uproot pegs planted by him In a process known as 'ho upella', herbalists would plant wooden stakes treated with herbs at the four corners of a homestead and at the entrance, to ward off evil and intruders.

About the translator

Johannes Malefetsane Lenake

Professor Johannes Malefetsane Lenake was born in January 1929 in Frankfort, Orange Free State. After acquiring a Primary Teacher's Certificate from Stofberg College in 1949, he started his teaching career at a tiny farm school in Theunissen. In the same year, 1950, he matriculated through private study and in 1952 became an assistant teacher at a community school in Frankfort, rising to the position of principal of the Fouriesburg Bantu community school in 1958. He completed his bachelor's degree through the University of South Africa (UNISA) in 1962 and took up a language assistant post in UNISA's (then) Department of Bantu Languages. In 1979 he was promoted to Senior Lecturer, in 1985 to Associate Professor and in 1987 to full Professor. His DLitt et Phil thesis was on the poetry of KE Ntsane. He has written, translated and edited books and manuscripts in Sesotho, English, Afrikaans and isiZulu. He has also won awards for his work from several institutions, such as the African Language Association of South Africa, South African Association of Language Teaching, South African Literary Awards, and Macufe Wordfest in the Free State.

To view the translators speaking about the Africa Pulse series, visit
www.youtube.com/oxfordsouthernafrica